CHRISTC
THE CASE OF THE

CHRISTOPHER BUSH was born Charlie Christmas Bush in Norfolk in 1885. His father was a farm labourer and his mother a milliner. In the early years of his childhood he lived with his aunt and uncle in London before returning to Norfolk aged seven, later winning a scholarship to Thetford Grammar School.

As an adult, Bush worked as a schoolmaster for 27 years, pausing only to fight in World War One, until retiring aged 46 in 1931 to be a full-time novelist. His first novel featuring the eccentric Ludovic Travers was published in 1926, and was followed by 62 additional Travers mysteries. These are all to be republished by Dean Street Press.

Christopher Bush fought again in World War Two, and was elected a member of the prestigious Detection Club. He died in 1973.

CHRISTOPHER BUSH

THE CASE OF THE HOUSEKEEPER'S HAIR

With an introduction
by Curtis Evans

DEAN STREET PRESS

INTRODUCTION

Labouring under Suspicion
Christopher Bush's Crime Fiction in the
Postwar Years, 1946-1952

Seven years after the end of the Second World War, Christopher Bush published, under his "Michael Home" pseudonym, *The Brackenford Story* (1952), a mainstream novel in which a onetime country house boots boy, having risen for some time now to the lofty position of butler, laments the passing of traditional English rural life in the new postwar order, as signified by the years in which the left-wing Labour party held sway in the United Kingdom (1945-51). The jacket description of the American edition of *The Brackenford Story* reads, in part:

> *The Brackenford Story* is the story of a changing England. William saw the political enemies of the Hall gradually successful, whittling away the privilege it stood for. He saw squire begin to sell his land, the taxes increase, the great Hall sold, the beautiful trees along the drive cut down. And then with a Second World War, nationalization, rationing, pre-fabricated houses and queuing. William recalled with gratitude the kindness of his masters and their sense of responsibility for others. He saw that the bad old days of Toryism were not so bad after all. And he never lost his sense of outrage at the loss of something he felt was worthy of preservation.

A few years earlier, in July 1949, Anthony Boucher, the postwar dean of American crime fiction reviewers and a highly socially conscious liberal (small "l"), wrote with genial bemusement of the conservatism of British crime writers like Christopher Bush, in his review of Bush's latest crime opus, *The Case of the Housekeeper's Hair* (1948), making topical mention of a certain anti-Utopian novel penned by a distinguished

CHRISTOPHER BUSH

dying tubercular English writer, which had just been published in June. "However much George Orwell, in *Nineteen Eighty-Four*, may foresee the forcible suppression of 'crimethink' under 'Ingsoc,' English socialism in 1949 takes pleasure in exporting mystery novels which disapprove of the Government and everything about it," Boucher observed with wry irony. "Like most of his colleagues, Christopher Bush is tartly critical of the regime; and an understanding of his unreconstructed Tory attitude is necessary if you're to hope to understand the motivations of this novel."

In both the detective novels and mainstream fiction which Christopher Bush published between 1946 and 1952, Bush, like many other distinguished mystery writers of the Golden Age generation (including Agatha Christie, Dorothy L. Sayers, Georgette Heyer, John Dickson Carr, Edmund Crispin, E.R. Punshon, Henry Wade and John Street), indeed was critical of the Labor government and increasingly nostalgic about a past that grew ever more golden in blissful, if perhaps partially chimerical, remembrance. Yet keeping Bush's distinct anti-left bias in mind, fans of classic crime fiction will find between the covers of the author's crime novels from these years--*The Case of the Second Chance* (1946), *The Case of the Curious Client* (1947), *The Case of the Haven Hotel* (1948), *The Case of the Housekeeper's Hair* (1948), *The Case of the Seven Bells* (1949), *The Case of the Purloined Picture* (1949), *The Case of the Happy Warrior* (1950), *The Case of the Corner Cottage* (1951), *The Case of the Fourth Detective* (1951) and *The Case of the Happy Medium* (1952)--fascinating observation of postwar social malaise in the age of British imperial decay and domestic austerity, as well as details about the rise of rationing, restriction and regulation, the burgeoning black market and, withal, that ubiquitous flashily-dressed criminal figure from Forties and Fifties Britain: the spiv (dealer in illicit goods).

Puzzle-minded mystery readers also will find some corking good no-nonsense "fair play" mysteries. "Few writers can equal Christopher Bush in handling a complicated plot while giving the reader a fair chance to solve the riddle himself," avowed the American blurb to *The Case of the Corner Cottage*, while Anthony Boucher applauded Bush's belated return to the American fiction lists after the Second World War, declaring: "It's good to have Mr. Bush back after too long an absence . . . he presents the simon-pure jigsaw-puzzle detective story with unobtrusive competence." Concurrently in the United Kingdom, author Rupert Croft-Cooke, who himself wrote fine detective fiction as "Leo Bruce," pointedly praised Bush's "urbane and intelligent way of dealing with mystery which makes his work much more attractive than the stampeding sensationalism of some of his rivals."

In the pages which follow this introduction by all means attempt, dear readers, to match your keen wits against those of that ever-percipient gentleman sleuth, Ludovic Travers. Frequently in tandem with his old friend Superintendent George Wharton and with occasional input from his smart and sophisticated wife Bernice Haire, the former classical dancer, Ludo continues to hunt, in his capacity as a sort of special consultant to Scotland Yard (or "unofficial expert," as he puts it), more not-quite-canny-enough crooks. Additionally Ludo, a confirmed fan of American crime films like *The Blue Dahlia* (1946) and *Call Northside 777* (1948), comes to find himself in ownership of the Broad Street Detective Agency, perhaps the finest firm of private inquiry agents in London. In these old and new capacities in the postwar world Ludo confronts his greatest cornucopia of daring and dastardly crimes yet.

THE CASE OF THE HOUSEKEEPER'S HAIR

REVIEWING Christopher Bush's *The Case of the Housekeeper's Hair* in the August 7, 1949 number of the *New York Times Book Review*, Anthony Boucher, the postwar dean of American crime fiction reviewers, enthusiastically declared: "You must bless Mr. Bush for his loyal conservatism in upholding the formal, leisurely, deductive murder novel. Ludovic Travers, his star amateur sleuth, is in fine form here. . . . there is one of those wonderfully intricate alibis . . . and it's all told with the quiet skill, not devoid of humor, which Bush has been developing in recent years." Yet despite his expressed admiration for Bush's latest Ludo Travers detective opus as an accomplished tale of mystery (an accurate assessment on his part), Boucher also wryly observed that the situation in the novel of "a young man of good family who faces disinheritance because he is a successful radio entertainer" might well strike bemused American readers "as justification not only for the general election of 1945 [in which the Labour Party took power], but for the more remote events of 1776." Since Americans of 2019--not to mention many modern Britons and citizens of other parts of the world as well-- who read this new edition of *The Case of the Housekeeper's Hair* likely will find the situation described by Boucher even more mystifying than did Americans of 1949, I will, in the afterword to this volume, explain why an heir's being a "successful radio entertainer" might conceivably have so much nettled a proper English gentleman of a certain age and class in the postwar years as to drive that man to contemplate the drastic sanction of disinheritance.

The Case of the Housekeeper's Hair opens dramatically with Ludo Travers divulging to his Scotland Yard friend of long standing, Superintendent George Wharton, that a man he recently met has confided to him, Ludo, that he plans to commit a murder—and Ludo tends to take him at his word. The ostensibly murder-minded man in question is Guy Pallart, a wealthy bachelor landowner in rural Essex who during the late war "got a lump of shell in his leg and had the bad luck to be taken prisoner at Dunkirk." Pallart was introduced to Ludo at the Regency Club in London by David Calne, son of steel magnate Sir Benjamin Calne and recipient of the George Cross, the second highest award in the United Kingdom's honors system, bestowed upon him on account of some hush-hush work in German-occupied France. Calne of late has rented a bungalow from Pallart, at a "tiny little spot" in Essex "on one of the little known creeks," where he plans on indulging his hobby of ornithology. Over drinks Pallart (whom Calne earlier to Ludo had pronounced "definitely a queer character" with quite possibly "a screw loose somewhere") boldly announces, after recalling that Ludo recently gave evidence "in that hotel murder case" (*The Case of the Haven Hotel*, 1948): "I'm interested in murder myself. As a matter of fact, I'm proposing to commit one in the not too distant future. . . . But I haven't the faintest intention of getting myself hanged."

At first both Calne and Ludo take Pallart's announcement in jest ("You're not just suffering a hangover after reading Edgar Wallace's *Four Just Men*?" Calne jokingly asks his landlord, referencing a once hugely popular early twentieth century English crime thriller.) However, Ludo begins to wonder to his consternation whether Pallart might just be serious after all. Unable as usual to resist sticking his nose into other people's business, Ludo soon finds himself in Pallart's lonely little corner of Essex, a brooding landscape of salt marshes and tidal flats. There he comes across some strange goings-on indeed.

Mysteries swirl round Ludo. Is Pallart really planning a murder, or was his boast just lordly bravado? Why was Pallart surreptitiously consorting in his shut-up summerhouse with an unknown Aryan-looking blond man? Why is that enigmatic Czech, Dr. Kales (pronounced Kalesh), staying at Pallart's home? Why is Pallart so out of sorts with his nephew and heir, young Richard Brace ("rather sallow looking with a decidedly weak chin")? Just what is it that Jack and Annie Winder, the kindly couple who shares the bungalow with David Calne, and Arthur Friske, Pallart's wiry old batman, know? Not to mention Georges Loret and Susan Beavers, respectively Pallart's highly Gallic French chef and his elderly hair-proud housekeeper, and that sneaking gardener, Fred Wilkins? ("Sometimes he fair used to give me the creeps," Susan Beavers, an avid filmgoer, confides, "Like that Boris Karloff on the pictures.") To find the answers to these and other questions Ludo, along with Superintendent Wharton, who joins the local scene after the first murder, must sort through one of the author's cleverest plots.

Curtis Evans

PART I
MURDER?

CHAPTER I
A QUESTION OF MURDER

"THERE'S SOMETHING I'd like to put up to you, George," I said.

George—Superintendent, to you—Wharton was paying a wholly unofficial visit to my flat in St. Martin's Chambers. It was an early evening of September and we were yarning over a couple of bottles of beer.

"Well, why not?" George asked amiably.

George is a man of many moods, and most of them ersatz, not that there is in them anything of the temperamental. But most of his life he has considered it necessary to practise various forms of guile for the due deceiving and ultimate undoing of innumerable witnesses, and now deception has become an ingrained kind of showmanship. I know well enough by now, after many years of association with him on murder cases, that there are times when he is wholly unaware that he is play-acting at all. But at the moment of my remark there was no need for acting. It was a warm evening and the beer was cold, and George, for once, was his natural self. He took a pull at his glass, wiped his vast walrus moustache with voluminous sweeps of his tablecloth of a handkerchief, and then graciously indicated that he was prepared to give his views on the particular problem I wished to put up.

"This is the point, George," I said. "What is the attitude to be adopted when you—or I or anybody—have a shrewd idea that a man is proposing to commit a murder?"

For a moment his eyes popped and his mouth opened. Then he gave a grunt.

"What's the idea? Trying something out on me before putting it up to the Brains Trust?"

2 | CHRISTOPHER BUSH

"The Brains Trust!" I said, and gave a little snort of contempt. "I'd as soon listen to the rumblings of a camel's stomach. Which reminds me. Why haven't you ever been invited to a session? Senior Superintendent of Scotland Yard. Doesn't the public want to know about crime?"

I admit a speciousness about all that, but George has to be handled carefully. A little flattery is never displeasing to George, and there are times when you can lay it on with a trowel. Now he gave what might have been a smirk, and while he was muttering something about regulations and unprofessional conduct, it was plain what was flashing through his mind. George, in fact, was seeing himself in the final, supreme, stupendous role. There he was, standing out from the ancient erudites and earnest bores and thrusters and pink intellectuals and mountebanks as Irving would have stood out in a crowd of supers. And millions of listeners would be hanging on his enchanted, if dignified and measured, words. There might even be a touch of the humorous or whimsical by way of deft relief, and a little smile wrinkled at George's eyes as he realised that dexterous need. And then he let out a breath and roused himself.

"Oh no, George," I said at once. "This is serious. Damn serious. Believe me or not, I have an idea that a certain man is going to commit murder."

"What's the evidence?"

"Just that he told me so—in so many words."

George gave another of his prodigious grunts. Then he took out his antiquated spectacle case and hooked on his glasses. The action must have been automatic. I've never been able to get those spectacles in my hands but I'm pretty sure they're plain glass. George knows they give him a kindly, paternal look, and then again he likes to glare at a witness over the tops of them.

"He told you so!" Another grunt. "Haven't you ever had your leg pulled before?"

"It wasn't leg-pulling," I told him soberly. "I think the chap was in dead earnest."

"What was he? A lunatic or a crank, or what?"

"As sane and sober as you and me," I said. "He's young, intelligent and wealthy—as far as we're allowed to be. And he treated the whole thing so cynically and casually that I'm all the more sure he was serious."

George gave me his first look over the spectacle tops.

"He was talking confidentially?"

"Don't know," I said, and frowned as I tried to think back. And then there was a tap at the door and in came the service dinners I'd ordered. My wife was away and George was staying on for the evening meal. Over that meal I told him all about it.

You will pardon perhaps, the briefest of words about myself. According to your political obsessions, you might describe me either as of independent means or a battener on the working classes, which means that I had the good luck to inherit some money and, before Comrade Dalton began running amuck, to put a little more to it myself. When I add that even in those circumstances I still think work the best thing in life, you will know that my mind is not altogether stable. But it is an agile mind for all that, backed by a queerly retentive memory; what, in fact, I would call a flibbertigibbet, crossword sort of mind that would be impatient of chess. Many years ago the Yard called me in as what they called an unofficial expert and since then I have automatically joined up with George when he is on a murder case, and maybe because the Yard has forgotten to strike me off its books.

George and I make a team of opposites. He is huge and lumbering with a back like a barn-end. I am six-foot three and lean at that, and once, when wearing my usual horn-rims, I was honoured by being caricatured as a secretary bird. George is reasonably patient and remorselessly inquiring; I persist in treating life more flippantly and am always on the look-out for short cuts and quick results. If I have a hobby, it is the busman's one of making a study of my fellow men, and if I am impatient, it is because a loose end or an unsolved problem will always gnaw at me like an aching tooth.

But about that September morning. My wife was away, as I have said, and there was nothing doing for me at the Yard. Service meals had already become boring and I proposed lunch at the Regency Club. In fact, I did lunch there, and it was just when I came back to the main lounge that I caught sight of David Calne.

Calne could, if he had wished, have been very much of a glamour boy. I had got to know him through a nephew of mine—killed unhappily over France—and I must say I liked him, as far, that is, as a man of my generation and outmoded views can like one so much younger and more virile than himself. I had also been something of a friend of his late father, Sir Benjamin Calne, the steel magnate, whose firm had ramifications in both Germany and France in that nightmare period between the wars.

David Calne hadn't been born with a silver spoon in his mouth; his had been a gold spoon studded with diamonds. But when war broke out—he was then in the late twenties—he was called up with his Territorial Battalion, and in the first spring went out to France. When he came back via Dunkirk he was taken for a hush-hush assignment. His mother, by the way, was French, and before the war he had had some sort of a job in France—decorative, I used to imagine—connected with the Calne Combine. What that hush-hush job had been I had only recently learned. He had been parachuted into France as an agent, and for his work he was given a George Cross. At the moment he was treating himself to an extensive holiday. In fact, as he was to tell me, he had no intention of reassociating himself with his late father's firm. His hobby was the study of bird life and he was proposing to make that hobby his life's work. It was work worth doing, and his parents were dead and he spoke of himself as a confirmed bachelor.

"You're looking quite an old stager," I told him. "What I might call mature."

"It's this moustache," he told me, but he didn't smile. That was one of the things that made me realise what worlds apart I was from a fellow like David Calne. It gave me a curious feeling of irritation or uneasiness, for we shouldn't have been that much apart. It was true we had not been to the same school but we had had the same college at Cambridge. But he didn't smile, as I said. I had rarely known him smile—at least with me. It was always as if the words he spoke had nothing to do with his intimate thoughts. And yet it was not—so far I could flatter myself—that he regarded me as a bore, for he never avoided my company. That early afternoon in the Regency lounge he could easily have avoided me, but when we caught sight of each other, it was he who came across to me.

"I'm thirty-six, you know," he was reminding me.

"A ripe age," I said, and again he didn't smile. When I asked him what he was doing with himself at the moment, it was as if he had to drag back his thoughts before he answered me.

"I've a flat in town," he said. "Most of my time, though, I'm hoping to spend at Wandham."

"Wandham?" I said.

"A tiny little spot in Essex," he said. "It's on one of the little known creeks. I've got a bungalow of sorts there and a kind of launch."

Before I could comment, he was craning his neck as if there was a something across the room that he faintly recognised. His voice lowered.

"See that fellow over there? The one talking to the fat chap in the brown suit?"

"Tall, good-looking fellow?"

He nodded.

"Extraordinary coincidence, but that's the chap whose place I have in Wandham. I rent it from him."

"What's his name?"

"Pallart. Guy Pallart. He lives at Ninford about a mile and a half from me. A very good fellow but—well, rather unusual. I'll get him to join us."

"Tell me more about him first," I said. I hinted to you that I have an insatiable and shameless curiosity, and if this man Pallart was unusual, then I was itching to know why.

"He's a cynical sort of cuss," he said. "About my own age but a Regular. Got a lump of shell in his leg and had the bad luck to be taken prisoner at Dunkirk."

That was all apparently that he had to say.

"But surely that doesn't make him unusual?" I said.

"Oh, but it does," he said. "He certainly *is* unusual. Very charming and so on but definitely a queer character. Sometimes I've even thought he's got a screw loose somewhere."

"And you put it down to his experiences as a prisoner of war?"

"Yes—perhaps. And that the Germans didn't handle his wound in time. He's definitely lame."

He gave a kind of peep round my chair and then suddenly got to his feet. Pallart must have caught sight of him, and I was getting to my feet too, for Pallart was almost on us.

"Hallo, young fellow. I thought it must be you."

Pallart had a delightful voice. My first quick squint at him showed as attractive looking a man as I'd wish to see: tallish, wiry and what old-timers would have called a sahib. His lean face was tanned with weather and it was only as he came still nearer that I noticed the limp. He was of the same age as Calne but seemed much older. His manner was more assured and his quick glance went from Calne to me, and back to Calne again. He seemed to be regarding both of us with a kind of amused detachment.

"You don't know Guy Pallart," Calne said to me. "Guy, this is Ludovic Travers."

"How are you, sir?" He smiled and nodded, then his eyebrows lifted quizzically.

"What, no drink? What'll you have, sir? Port? And you, David?"

I said a glass of port would be excellent. Calne said he'd see to it.

"Oh no you don't," Pallart told him. "This is my show."

We had lunched early and the waiter problem was acute. That was why Pallart had moved off to the bar to fetch the drinks.

"Seems a very nice chap?" I said tritely as I settled to the chair again.

"Charming enough—yes. But he's got queer ideas," Calne said. "Of course he may not trot any of them out today. What I mean is that there are times when he's the most normal person in the world."

"Weren't you saying he was your landlord?" I asked him, and passed my cigarette case.

"I won't, thanks," he told me. "Not till after the port."

"Foolish of me," I said, and somehow I couldn't help wondering what Pallart would have done in the same circumstances. He'd have taken the cigarette and damned the port, even if he'd had the private idea that I hadn't much of a palate. I think too that Calne was realising that I was a bit huffed, for he began telling me more about Pallart, and while he was talking I was thinking how different the two men were: Calne, shortish and thick-set, punctilious and even preciously correct. Maybe natural born bird-watchers had that particular attitude to things, I thought to myself: the aloofly studious attitude and the self-absorption.

But to get back to what Calne was saying. Pallart's people had always been connected with the church. His parents were dead but he still lived in the old vicarage at Ninford, the present incumbent occupying a new vicarage recently built. Pallart had plenty of money.

"You find him a good landlord?"

He hesitated for a moment, then shrugged his shoulders. "I wouldn't say that. What I mean is that I pay a pretty stiff price for the Wandham place."

"Everything's dear nowadays," I said sententiously. "A bachelor, is he?"

"Absolutely. A very queer *ménage* he has at Ninford. Keeps a French chef for one thing."

"Lucky man!" I said feelingly. "Wish to God I had one, and something for him to cook."

He made no comment on that. There was an ancient female retainer, he was going on, who did the housework. An extraordinary old lady with the most astounding vitality. And there was a gardener. And again there was something unusual—the happy-go-lucky way the place seemed to be run. Even Pallart's man, who lent a hand in the house as well as out, seemed to do very much as he liked.

That sounded rather attractive to me, and then it suddenly struck me that Pallart was being the very devil of a time fetching those ports.

"He's probably stopping to yarn to someone," Calne said. "An extraordinary cove. Sometimes he seems to have not the faintest idea of the importance of time."

"Lucky man," I almost said again. But what I did ask was how Pallart got on with the French chef. Did the chef speak English or did Pallart speak French?

"The chef speaks a little English," Calne said. "And that reminds me of something else. Pallart speaks the most excruciating French. He goes out of his way to speak it with me."

"You're bilingual, of course."

"Well, I suppose I am," he told me deprecatingly. "I think Pallart just tries to get my goat. You can sort of feel he's pulling your leg. Here he is, by the way."

And there he was, steering his way past people and chairs, the tray held aloft on his fingers in the best professional way. He gave a cheerful grin as he set the tray down.

"Your drinks, gentlemen."

We took sips of that excellent club port and Pallart drew up a chair.

"You a member here, sir?" he asked me.

"Quite an old one," I said.

"Dammit, Guy, you've surely heard of Ludovic Travers?" Calne told him, and it was the kind of remark that makes me feel both a bit of a fool and a highly exasperated one.

"Sorry," said Pallart. His head moved quick and bird-like and he was giving me that whimsical smile. "Are you anyone really important?"

"Not a bit of it."

"But I should have known your name?"

"Not at all," I told him. "The fewer people who know my name, the better I'm pleased. Cryptic, perhaps, but let's leave it like that. Finish that port and let me get you another."

"Not for me, sir," he said, and then Calne was cutting in.

"Mr. Travers is associated with Scotland Yard."

"But how interesting!" Then he was giving a look of dismay. "How stupid of me! I do remember your name now, sir. You were giving evidence in that hotel murder case."

He was about to take a last drink from his glass, and then he paused. He set the glass carefully down.

"Funny, you know, sir, that you should be a murder expert—"

"I'm not," I said.

"You're too modest," broke in Calne.

"As I was saying," Pallart went on patiently. "It's extraordinary, in a way, that we should run across each other like this. I'm interested in murder myself. As a matter of fact, I'm proposing to commit one in the not too distant future."

He picked up his glass as if the remark had been merely about the weather. Calne caught my eye. His eyebrows lifted. He actually smiled—or was it a grimace?—and he gave a wink.

"What's the idea?" I asked Pallart. "Are you writing a book?"

"Good lord no, sir!" he told me. "I'm perfectly serious."

"Splendid," I said. That look of cynical amusement had been in his eye and I was anticipating some elaborate leg-pull. I was in no hurry, and I was finding myself liking Pallart. He was definitely unusual, which was right up my alley. I'm always on the look-out for unusual types.

"Splendid," I said again. "If it isn't too cold a morning I'll come and see you hanged."

He laughed gently as he passed his cigarette case. He was still chuckling as he held the lighter for Calne and myself.

"But I haven't the faintest intention of getting myself hanged."

"Good," I said. "It's refreshing to meet an optimist. Besides, crime does need a bit of gingering up."

"Take this morning," he was going on. "I could have murdered both you and David, here. Why shouldn't there have been poison in that port?"

"Why not indeed?" I asked amiably. "But you collected the port at the bar and brought it here. Wouldn't Scotland Yard want to know about that?"

"Not at all, sir," he told me patiently. "Just as I was coming out of the bar I saw a man I knew, so I set that tray down on the hall table. Anybody could have popped some poison in while it was there. I wasn't looking at the tray and neither was the man I was talking to." He beamed cynically at us and waved a hand. "Besides, even Scotland Yard would know that I haven't the remotest reason for poisoning either you, sir, or David."

"Delightfully facile," Calne said. "You've poisoned the port and we're dead. Now what?"

Pallart frowned as if in pain.

"My dear fellow, must you always be so matter-of-fact? That was merely an illustration."

"And what about moral inhibitions—not that that's the right term. Still, you know what I mean."

"Let me give you another hypothetical case," Pallart said, and drew his chair in. Then he was asking me with the most charming smile if he was being a bore. I assured him he wasn't.

"Well, then, take one of those cases where a man's tried for murder and gets away with it. Let's say he murdered my mother. A brutal murder, but he's found not guilty. Later he comes to me and boasts that he did the murder. He even tells me just how he did it, and I know that he can't be tried again for the same crime. So I calmly pull out a gun and blow his brains out. What's immoral or unsocial about that?"

"Sophistry, my dear fellow," Calne told him.

Pallart looked surprised. He looked appealingly at me.

"If that's the kind of murder you're going to commit, then good luck to you," I said, and hastened to add that my blessings were entirely unofficial.

"But you said the case was hypothetical," Calne fired at him.

"My dear old ass, of course it was hypothetical," Pallart told him patiently. "But the murder I'm going to commit isn't hypothetical. I admit it'll be just as much an act of justice as the hypothetical case of the man who murdered my mother."

"But what's the law for if it can't give justice?" I asked him. I admit I asked it to keep the conversational ball rolling. Or was it that I was having the peculiar feeling that Pallart wasn't pulling our legs after all?

"I've just given you a case where the law couldn't do a thing about it," he told us. "There are plenty of similar cases. Men can laugh at the law in spite of the fact that they've done things for which they ought to be trodden on like scorpions or snakes."

"You're not suffering from a hangover after reading Edgar Wallace's *Four Just Men*?" Calne asked him amusedly.

"No," said Pallart, "but it's quite a sound idea." He let out a breath and slowly shook his head. "Still, there we are. And just one other little thing, sir. If you use such a phrase nowadays as 'playing the game', you're put down by the hoi polloi as a Colonel Blimp. But I'm going to play the game over my murder. I shall give my man good and sufficient warning of what's coming to him. Then, as far as I'm concerned, I've no further moral obligations. The rest will be up to him. He can look after himself." The cynical smile came again. "What's it that Frenchman said: *'Cet animal est très malin. Quant on Vattaque, il se défend.'* Sorry for my frightful French and all that."

It was the accent that had been so appalling. The words had been there right enough. Calne was still wincing.

"So you're warning this chap, are you? How're you doing that? I mean, you're not telling him your name?"

"Oh no," Pallart said airily. "I shall simply ask him to take a good look at his conscience and ask himself if he hasn't done anything for which he deserves killing. I shall say that in my opinion he has, and I'm the one who's going to do the killing." He smiled charmingly once more at me. "I think that'll all be fair and in good order, sir, don't you?" He hoisted himself to his feet. His game leg must have hurt, for he made a face as he moved.

"Damn good of you to listen to me, sir."

"Not at all," I said, and I tried to give a smile as friendly as his own. "It's I who am grateful to you. I don't often meet a murderer before the crime."

"Good for you, sir," he told me, and chuckled. "You coming now, David?"

A minute and the two had moved off and my eyes had followed the tall figure of Pallart as he limped across the room. Then I dropped into my chair again and suddenly I knew that I had had a most unusual experience. In other words I knew that Pallart had been in earnest. I can't explain why I was all at once so sure, but sure I was. Maybe I've made a bad hand of accenting his words in the right places or in showing you the brief flashes of this and that as they lighted his face and the ironical—yet far from bitter—twist of that friendly mouth.

I sat there for perhaps five minutes and then made my way to the cloak-room. When I came out I walked clean into Pallart again. It was as if he'd been waiting for me.

"You still here, sir?" he said cheerily. "What about another quick drink before you go?"

"Not for me," I said. "I'm a most abstemious cove. But if you'll have one—"

"Thank you, sir, but I won't." He waited for a moment. "Which way are you going, by the way? I mean, I might give you a lift."

"Not worth it," I said as we moved off down the stairs. "I'm only going a few yards."

His voice came quite low and there was no reason for it. There was no one on the stairs.

"You mentioned the word 'unofficial' just now."

"I believe I did," I said.

"Yes," he said, and gave himself a nod. "It's a good word. It's a word I like."

It was a queer way of telling me that what he had said that afternoon had been in confidence—if that was what he was really telling me. But by then we were at the door, and I held it for him to go through. He thanked me gravely, and as I came out to the pavement, I saw his car at the kerb. A youngish man—ex-soldier by the look of him—was standing by and I recalled what Calne had told me about things at Pallart's Ninford place being free-

and-easy, for the man had on a chauffeur's cap but his clothes were sports clothes and he was smoking a cigarette.

"Goodbye, sir," Pallart said and lifted a hand in a kind of salute.

"Goodbye," I said, and then the man took his arm and eased the game leg into the driver's seat. I watched the back of that car till it was out of sight among the traffic by the Park.

That was roughly the story I told George Wharton, and the meal was over before the recital had ended.

"And you still want me to take this seriously?" George asked me and he was peering along his nose as if the antiquated spectacles were still there.

I could only shrug my shoulders and leave it to him. After all, I did know that he had had a good meal and a good drink and that meant he was likely to talk horse sense and leave the play-acting out.

"Even assuming your opinion is correct, there's nothing you can do," he said. "You don't know whether he was speaking in confidence, but even if you assume he wasn't, what can you do? Let's say you consider it your duty to lay information. You suspect him of—well, no matter what. Say, acting to the public danger. If he's questioned, he'll say it was a leg-pull and you'll simply look a fool."

"All the same, I don't like leaving it quite like that."

"Why not?" asked George with just a touch of belligerency. "This is a case where it's better to be wise after the event than wise before. If what you think is correct"—a shrug of the shoulders showed that he was still of the opinion that I'd had my leg pulled—"and this man Pallart does do something along the lines he mentioned to you, then he'll be a goner. It'll be child's play for you to get a conviction."

I had opened in his honour almost my last pre-war bottle of whisky, and he took an appreciative swig.

"Nothing else happened I suppose?"

"Not very much," I said. "About an hour before you arrived David Calne rang me here. Wanted to know if what he'd told me about Pallart beforehand had been confirmed. I told him it certainly had."

"You don't mean you think this Pallart is slightly off his rocker? Mind you, ex-prisoners of war very often are. Not what you'd call out-and-out balmy perhaps, but queer." He nodded to himself. "Poor devils. Five and more years of it. It must have been a hell of a time. I'd have gone balmy myself."

"Pallart's sane enough," I said. "He's the owner of a damn good brain, in spite of that cynicism stuff. Murder or no murder, I can't help liking him. I don't know when I've been so attracted to anyone before."

"Well, there's nothing to be done about it," George said. "All you can do—assuming you're right—is to wait and see."

"There *is* something I have done," I said. "I've made up my mind to learn a whole lot more about Pallart."

George's glass stayed an inch from his lips.

"How're you going to do that?"

"Well," I said. "I'd made up my mind to do it even before David Calne rang me this evening. I mentioned to him casually that I had business in a day or two near Colchester—"

"What business?"

"Imaginary business," I told him, and he chuckled. George isn't such a fluent liar that he can't admire the talent in others—at least where justice is concerned.

"He rose to it as I'd hoped he would," I said. "Since I was so close, I simply must come down to that place of his at Wandham. I said I'd give him a ring some time."

"And when are you going?"

"Tomorrow as ever was," I said. "I'm going to a little town called Drowton, to a pub called the Ostlers. When it suits me I'll ring Calne from there. All I'm wanting is an excuse to learn a bit more about Guy Pallart, and Ninford's quite close."

That was all, except when George was leaving that night he gave me a dig in the ribs and one of his specious chuckles.

"You're always offering to bet a new hat about this and that. Tell you what. I'll bet you a new hat nothing ever comes of all this business."

"No betting this time, George," I said, and he gave a contemptuous snort.

"You know you're going to lose."

"No," I said slowly. Then I found myself polishing my glasses, which is a nervous trick I have when at some mental loss or on the edge of discovery. "Not because I'm going to lose, George. Because something will keep telling me I should win."

CHAPTER II
THE OLD VICARAGE

IF I HAD cared to be specious about that short stay I was proposing to make at Drowton, I should have argued something like this. I had time on my hands and I really needed a holiday. The study of men like Pallart was fascinating work. People spent money and time on their hobbies and that was precisely what I was proposing to do in the matter of Pallart.

You may wonder where the speciousness lies in anything so logical as that, and I may as well admit at once that the motive I have given—interest in my fellow men and in Guy Pallart in particular—was clouded over with various confusions and doubts. I didn't face up to them in fact till I was talking with Bill Ellice. Soon after Wharton left me that night I rang Bill at his private address and made an appointment for around eleven o'clock the next morning.

That next morning—a Wednesday—I went to the Regency and unearthed some old Army Lists. In the one for 1939 I found Guy Pallart. I won't mention his Regiment except to say that it was a famous Scottish one and that he then held the rank of Captain. I felt gratified in a way to know his Regiment, for I had wondered why a man of his obviously keen mind and alertness hadn't preferred anything to capture and the prospect of life in a prisoners' camp. There was his wound, it was true, but I didn't know when he had received that wound. But what I did know now was that his had been that famous Division that had found itself cut off on its way out of the Maginot Line. It had never had a hope of reaching Dunkirk and Pallart had never had a chance to escape.

Eleven o'clock found me with Bill Ellice in that Broad Street Detective Agency which I was still hoping one day to acquire. I said the job was highly confidential as usual and for me personally, then I told him all I knew to date about Guy Pallart.

"Is he sane or is he not?" Bill asked bluntly.

"In some ways that doesn't matter," I said. "It's what he is or is not going to do that really matters."

"All the same, it might help if we knew."

I could only shrug my shoulders.

"That's one of the things I'm going to Drowton to find out. At the moment I'm sure he's sane enough. A bee in his bonnet? Maybe, yes. Most of us have private apiaries, Bill, and yet we're regarded as perfectly sane."

"We'll take that as read," Bill said resignedly. "Now what is it you want us to do?"

"Locate a fellow officer or officers and find out what Oflag or Oflags he was in. Find out just what he did with himself there. To put it comprehensively, get his complete history during captivity."

"A pretty tall order," Bill said as he wrote it down. "Still, we'll do what we can."

I gave him a list of Pallart's brother officers in 1939 and said it might help. So might the Red Cross.

"Something else I'd like to know," he said. "You needn't tell me unless you like, but suppose you find out what murder this man Pallart is thinking of, just what do you propose to do?"

"That's a bit of a facer," I said. "I think perhaps I should go straight to him, tell him what I know, and make it clear that I have no option but to go to the police. What will emerge from that remains to be seen."

Bill nodded as if in agreement. Then he had another question. Had I any ideas on the kind of murder it might be.

"Not exactly the kind of murder," he said. "The reason for the murder—that's nearer what I mean."

"The answer's in what I've asked you to find out," I told him. "You may think me a fool, but I'm taking Pallart as he showed himself deliberately to me. I think in his own mind—even if he talked about murder—he's thinking of something more in the nature of an execution. He's proposing to step in where the law either can't or won't."

"Where's that get us?" Bill asked bluntly.

"To his life during the war," I said. "Either something happened then or something has recently arisen out of what happened then. Let me be more concrete. Suppose he knew of some treachery or treason of a fellow prisoner in that camp. Suppose he discovered some treachery before he was actually captured."

"I see that," Bill said. "And he might have been waiting for this particular officer to arrive home. Or he might have been getting all the facts together."

"There's just one other possibility for the murder," I said. "There might have been some brutal German Commandant or doctor or official in one of the camps. I'm not specially enamoured of that theory because I don't quite see how Pallart could get that particular person to England."

"But why shouldn't Pallart be going to Germany? Nothing he told you excludes that possibility."

"Yes," I said ruefully. "I'm afraid you're right. And if he eliminates some Hun or other in Germany, then it's no business of mine. If he does leave England, of course, then I shall know that that theory is true and I can wash my hands of the whole thing."

"But you hope the theory *isn't* true," Bill said dryly.

"Who made you a thought-reader?" I said, and then I had to laugh. "But you're right. What I'm hoping is that I'm going to be engaged on the most curious murder case that ever was. A murder case in reverse. Find out how and why and when and then step in before it actually happens."

Bill gave an apologetic cough.

"And if you don't mind my mentioning it, there's still the chance that there's nothing in the whole thing."

"Maybe," I said, and got to my feet. "All the same, something tells me I'm going to have quite a bit of fun. And a good run for my money."

That was that. I gave him the telephone number of the Drowton hotel, had a quick lunch in town, and an hour later set off in my car. It was only an hour and a half's steady run to Drowton. If you like maps, here is a rough one that I drew of the country beyond Drowton and around Wandham Creek.

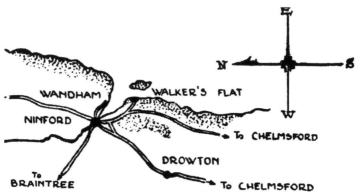

The dotted areas represent marshes or sandy hummocks covered at very low tide. Two of the roads—from Ninford to Wandham and the northern coast one to Chelmsford—are open but narrow lanes with none too good a surface. As for distances, from Ninford to Wandham is under a mile and a half, which shows that the total length of Wandham Creek is no more than three miles. From Ninford to Drowton is about six miles and the road is particularly good. Inland from the marshes the land is typically Essex, slightly undulating, fairly well wooded countryside with scattered farms and roadside cottages.

I was some ten miles from Drowton when something went wrong with my starter. I had pulled up at the roadside to admire a particular view and when I got in the car again and pressed the starter, nothing happened. I had had slight trouble before with that starter but now it seemed absolutely dead. Luckily I had halted on the top of a rise, and so, by giving the car a push and then nipping back in, I got things going again. But I didn't dare risk another stalling of the engine—like a fool I'd left the starting-handle behind—and as soon as I ran into Drowton I was looking for a garage and at the first one I saw I pulled up.

A highly intelligent mechanic diagnosed the trouble as being in the solenoid, which would mean getting an entirely new one. The upshot was that he was to make a thorough test and I was to call round in the morning. So I carried my bag the couple of hundred yards to the Ostlers and, though it was a fine September afternoon, life had for me a sudden depression. I had proposed that very evening, just before dusk, to pay a visit to Ninford, and now it looked as if a whole day would be wasted. And to spend an idle day in Drowton wasn't too good a prospect. Its population was about four thousand and after one had had a look at the church, the rest of the hour could only be dragged out by an inspection of the far from exciting shop windows. There was a cinema, but with a programme to make one shudder, for the main picture was HER NIGHT OF ROMANCE. Which was a pity. A matinée was on—Wednesday was market day—and the second house began at four-fifteen, which would have suited me after a hotel tea.

I was not to know it, but everything was going to work out for more than the best. But for that tricky solenoid I should never have had a preliminary view of Susan Beavers. What happened, in fact, was this.

Quite a charming, middle-aged couple were having tea with me in the hotel lounge and we naturally got into conversation. Then I learned that there was no need to worry about my car. A regular service of buses plied between Ninford and Drowton, and when I had a look at the time-table, I found two timings that might have been made for me. One bus left Drowton at half-past seven and another left Ninford at nine-forty-five. That meant that I might have well over an hour and a half in Ninford, and a goodish bit of it in the dark.

Dinner was at seven o'clock, which suited me exactly, and just before the bus was due to leave, I was waiting for it. But I was at the end of a queue, for the second house at the cinema was over and I began to wonder about my chances of a seat. But there was room enough. It was a double-decker and I found a seat downstairs with a fattish, elderly woman occupying the inside berth. And before the bus was out of the town, I was realising that the journey was very much of a family affair. Everybody seemed to know everybody else and the conductress knew them all. To stand on one's dignity would have been not only foolish but impossible. Gossip was being exchanged between back seats and front, and the conductress herself had a nice line in wit. As we were approaching a hamlet about a mile out of the town, a woman asked to be dropped just short of the corner.

"Don't you worry, Mrs. Quick," the conductress told her. "Which would you like? Your front door or your back?"

The joke must have been old but everyone laughed. Then when the bus was on the move once more and there was a bit more room, the gossiping began again.

"How were the pictures today, Mrs. Beavers?" the conductress was asking, and suddenly everyone seemed to be listening.

"Very good, my dear. Very good."

The speaker was obviously an elderly woman but I could catch a glimpse of only her head and shoulders.

"Plenty of love in it, wasn't there?"

The old lady gave a snort.

"And why not, my dear? A little bit of love never did no one any harm."

Everyone laughed. My seat companion leaned towards me and whispered.

"A wonderful old lady, she is. Never misses a Wednesday at the pictures. Comes all alone from Ninford and has tea with her daughter and then goes to the pictures. Enjoys it all too."

"Good luck to her," I said, and I could hardly hear myself speak, for something must have been said up in front where the old lady was and everyone was laughing.

"You wouldn't take her for much over fifty," my neighbour was going on. "And how old do you think she is? Just gone eighty! And as spry as ever she was."

Another moment or two and she was getting off the bus. I was sorry about that for I was thinking of asking her about Ninford and the old vicarage. But there was more room now in the bus and I moved to a forward seat. I knew we were nearing Ninford and I wanted to ask the conductress just where the old vicarage was. But the conductress was engaged in a conversation with old Mrs. Beavers and her seat companion. I was in the seat immediately behind.

"I can't say as I mind them gangster pictures," Mrs. Beavers was saying. "We don't see much life in Ninford, you know, and we might as well see a little when we go out."

Her voice was brisk and lively, like herself, and she had the most infectious little laugh.

"I like the musicals," the conductress said.

"The musicals? What are they, my dear?"

"You know. Singing and bands, and so on."

"Oh them!" the old lady told her scornfully. "I don't understand half what they're singing about. All this—what do they call it—boop-a-doop-doop."

The conductress seemed tickled to death. Mrs. Beavers' seat companion thought that they sang because they were supposed to be in love. Mrs. Beavers snorted.

"I didn't do no singing when I was in love—as they call it. Too much worried whether I was going to get him or not."

Then she was looking hurriedly round. But she needn't have been alarmed. The driver apparently knew who was aboard and the bus was already slowing and Mrs. Beavers was getting to her feet. She was shorter than I had thought: little over five feet, perhaps, but upright as a ramrod. She had a round face and though her body was slight, the cheeks were plump and rosy. Her eyes were twinkling as she said good-night.

"See you Wednesday," the conductress told her.

"I don't know, my dear. I may be earlier Wednesday. Going to have my hair done."

The bus moved on.

"She's as good as a tonic," the conductress said. "And will she let anyone help her out of the bus? Not she! Wonder what she's having done to her hair?"

"She's very proud of her hair," the other woman said, and then I noticed we were at the first houses of Ninford.

"Would you mind telling me where the old vicarage is?" I asked the conductress when I had got to my feet.

"Just back there," she said. "Where we last stopped."

Her finger went to the bell but I said it didn't matter and I'd get off at the usual stop. And I was remembering something that David Calne had told me. That Mrs. Beavers, then, was Pallart's ancient retainer, as he had called her, and that was all I had time to remember. The bus was slowing and it drew up outside a pub called the Wheatsheaf.

When it moved off I had a look at the lie of the land. Ninford lay in a slight depression and before me was the rising ground down which the bus had come to the village. The church tower stood clear among the elms three hundred yards back, and just beyond it was the Old Vicarage. I had caught a glimpse of it as we had waited for Mrs. Beavers to descend, and again as we had moved off. It was a typical early Georgian house, disfigured, as I thought, with ivy. It had twin double gates for a car to enter and leave along the semi-circular drive, and it seemed to have ample lawns and plenty of trees.

Then it struck me that I must look conspicuous standing there peering about me, and the last thing I wanted was to run into Guy Pallart. Dusk was barely in the sky, so I made my way into the pub. Only one man was there, besides the landlord, when I asked for my tankard of bitter.

I didn't want to do much talking in that pub. Ninford was a village of about four hundred inhabitants, each of whom would know the business of everyone else. For all I knew Guy Pallart might drop in, and the landlord might say, 'There was a man in here the other night asking about you.' When my description followed, then Pallart would have good cause to wonder. Or would he be merely cynically amused?

There was some talk, of course, though I dropped out of it when another couple of men came in. Then I pricked my ears.

"Pity we ain't got a fourth or we might have a game of darts," one man said.

"What's wrong with a single-handed game. You play Harry, here."

"Don't seem so friendly," the other protested.

"Frenchy may be in at any time now," the landlord said.

"He don't often miss a night. Soon as dinner's over, in he slips."

"This is just about his time," the landlord said and then the man who'd been in when I arrived said he'd just seen the Major go out in his car. The Colchester Road, and he was driving himself.

"Arthur was digging in his garden not so long ago," the third man said, "so he couldn't be driving him. Wouldn't be surprised if he drop in in a minute or two."

Arthur, I thought might be the chauffeur I'd seen in town. Frenchy was probably the chef.

"I used to know a Mr. French round this way," I remarked to the man nearest me. "You were talking about a Mr. French, weren't you?"

He laughed.

"Not a Mr. French. Frenchy's the name we have for that chef that Major Pallart have. We don't call him that to his face, of course. George is his name."

"Georges," the landlord said importantly.

"Well George or Georges or whatever it is. He don't seem to mind. Rare good-tempered chap."

"And don't he throw a rare good dart!"

"What about his English?" I asked.

"That ain't half bad."

"I wish I could speak French as well," the landlord said.

"Oh, Frenchy's all right. He know enough to order a pint of bitter. And he know his way about the dart-board."

The talk shifted to gardening. Another quarter of an hour went by. I finished my second tankard, gave the room a good night and went out. Now dusk had almost gone but I turned left towards the bridge and not by the way I had come. I heard the voices of two men and then their footsteps stopped.

"Coming along to the Wheatsheaf?" one said.

"Not tonight, Arthur. Tomorrow, perhaps."

"Well, cheerio, Frank."

"Cheerio, Arthur."

I stepped back in a yard entrance and Arthur passed within two yards of me. The night was not dark. The sky above me was thick with stars and the darkness had a kind of luminosity and I saw him clearly. After a moment or two I followed him to the Wheatsheaf. He went inside and I saw him still more clearly in the light of the opened door. Then I went on up the slope.

I didn't know just what I wanted or hoped to see at the old vicarage. Perhaps I was doing something for the mere sake of doing it or carrying out the usual routine of creating a background. Or since there's no fool like an old fool, maybe I had a sudden urge for a spot of adventure, even if that adventure was no more than making a private survey of another man's house and garden. Not that there was any great risk or daring. If I were seen I had only to say that I was staying in Drowton and thought I'd pay a belated call after dinner, and had missed the path in the dark. A footling excuse no doubt, but adequate.

As I neared the house I walked on the grass verge. The first main gate was open wide. Pallart, as I'd heard, was out with the car, and on his return he would wish to drive straight in. I nipped round the gatepost and my steps made never a sound on the mown grass of the lawn. I stooped till I could see the dark bulk of the house against the sky and the stars. A minute or two and I could distinguish individual windows and the greyish-white pillars of the porch were clear.

As I neared the house I saw that the drive continued straight on, and to what I guessed must be the back premises and the garage. It was tricky going that way and I had to tiptoe for fear my footsteps should be heard on the gravel. To my right was the west wing of the house and to my left a shrubbery. The house itself was in total darkness but just as I recognised the garage and was nearing its open doors, I saw a light a few yards along the house and it seemed to be coming through an open door. At once I stepped back and wriggled my way among the laurels of the shrubbery.

A darkness crossed the light. Then I saw something white approaching me in the air. Someone was humming or singing quietly and in a moment I caught the words.

> *Auprès de ma blonde*
> *Qu'il fait beau, fait beau, fait beau . . .*

The footsteps neared and I knew it was the French chef. That white thing in the air had been his cap, and just as I realised that, there was another voice, and coming from the opened door which he had just left.

"Mr. Loret!"

Loret—that was his name—whipped round.

"Allo!"

"See that Mr. Guy has his coffee."

"I will see," he called back to her.

"I'm going to bed now."

"Good night and good dreams."

There was a smile in his voice. Her voice came tartly.

"Never you mind about dreams. You tell Mr. Guy he's to drink that coffee."

The door closed. Loret began singing gently to himself again and his voice was lost towards the gate. I tiptoed out and along the side of the house and past the closed side door. A glint of glass from the greenhouse caught my eye and I was in a closed yard bounded by out-buildings. Near the house was a side door in the wall. It was ajar and I went through and stood for a moment with my back to it. Now there was a choice of two ways. A wide path ran by the east end of the house to the front and the main drive. A second path led along another shrubbery and on its right was a great stretch of lawn—the same lawn that fronted the house and ran for a good fifty yards along the Drowton Road.

I took that narrow path and then almost at once I stopped, for a flash of light had come from the main gate by which I had first entered. Then I knew that Loret was lighting a cigarette, but I stood motionless all the same, and soon I heard his steps on the road. They halted and there was silence for a long minute. They turned back and I knew he was making his way to the house again. I thought he had been listening for the sound of Pallart's returning car.

I moved on along that path and soon I had shrubbery on both sides of me. But only for a yard or two. Then I was up against a new blackness that turned out to be a kind of summer-house. There I drew back my glove and the luminated dial of my wrist-watch told me that in another five and twenty minutes I should have to catch my bus. It was very dark there in the thick shrubbery and as my hand went up to feel the side of that summer-house, I found I was feeling the glass of a window. But the walls were brick and when I moved round to the front I could discern in the better light that the roof was thatch and that a verandah ran the full length.

I listened for a moment and then tiptoed to the door and tried it. It was locked. I peered at one of the two large windows and found that its blind was drawn down inside. The other window was the same and that struck me as odd. And just why I hadn't time to assess, for it was just then that I heard the sound of a car.

Its lights were coming towards the house from the village. They turned to the open gate and before the car was through it, they were switched off. The car moved quietly on. It passed the porch and was making apparently for the Drowton-side gate. Then it stopped and I was nipping back to the summerhouse side.

Two figures emerged from the car. One was limping, and his hand held the arm of a somewhat shorter man. They were making for the summerhouse. Steps were on the verandah.

"*Un moment—*"

That was Pallart's whisper, and then there was the sound of a key in a lock.

"*Vite alors!*"

That was Pallart's whisper again. A light flashed on inside the summerhouse. Pallart was inside already and I caught a glimpse of the second man. He was hatless and his blond hair looked paper white. And the clothes he was wearing were those of a German prisoner of war!

It was in a fraction of a second, perhaps, that I saw all that, and in the same second the door was closed again and everywhere was darkness. In a flash my ear was against the brickwork of the wall but never a sound could I hear. Then as I half-turned, I saw something else. A man—and he was almost on me—was running towards the summerhouse and his feet made no sound on the grass of the lawn. My heart went to my mouth and I stood like a rabbit before a stoat. But I needn't have worried. It was not with me that this newcomer was concerned. He was tiptoeing with infinite care across the verandah, and I saw him kneel by a window corner.

It was the window furthest from me, and he seemed to be manipulating something at the window corner. I saw an infinitesimal streak of light, and then it was hidden by his head. And then nothing happened and the moments went slowly by. The snooper was motionless at his peep-hole and all at once I remembered my bus. In another five minutes it would be gone!

For a moment I thought that I'd walk the six miles back to Drowton, and then I knew I should be a fool. Tomorrow, I could tell myself, would be another day, and with that I began making my way along that narrow path again. Then I took a risk and moved more quickly and at the side door I halted and listened, but there was never a sound, and in the gloom beyond, the summerhouse was now invisible. So I didn't take the way I had come but went like a streak across the open lawn.

I took the grass verge until I was well away from the house and then jog-trotted down the hill towards the Wheatsheaf. As I came round the bend there was no sign of the bus, and it was then that I had a sudden idea. So I opened the pub door and gave a quick look in. Luckily the landlord had his back to me and the dart-board faced the other way. Four men—Arthur among them—were playing and two other men were watching. I closed the door as gently again and almost at once I saw the approaching bus.

It was a conductor who punched my return ticket, and there were only three of us in the downstair part of the bus. I changed my mind and made my way upstairs and there lighted my pipe, and for once in my life I was utterly at a loss. Usually I'm never at a loss for a theory, in fact my fluency is one of the things that exasperate George Wharton when we're working on a case. Not that George has cause to complain. At the worst computation my theories are right a third of the time, and that's a good average, and I'm the only one who should be exasperated. For when a theory proves wrong, George always reminds me that that theory was mine. But if there's a certain amount of value to be attached to it, then it becomes 'ours', and if it proves a winner, then it's more than likely to become George's own.

But now I was flummoxed. What the devil was Pallart doing with a German prisoner? Or had my bat eyes deceived me in that more than tricky light? And why the secrecy of that blacked-out summerhouse? And, above all, who was the man who had waited for the car, and had peered through that window corner? He couldn't have been Arthur, the chauffeur—that was the only thing of which I was certain.

I thought of a lot of things as that bus moved on in the quiet of the countryside. And there was one thing which I was wishing I'd done, and which it seemed I must somehow contrive to do. I'd had the chance and, like a fool, I'd missed it. Calne had rung me and asked for my opinion of Pallart. It was then that I should have said, "By the way, did you ever hear him talk any of that murder stuff before?" If the answer was yes, then one would have to consider the matter of an obsession. If it were no, then a wholly new set of problems arose. Just what those problems were I was to realise a bit too late.

I HAD the whole day on my hands, so I breakfasted late. Then I lingered out the time over the newspapers and did my crosswords, and it was about ten o'clock when I went round to the garage. The mechanic had a reasonable report for me. There was a faulty connection to do with the solenoid but the starter was operating nine times out of ten. If it went out of action, all I had to do was to give the solenoid a smart tap and the connection would be made again. But he strongly advised me to have a new solenoid in any case, and I gave him the order.

I paid his bill and was moving out backwards to give the road to the man who was getting the car out for me, when a voice sounded at my ear.

"Good God, sir, what are you doing here!"

It was Guy Pallart, and it wasn't hard for me to simulate surprise.

"Good lord!" I said. "And if it comes to that, what about you? What are you doing here?"

"Dammit, I live here," he told me amusedly. "At least I live at Ninford which is only six miles away."

I explained about the car and he seemed most interested. I also said I had business at Colchester but as I'd had to put up at the Ostlers on account of the car and had found it so comfortable, I was thinking of staying on there till my business was finished. That oughtn't to be more than a day or two.

"You must drop in on your way," he said. Then he seemed to have an idea. "You coming back from Colchester this evening? If so, why not drop in for a meal. Come as early as you like and we can have a yarn."

I made the usual protestations and pleaded that I couldn't get to Ninford till about half-past six.

"Excellent," he said. "We feed at seven. I'll be on the lookout for you."

He'd come to Drowton to do some urgent shopping, he said, and would have to be getting back at once. A nephew was arriving that afternoon for a day or two's stay, and there'd be a young Czech doctor whom he'd known in Paris.

"He's an interesting cove," he said, "though you mayn't think so."

Then he gave that incipient salute of his, said he'd be seeing me, and away he limped. I drove my car to the hotel yard and once more, though the morning was the perfection of early autumn, I was feeling an annoying depression. Pallart, you see, had been so vastly different. Charming, delightfully mannered—yes, but perfectly normal. No cynical quips or ironic remarks about crime. My presence in Drowton and my explanation accepted with never a lifted eyebrow. Never a mention of our first meeting at the Regency or the vaguest of references to that talk we'd had. No mention of David Calne, though the two had seemed very friendly, and Calne was living almost on Pallart's doorstep. Maybe then, I thought uneasily, Pallart is dissociating himself, consciously or unconsciously, from that talk at the Regency. He's showing that there can be a Philip drunk and a Philip sober. In other words, he's taking it for granted that I knew the murder talk must be a leg-pull.

That depression didn't altogether go when I remembered something else. That morning I had seen bus loads of German prisoners passing through Drowton on their way to the various farms of the countryside. At the hotel a fellow guest had told me that some farmers had permission to board the prisoners. Quite a good few prisoners, in fact, were living in. And if that were so, it made far less of a mystery of that blond German I'd seen with Pallart at the summerhouse. There might be a score of reasons why Pallart should want to make use of him. And then I cheered up as I remembered two other things: the haste with which Pallart had hustled the German through the door and the fact that the windows were carefully blacked out. And there was also the more than queer episode of the crouching snooper. It would need something unusual to explain *him* away.

After lunch I went to Colchester by a roundabout route. I hadn't seen the town since I was stationed there for a time in the last war and I found it little changed. I had tea and watched a game of bowls in a park and it was just before six o'clock when I set off for Ninford. It was half-past to the dot when I passed the Wheatsheaf. A hundred yards up the slope a roadman was trimming the grass verge. I pulled the car up.

"Can you tell me where Major Pallart lives?"

"You're right on it, sir," the man said. "Just where them elms are."

I thanked him and added that I had business with the Major. "What's he like?" I said.

"Major Pallart? A rare nice gentleman, sir. One o' the very best."

"Married, is he?"

"Oh no, sir. He ain't married. They reckon he ain't never got over that young lady of his dying when he was a prisoner."

"That was bad luck," I said, and heaved a sigh. "Well, I must be getting along or the Major will wonder what's happened to me."

So Pallart had been engaged and had lost his fiancée while he was in a German prison camp. Maybe that was the cause of his cynical outlook on life, though I confess it was David Calne who had harped on that side of Pallart's character, for I hadn't seen overmuch of it myself. *German prison camp.* I thought of that again, and the vague connection there seemed to be with the German prisoner of the previous night. Then I realised I was overshooting the entrance to the house and I hastily trod on the brake. The gate was open and there were three deckchairs on the lawn before the porch. Pallart came across to greet me.

The two men were standing waiting.

"Travers, this is Dr. Kales." Kales—he pronounced the name as Kalesh—gave a shy little bow and a how-do-you-do.

He was a black-haired, nervous man of about Pallart's age, clean-shaven with a little scar on the side of one nostril. He seemed stiff in his joints and awkward with his hands.

"My nephew, Richard Brace."

Brace looked no more than twenty-two or three. He was rather sallow looking with a decidedly weak chin and I could see no resemblance whatever to Pallart. He also seemed none too self-assured. It seemed curious too, to think of Pallart as an uncle, but maybe Brace was finding that uncle rather overwhelming. He gave the usual how-do-you-do and a bit of a grin, and was about to say something else when Pallart cut testily in:

"Get Mr. Travers a drink, Richard. Kales, you get another chair. There're some in the hall. The hall—there. What'll you have, Travers? Whisky?"

I said that would be admirable. Kales appeared with a chair and the four of us sat down in the pleasant shade of the house.

"It's been a grand day," I said.

Pallart agreed. Brace said that when an English day was good, it *was* good.

"You living near here?" I asked him.

"Unfortunately no," he said. "I'm working in town. In North London."

You had only to be in Pallart's company to know that he was an aristocrat to the finger-tips, as they say, or county to the last inch of him. He had a natural suavity and almost an elegance and there was nothing forced about his charming manner. But this nephew of his wasn't quite off the top shelf, I was thinking, though why I couldn't quite say, unless it were that he looked callow and awkward.

"Dick is an incipient house-agent," Pallart said. "I hope he sticks to it."

"There's certainly money in it," I said. "And what about you, Dr. Kales? You know England pretty well?"

"I have spent some years here," he told me with careful intonation. "But I don't speak the language very well."

"But you do," I said. "And what about your own country these days?"

"It is not a good country," he said, and gave a mournful shake of the head. "It is—what you say?—too political."

"You've hit the nail on the head," I said. "But I'd like to see Prague again. It must be twenty-five years since I was there."

"It is still much the same," Kales said, and then Pallart was getting to his feet.

"Like a clean-up before another drink?" he was asking me. "Dinner should be on in a quarter of an hour."

He took me to the downstair cloak-room and when I came out suggested I might like a look at the garden while it was still light. We went out by a side door and into the kitchen garden first.

"Too big for one gardener," he said. "The devil of it is you just can't get help."

"What about a German prisoner?" I asked casually. "Aren't they available nowadays?"

I didn't look at him though I felt his eyes suddenly on me.

"I did toy with the idea," he said. "But this place isn't regarded as essential work. If I turned it into a market-garden, that'd be different. I may do so even yet. Not that I'm absolutely desperate. I have a man of sorts. Lucky to get him too. David Calne put me on to him."

"How *is* Calne?" I said.

"I expect he's flourishing," he said. "Nice chap, Calne. Damn plucky one too. You know what he did in the war?"

"Parachuted into France, wasn't he?"

He nodded as he opened the side door for me—the door by which I'd made for the summerhouse in the dark of the previous night.

"Sorry we can't show you many flowers. Bad time of the year. Those dahlias are rather nice?"

We were moving towards the summerhouse.

"This is quite an ornate place," I said. "Quite well built."

"It's a white elephant nowadays," he said and gave a contemptuous sort of wave of the hand. "All very well in the old days when there was a tennis court in front of it. No more tennis for me. I used to be rather good once, too."

"You look the type," I said, and then I was admiring a bed of pink roses. Then I noticed that the chairs had gone from the front of the house. He was looking that way too, and afterwards I knew I ought to have anticipated his question.

"You any children, by the way?"

"Unluckily, no," I said. "I do own up to having been wet nurse to nieces and nephews in my time."

"Funny you should have said that," he said.

"Why?"

"Well,"—he paused and frowned—"I don't know that there'll be time to tell you."

We moved on towards the house and then halted again. "What did you think of Brace? My nephew? I should say, my only nephew?"

"An awkward question," I said. "Perhaps you'll let me counter with another. What sort of answer do you want?"

"Well—frankly . . . well, what do you think of him?"

I temporised too.

"He doesn't seem the athletic type."

"He isn't," he said bluntly. "He's been a damn young fool in his time. Not that the fault was all his. He doesn't know it, but I asked him down here because—"

There was the sound of the gong.

"We'll leave it till some other time," he said. "But I'd like your advice. I may have to take pretty drastic action and I'm damned if I like doing it off my own bat."

We moved on towards the house and then suddenly his hand went to my arm, and as we halted again, he was giving an apologetic smile. There was more in it too than that. It was quizzical and warm and friendly.

"I wonder why I should have worried you with my family affairs? Damn bad manners on my part. But you don't think I asked you here to—well, to make use of you?"

"I never had any such thought," I told him, and I hoped my smile was as friendly as his own. "Yours was a perfectly natural question. Besides, I can't imagine there're many people in Ninford in whom you would care to confide."

"How right you are," he said. "But you ought to give yourself some credit too. Funny thing to say after knowing you only a couple of days, but ever since I left you this morning I haven't been able to get away from the idea that you were the very chap I ought to talk to—about Richard, I mean."

He broke off with a grimace of humorous exasperation.

"I forgot that damned gong. There's Susan after us already."

Susan Beavers was at the front porch, and looking like a family servant of fifty years ago. Quite a dignified old lady she was in her long black uniform buttoned high at the neck, and the white apron spotless against it. She was wearing no cap and there were little yellow streaks in her mass of silvery hair.

"No panic, Susan," Pallart told her amusedly.

"It's not fair, Mr. Guy," she began. "All that time to cook a meal and have it ready for the table—"

"This is Susan," Pallart broke in. "Worth her weight in gold, even if she has got a horrible temper. Susan, this is Mr. Travers."

I thought there was an impish look in her eye as she gave me a little bob of a bow.

"He's the one with the temper, Susan," I said. "Don't you let him bully you."

"I'll see to that, sir," she told me grimly. "Come on in both of you. Food all spoiling and . . ."

Her voice trailed grumblingly away.

"She's a great lass," Pallart told me. "I hope to God she lives to be a hundred."

In a room on the left—part drawing-room, part lounge—Kales and Brace were having a drink.

"Sorry, Uncle," Brace said, "but I didn't like to disturb you and Mr. Travers."

"That's all right, my boy," he told him amiably. "Sherry, Travers? Or perhaps we'd better take it in with us and sample it with the soup."

It was a quiet meal, and a good one. We had a boiled fowl and an apple tart and a really superb savoury. As for the talk, it might be described as placid. Pallart was an excellent host and garrulous, like myself. Young Brace seemed to me a bit nervous. Just why his uncle had asked him down I hadn't the least notion, but I did have a suspicion that Brace was aware that the Riot Act was shortly going to be read. Kales was quiet and shy, which was not unexpected in a foreigner paying—as I gathered—his first visit among strangers in a strange place. But he told me a whole lot about Prague. He had been there, it seemed, when the Germans marched in, and I gathered that he had escaped to France and from there to England. Like most continental intellectuals he spoke several languages. German was his weakest, he said. I had the opinion that if he could be got out of that constant nervous awareness of his, he would be quite an interesting chap. He was not a doctor of medicine, by the way. Physics was his line, and that made me think that he was or had been one of the hush-hush foreigners employed by our Government. If so, his nervousness might be explained by a dread of opening his mouth too wide.

It was Susan who brought in the coffee tray and Pallart whispered that this was ancient ritual.

"There's only one cup each," she announced. "I told them we should want some more milk and of course they had to go and forget it. About time they had a piece of my mind."

"A really excellent meal, Susan," I said. "Perhaps you'll tell the chef I said so."

"Tell him to come in, Susan," Pallart told her. "He'll be very bucked about it. By the way, I ought to tell you that Susan's a magnificent cook herself."

"Get along with you, Mr. Guy," she told him, but was beaming nevertheless.

I was realising why, to the punctilious Calne, things at Ninford had seemed free and easy. But Pallart was telling me about Susan. She'd become a member of the Pallart household at fourteen and had left to get married. She'd had a daughter and then her husband had died. As soon as her daughter left school and went into domestic service, Susan returned to the old vicarage and she'd been there ever since.

I recognised Georges Loret as soon as he stepped into the room. He was wearing his chef's hat and had apparently donned a clean apron. He was just above medium height, tremendously sturdy, and with a smiling, fattish face with a streak of moustache.

"Messieurs?" he said enquiringly, and spread his palms.

"There you are, Georges," Pallart said. "We've all enjoyed your dinner and we wanted to tell you so."

Loret bowed and told us in French that he was at our service, as always.

"A magnificent meal," I said.

Loret thanked me and backed out with a face all smiles.

"What about a glass of port?" Pallart called to him. "Or am I too late?"

"Monsieur will have his little joke," Loret told him in English, but was evidently pleased as Punch.

"Take the decanter in," Pallart said. "Give Arthur a drink too. I expect he's going to earn it."

Out the decanter went. Pallart was still chuckling.

"I expect you think we're all mad here," he told me. "In my father's time things were a bit more ceremonious. I'm all for the other way."

"Hasn't one got to be these days?" I said. "Domestic help is hard enough to get and harder to keep."

"Don't think me rude," he said, "but that isn't so here. I'm lucky perhaps but I do like to think it'd take a goodish deal to get our people out of the house. Look at Susan. This is her home and she's boss in it—and why not? Then there's Arthur—that's Arthur Friske, my old batman. He's got a cottage in the village, but he spends most of his time here. When there's any sort of show, like tonight, he comes in and lends a hand with the wash-ing-up and so on. Happy as a bug in a rug."

We were moving out to the hall. I'd refused a cigar and Pallart was passing round his lighter for the cigarettes.

"What about taking Kales for a short walk, Dick?" he asked his nephew. "Go round by the river. Would you like a walk, Kales?"

Kales said he would love a walk if it wasn't too far. Pallart and I went on through the porch to the lawn. It was a lovely quiet evening and still warm. There was a rustic seat in the lee of the tall clipped hedge and we sat there till the dusk was there and the midges became a pest. Kales and Brace had returned after a short half-hour and were in the house. Pallart had been telling me how he had run across Georges Loret in Paris and had induced him to come to Ninford. Then he had apologised again and reverted to the question of the nephew. I heard the family history.

Guy Pallart's sister Helen was ten years older than himself. He hadn't known of the scandal at the time but she'd horrified the family by marrying Henry Brace. He was a composer, claimed by his wife and himself to be a neglected and unlucky genius, but given to lifting the bottle. He made something of a living by hack conducting and was not above giving music lessons, but it was Pallart's father who in the long run kept the family reasonably solvent. It was he who had sent Richard to his school and afterwards to Cambridge.

"Henry was a bad egg," Pallart said, "but my sister was so besotted that she just wouldn't see it. I was in the pen, of course, when everything happened. My father died and he did the very thing he oughtn't to have done—left her her money personally and not on trust. She was killed not long afterwards in a London blitz and Brace proceeded to drink himself to death on the money. Richard left Cambridge and there was I, only getting the news through the solicitors and not knowing what the devil to do for the best. When I did get home and ran Richard to earth, what do you think he was doing?"

I couldn't even guess.

"He was playing in a dance band up north!"

I gave a non-committal grunt, though evidently the discovery had been a nasty shock.

"I had the devil of a job to make him see sense," Pallart went on. "The whole thing was repulsively indescribable. You probably guess the life such people lead. Still, I got him out of it and up to town, and I arranged an allowance. After all, he's my only living relative."

"What was he like at school and Cambridge?"

"Never did a damn of anything," he told me. "Nothing reprehensible. Just slacked generally. Supposed to have a weak chest and that kept him out of the Services."

"And what's the particular trouble now?"

It was difficult to explain, he said, unless one appreciated the fact that Richard was, as it were, the Pallart heir. His uncle had asked him what he wished to do and he finally announced that he'd like to take up music seriously. So while Pallart didn't regard that choice too favourably, he wanted his nephew to be steered rather than pushed, he arranged for special coaching for the entrance examination to one of the best Schools of Music. Then Richard suddenly announced that he'd changed his mind and wanted to be a house-agent. He'd renewed the acquaintance, apparently, of someone he'd known at school and this fellow was getting him into his father's firm.

"I had lunch with this chap and Richard in town and everything seemed all right," Pallart told me. "Richard isn't anything of a correspondent but whenever he did write he was liking things pretty well. Then a few days ago I happened to discover in a roundabout way that Richard was spending a hell of a lot of money—far more than what I allow him and what he's getting as a beginner from his firm."

"You think something fishy's happening?"

"I'm damn sure of it," he said. "That's why I asked him to run down here and see me, though he doesn't know it yet." He frowned. "Now you see my problem. I can't go on doing things if I can't trust him. There's a streak of craftiness in him which I absolutely abominate. He gets it from his father. But I can't go on for ever. I've either got to be dead sure of him and he's got to show himself worth it, or else I'm cutting him right out. I'm damned if I'm leaving this place and whatever I have to be chucked down the drain."

"I think you're right," I said. "And you're going to put that up to him?"

"It's got beyond that," he said. "He's had it put up to him already. It depends on what he tells me whether or not I do as I said. Let him go to the devil his own way. Not that I think he'd ever starve. He's clever enough in his own disreputable way."

It was then that the midges drove us indoors. As we came into the hall there was the sound of music from the lounge. A low, husky voice was crooning to what sounded like a guitar accompaniment underneath. I thought it was a woman but it turned out to be a man. Pallart looked at me and his face was a thundercloud. Then he was striding forward. The words rasped out before I was in the room.

"Damnation, Richard, haven't I made it clear enough that I object to that bilge in this house. Turn it off at once!" Kales had got rather sheepishly to his feet.

"Sorry, Kales," Pallart said. "I hope I'm not being rude but I happen to feel rather strongly this—"

The words wouldn't come and he waved an impatient hand. Then who should appear but Susan. I think she had whisked out of the room and had heard what was said.

"Now don't you blame no one but me, Mr. Guy," she said. "It was me as much as anyone who wanted the wireless on."

"But you've got your own wireless in the kitchen?"

"Mr. Loret always want them French stations on," she told him, as one might explain to a child. "And it wasn't rubbish either we were listening to—"

"Oh?" said Pallart ironically. "And what was it?"

"It's what they call The Voice In The Night," she told him. "It's only a quarter of an hour once a week on the Light Programme."

"The Voice In The Night—my God!" His face screwed up as in pain.

"Well, I like it," she told him. "It isn't all that boop-a-doop-doop stuff. And he's got a rare nice voice."

"Oh, my God!" Pallart said again. His shoulders shrugged in a gesture of hopelessness, and he turned to the door.

"Sorry about all that," he told me when we were in the hall again, and just then the telephone went. He gave a quick, 'Pardon me', and I went on to the dining-room. It was a good five minutes before he came in.

"Extraordinary thing," he said. "That was David Calne. He was suggesting we should have a day in that new boat of his. He was staggered to hear you were here."

The weather report had apparently announced that fine weather might be expected for a few days, and Calne was proposing a trip along the coast.

"When's it to come off?" I said.

"Tomorrow," he said. "And you're in it. I said I thought you'd like to go and you'd ring him the first thing in the morning if you couldn't make it."

"I think I'd like it very much," I said, "though I'm the world's worst sailor. What time is all this, by the way?"

"We're to be at Wandham at about eleven," he said. "I said I'd be bringing Kales and Richard and I rather gathered we'd be lunching on board."

That seemed an excellent moment for saying good night. As I told him, if I was having a day's holiday, I'd have to get back to Drowton and make an arrangement or two. I said good night to Richard Brace and Dr. Kales—each looking none too happy over a couple of books in the lounge—and Pallart went out with me to the car.

"I'm afraid we haven't given you too good a time," he said. "Perhaps you'll have a better one tomorrow."

"On the contrary, I don't know when I've enjoyed an evening more," I told him. "And I'm looking forward to tomorrow."

"I still think it was unpardonable of me to pester you with that nephew of mine," he said.

"Nonsense," I said. "I regard it as a compliment that you should have confided in me as you did."

I switched on the headlights and I could see the gloomy shake of his head.

"Which reminds me," I said, and tried to make it sound flippant. "What about that other confidential matter?"

"Confidential matter?"

"Yes. Just a little matter of a private murder."

"Oh, that," he said slowly. Then he let out a breath. "I was hoping you'd forgotten about that."

Then he stepped back. It seemed a kind of gesture of finality and I could no longer see his face. I pressed the starter and it worked. The gate was open and I waved my hand as the car moved on.

As I drove towards Drowton that night I had a feeling that was part shame and part humility, and neither could be wholly explained. But Pallart had been the perfect host and there was the knowledge that I had somehow forced my way into his house and hospitality. I had loved the house, too, and its occupants, and I even felt no special dislike of the sallow-looking, weak-chinned Richard, for after all he doubtless had a point of view which I should never hear. As for that talk in the Regency, it was seeming little more now than provocative chatter over a glass of excellent port. And yet somehow it was not to be dismissed as easily as that, and then again, as I neared Drowton, I was sure that Wharton had been right. What I couldn't possibly surmise was that in a very few hours I was to know a great deal more. And curiously enough, I was to know a great deal less.

Chapter IV
THE RIGHT MURDER?

I woke earlier than usual and because I had something on my mind. David Calne ought to be rung in good time, so I slipped into a dressing-gown as soon as I'd had my eight o'clock cup of tea and went down to the telephone. I was expecting he'd be up, and he was.

"Delighted you're coming," he said. "Why not make it early and have a preliminary look round?"

"What do you mean by early?" I asked him.

"Half-past nine, or tennish?"

I said that would suit me fine, and then as soon as I'd rung off, I knew I'd been too precipitate. My car would be passing Pallart's very door and it had ample room for the four of us. Now, if his party was arriving at eleven, he'd have to bring his own car. Then I realised that Wandham was the shortest of trips from Ninford and there wouldn't be much of a waste of petrol.

As I ate my breakfast that morning I was making up my mind to leave Drowton the following day. Night had brought, if not counsel, at least a settled point of view, and I was now of the opinion that in the matter of that talk at the Regency I had taken both Pallart and myself too seriously. Why I was now of that opinion was largely because of those last words that Pallart had spoken the previous night. "I was hoping you'd forgotten all about it," he had said, and referring to that murder talk, and it seemed to me now that what he had implied was that he had been guilty at the Regency of a certain amount of idle chatter which he wasn't too keen on recalling.

Another matter about which I was thinking was the trouble between Pallart and his nephew, Richard Brace. As I've said, I'd heard only one side of the argument, and at breakfast that morning I was trying to see something of the other side. I held no particular brief for young Brace. I didn't like him or dislike him, and if only because we had precious little in common, but it did strike me that even a youth who'd only mooned about at a good school and at Cambridge must at least have acquired something that might go to the making of a man. His home environment must have been pretty bad and the fact that he was earning his own living when Pallart came home from Germany, showed, to my way of thinking, that he wasn't quite the wash-out that Pallart was disposed to imagine him.

I've always been irritated by people who take themselves too seriously, and Pallart certainly was showing snobbishness and even horror at what he considered a loss of family face. To play in a dance band isn't quite the profession I'd choose for a nephew of my own, but it is at least a step above crooning. I remembered that dreadful voice we'd heard the previous night— The Voice In The Night, Susan had called it ecstatically—and I remembered, too, a remark I had once made myself, and not, I should add, in a drawing-room. Someone asked for my opinion of crooners and I said I'd cheerfully witness their execution. Young Brace looked callow, I could tell myself, and even a trifle shifty, but looks aren't a true test. And then I was thinking that during the day's cruise I might have the chance of a word with him myself. Just a tactful lead or two and I might be hearing his own side of the story.

Just after half-past nine I was on my way. Calne had said we mightn't be home till dark, and though the morning gave promise of a hot and even sultry day, I took a sweater with me. As I passed the Old Vicarage at Ninford I saw Pallart's car standing at the porch. Five minutes later I was nearing Wandham. Even before I reached the hamlet, the narrow road was making its way over marshland and its metalling was beginning to peter out. To my left was a tiny church and half a dozen houses, so I took the fork to the right where a long white building stood just above the Creek. Just short of it I was on a private concreted road and then I caught sight of Calne himself. He waved to show me where to park the car.

"This is more than a bungalow," I said. "I'd call it a good-ish-sized house."

"I don't know," he said. "When you consider that Jack Winder and his wife have their own quarters, that doesn't leave too much for me."

He had breakfasted very early and now he was suggesting a cup of coffee. While Annie Winder was bringing it we had a look over Calne's side of the house. I preferred to call it a house, even if it was on only one floor.

The Winders' quarters, he said, consisted of a kitchen, living-room and two bedrooms. The kitchen was next to his own lounge-dining-room by which we went in. Beyond it was a cloak-room and then what he called a work-room, in the corner of which was a dark-room. He showed me his three cameras, any one of which I'd have loved to buy. Next came two bedrooms, and his own had a bathroom annexe.

Mrs. Winder was just bringing the coffee as we came back to the lounge. She looked a pleasant, competent woman of about forty, and Calne didn't dream of introducing me. I couldn't help thinking of the atmosphere at Ninford, and how it took all sorts to make a world.

"What do you call this place?" I asked.

"Walker's Ferry," he told me. "No one seems to know who Walker was. Probably someone a pretty good way back who used to ferry people from here across the Creek and back."

"The same Walker of that island at the mouth of the Creek?"

"Walker's Flat? I suppose it would be," he said. "But I don't know that it's really an island. It's not much more than a mud flat. It's practically covered at high tide."

There was a fine view across the Creek from the window where we were, though the sun was already too south to make for good visibility towards the open sea. But the coastguard cottage was plain enough across the Creek at the Point, and the tide was sufficiently out to show the grey line of Walker's Flat.

"What's the name of your boat?" I asked.

"Something quite trite," he said, "*Avocet*. Only because it happens to be a favourite bird of mine. Like to have a look over her?"

Let me make something perfectly clear. I know a lot about very few things, and a little about a good many things. But about boats—should I say ships?—and their machinery and gadgets I am ignorant to the point of utter blankness. I suppose I could identify a yacht or a rowing-boat, but try me on the kinds of sailing craft and my knowledge is nil. But I wasn't wholly to be blamed for the surprise I showed when we stepped out to the little jetty and I saw the *Avocet*.

"Good Lord!" I said. "This is terrific. It's a young steamer."

He had to smile at that. I told him I didn't in the least mind being thought an absolute fool.

"As a matter of fact, she's unique," he said. "She's a war experiment, designed really for the Far East and never actually put into service. I managed to buy her—"

"Influence?"

"Why not?" He smiled dryly. He was more pleased with life that morning than I'd ever known him, and maybe because he was in his element. "There was the usual landing-craft mechanism at the stern there, but I managed to get that removed and redesigned. You'll see for yourself."

I'd only be talking like a parrot if I repeated a tenth of what he told me. Purely as a layman, so to speak, I may say there was a double-berth cabin and galley forrard, and mess-room and a lounge amidships, and two double cabins aft, and I hope to heaven the terms are correct.

"But why do you need all that room?" I asked. "I should have thought that a much smaller craft would have been more in your line."

"She's heavy on fuel," he said, "and that means I can't take her out much. But I never intended to. The thing is that I can go anywhere and stay as long as I like. There's living and sleeping and cooking space for the Winders, and the lounge will be my workroom aboard, and one of the cabins will be a dark-room. It's not any too large, really."

"What do the Winders think of it?"

"They love the idea," he said. "Jack's an old fisherman, and Annie's a fisherman's daughter. We'll have a word with Jack if you like."

He gave a holler and Jack Winder appeared—a shortish, weather-tanned man of fifty. He was wearing blue dungarees and a peaked cap and rubbing his hands on a piece of oily waste. I liked the look of him. His eyes wrinkled with a grin as we shook hands.

"Everything all right, Jack?" Calne asked him.

Jack said it was.

"What's Tom think of it?"

Jack gave a chuckle.

"Between ourselves, he told me, sir, that instead of you paying him for the day, he ought to be paying you."

"Fine," said Calne. "We shall know what to do then, Jack."

He gave a nod and Jack flicked his forelock and went. Calne explained. Tom Pike was a local man and he and Jack would share duties and so leave Calne himself free. Pallart was bringing his man Friske, who would act as steward.

"They ought to be here at any minute now," he said as he went up on deck. I had another look round me. If Calne was going to live on that boat, I thought, he needn't altogether lack for exercise, for it was quite a goodish way round the deck.

"I think that's Guy's car now," he said, and it was. A moment or two and there was handshaking and introductions. Kales was as shy as usual and young Brace less nervous, or so it seemed to me. Guy Pallart was in great form. He was apologising for having brought along a crate of ale. Then he was introducing Arthur Friske, a raw-boned young fellow of about thirty whom I'd already seen. Calne called Annie Winder and the two began taking food aboard. In ten minutes we were aboard ourselves.

* * * * *

I shall not bore you with the events of that day, though it will be necessary to mention certain things that had a bearing on subsequent events. Throughout I must apologise again for my lack of nautical knowledge. But provided you can follow what I happen to be trying to convey and can visualise what I want you to see, an error or two in terms is of no particular moment.

The boat—large launch is perhaps a better word—was steady as an armchair. Even outside the Creek the sea was incredibly calm. When we had all taken a turn at the wheel—Jack Winder was in charge—we lounged in deck-chairs which Friske brought up from below and drank cold beer and watched the passing shore that lay drowsing in the full morning sun. We were throttled down, as I call it, to preserve fuel and were doing, I believe, eight or ten knots, and it was fine sitting there in the breeze with never a care in the world.

It was one o'clock when we were abreast of Landguard Point and Friske was announcing that lunch was ready. It was a first-class meal and we were hungry and that was why there was precious little activity in the early afternoon. Kales was talking to Calne who was relieving Winder at the wheel, but Pallart and I dozed shamelessly in our chairs. Kales and Came had cottoned to each other from the start, and perhaps because Calne's French was so good. What Brace did with himself I don't know but I think he was below deck.

Guy Pallart and I seemed to rouse ourselves at much the same time. I passed my cigarette-case and he was saying it was perfectly disgraceful of us sleeping away such an afternoon. Jack Winder came back and Calne and Kales appeared.

"A pity we didn't all have bathing costumes," Calne said. "We might have had a swim before tea. Do you swim nowadays, Guy, or not?"

"A bit lop-sided," Pallart told him. "But probably good enough to give you a start in a hundred yards."

"I'd be damned lucky to get a hundred yards," Calne said. "Travers looks as if he might be one of those long-distance chaps."

I told him I didn't mind how far I swam out to sea provided I had one toe on the bottom. Brace said that was about his standard.

"Anyone like to come and have a look at the works?" Calne said.

Pallart said he felt too lazy to move. I was well dug in, too, so the three left us to ourselves.

"You might like to know," Pallart was telling me in a minute or two, "that I had a word with our young friend before we turned in last night. I said I was giving him his final chance."

"I think you've done the very best thing," I told him. "When I look back on my own youth I still blush up to the eyebrows. Some of us take a hell of a time to settle down."

Then I remembered something.

"How did he explain that extravagance, or whatever it was, that you'd discovered?"

"The old tale," Pallart said sceptically. "A friend gave him a tip on a horse and he had a good win."

Then he was asking where we were. I said I thought we'd passed Orford Ness. There had been talk of tea off Southwold and then a turn for home. Then Brace and Kales came up again and I went below. Calne was just coming out of the lavatory as I went to go in. He was waiting in the corridor as I came out.

"Tea won't be long," he said. "You're not bored with the trip?"

"My dear fellow, I'm enjoying every minute of it," I told him.

"Well, we haven't finished yet. I've got a surprise up my sleeve—or so I hope."

"I love surprises," I said. I had taken his arm and my voice lowered. "Something I've been wanting to ask you and this is the first chance I've had. That talk there was the other day at the Regency. Surely Pallart wasn't serious about that murder stuff?"

"Serious!" He gave a little snort. "I've told you he was unusual, and that's one of the forms it takes. He loves to be— well, the least bit outré. You were a good listener. But you tell me something," he was going quickly on. "What did you think of the Old Vicarage? The atmosphere, I mean."

"I thought it was highly diverting," I said. "I love old Susan. That French chef looks as if he might be interesting, too."

Friske came up then and wanted to know if tea was to be on deck. Calne said it was, and he was telling me to go up. I was wearing rubber-soled shoes and they made no sound as I went up the stairs. Pallart and Kales were talking and for some reason or other I stopped dead in my tracks. Maybe it was the French: the realisation that Pallart was talking such perfect French and with so excellent an accent,

"*Et tu l'as reconnu?*"

"*Absolument.*"

"*Pas de doute?*"

"*Pas de doute. C'est lui lui-même.*"

"*Et toi?*"

"*Mais non. Je vous l'assure.*"

I took a step or two down and noisily cleared my throat.

"Tea's just coming," I said, and there was Friske on my heels with a couple of folding tables. I went over to the rail to have a look at Southwold and I saw Richard Brace leaning over the rail astern. He was smoking a cigarette and apparently looking at the wake.

But I was thinking about two curious things. I wasn't interested in *what* Pallart and Kales had been so earnestly discussing, though with my usual readiness to produce a theory I thought I had an idea. Kales had been telling a story about himself and some man or other—an episode perhaps to do with the war. Kales had recognised the man but the man hadn't recognised him.

But that, as I said, didn't interest me more than academically, so to speak. I wondered why Pallart should be capable of such perfect French, when in the Regency he had spoken with so execrable an accent. And then I had an answer. That was just an example of the *outré* of which Calne had spoken. Calne and Pallart were vastly different types. However friendly the two might be at heart, each had the capacity for rubbing the other the wrong way. Pallart, with his ironical twist of mind, took a secret delight in talking bad French to one who prided himself on speaking the language like a native.

But the other thing was more interesting. In that short talk I had overheard, Kales had been a different man. His words had been quick, lively, alert. They had been the words of a man of action, and that was the last thing one could have imagined him to be. In fact, if I hadn't seen it was Kales—

"I love the sound of bells, don't you?"

Pallart had joined me at the rail and I was aware that a bell was ringing intermittently. The boat gave a sort of shudder and I saw that we had come closer inshore. The multi-coloured speckling of the beach was no longer vague. One could discern individual bathers and the sun-bathers and the family groups. Then the ship wasn't moving and Calne was calling us to tea.

The late afternoon was perfect. I was wondering what Calne's surprise was to be and it was not till we were nearing Harwich again that I knew. We drew more inshore on the Dovercourt side and then made for a tiny creek. In a few minutes we were drawing alongside what looked like a private landing-stage and Tom Pike was coming on deck and helping Winder to make all fast.

"Stopping here?" asked Pallart. Calne had been at the wheel and now he had rejoined us.

"Dinner," Calne told him. "There's the hotel."

He was looking quite pleased. Pallart rather gaped.

"But will they be able to feed us?"

"All arranged, my dear fellow. Fixed up yesterday."

"That's what I call staff work," Pallart told him. "You and I will have to come out with this chap again, Travers." We did ourselves remarkably well. By the time we'd drunk Calne's health for the last of umpteen times, it was getting on for eight o'clock. We had intended to be back at Wandham by nine and Calne said we might open out a bit and be there soon after. Pallart said there was no hurry. It wasn't as if one of Susan's meals would be spoiling. All she'd had instructions to leave was a cold supper, and now even that wouldn't be wanted.

The evening was incredibly beautiful and I didn't need that extra sweater I'd brought. Brace said it would be a grand night for a moonlight swim, only there wasn't a moon. The sea at Dovercourt had been absolutely warm.

"What a thing it is to be young," Pallart told me ironically. "A couple of drinks and you're ready for anything."

"I think Richard's was a damn good idea," I said. "I wouldn't mind splashing about myself, if there was a moon."

> Moon, moon, serenely shining
> Don't go in so soon. . . .

That was Pallart, actually singing. It showed, as I said, what a couple of drinks could do.

"A damn good song that," Pallart said. "Better than all that bloody drivel you hear nowadays."

"Surely some of it isn't so bad?" ventured Brace.

"I don't mind some kinds of jazz myself," I said.

"Keep to the point, old-timer," Pallart told me. "We were talking about songs."

"That's rather jolly," put in Calne. It was dusk and he was pointing to a twinkle of lights along the shore. That broke the chatter up and we watched for a few minutes. Dark was beginning to close in. Light shone through the portholes beneath us and gave an eerie colouring to our wake.

"We shan't be long now," Calne said as the boat suddenly lost speed. A bell sounded and the boat checked again. "What about going down for a nightcap. You people may want to get away in a bit of a hurry."

"Sounds all right to me," Pallart said.

"We might get some of these things down," Calne said, and I gathered that he meant the chairs. "Dr. Kales, I wonder if you'd mind bringing me those binoculars from the cabin? They're just above those books we were looking at."

I unfolded a couple of chairs and Trace did the same. Pallart disappeared, and he said afterwards that he'd gone to look at the wake. Brace and I met Kales coming up with the binoculars and Friske was just behind him. In a matter of seconds Friske was below again with the remaining chair and the tables. I heard a kind of holler from the deck as if someone was calling. Kales suddenly appeared.

"Mr. Calne? He is not here?"

"He's on deck," I said.

"But I looked," he said, "and he is not there."

"He must be there," I said, and then Pallart came in.

"Did you leave Calne on deck?" I asked him.

"Calne?" he said. "I didn't see him."

Kales went up again. Friske was bringing out the whisky and a siphon and glasses. He looked natty in his short white jacket.

"Better wait till Mr. Calne comes," I told him. "Leave everything here and we'll look after ourselves."

Two or three minutes went by. Kales came down again. You could see his feet before they touched the floor, for the stairs ended just outside the door.

"Did you find him?"

"He was nowhere," he told me.

"A damn queer thing," I said. "I wonder where the devil he's got to. I'm certain he never came down here."

"But he must have done," Kales said. "It is impossible for anyone to be on the deck and not to be seen."

"He's playing some damn silly trick," Pallart said. "You and Richard go that way, Travers, and Kales and I'll go this. We'll soon winkle him out."

But there was never a sign of Calne.

"There isn't anywhere he could have hidden," I said. "Besides, Calne isn't the sort to play a silly trick like that." Then suddenly I went on deck. Jack Winder looked back over his shoulder.

"Oh, it's you, sir," he said. "Another couple of minutes and we'll be tying up. You can see the Ferry now."

"Seen anything of Mr. Calne?" That was Pallart who was all at once at my elbow.

"Never a thing, sir," Winder told him. "I haven't seen nor heard of him since he gave that holler a while back."

"A holler?" I said. "I heard a holler. A quarter of an hour ago or more. What did it sound like to you, Winder?"

"I thought it was Mr. Calne hollering to someone."

"My God!" I said. "I wonder if he went overboard?"

"But how could he?" Pallart said. "You didn't hear a splash, did you, Jack?"

Winder waved a hand as if he didn't want talk. The boat was coming alongside and I suddenly heard a noise. It was Tom Pike throwing over the fenders and in another minute the boat was alongside.

"Now what's all this, sir?" Winder asked me, and Pallart and I began to talk at the same time. He gave way and I was telling Winder what I knew.

"Funny," he said. "I did hear something like a splash. Couldn't have been, though. I shouldn't have heard it where I was."

Then he was giving a little laugh.

"Don't make sense, sir. How could anyone fall over them rails? He must be down below, somewhere."

We wasted time over another look. Curious how people refuse to believe the evidence of their own eyes. Calne couldn't possibly have come down. I'd left him on deck and the stairs had been all the time under my eyes. And it had been just after I'd come down myself that I'd heard that holler.

"Looks as though something must have happened," Winder had to admit. "Tell you what, sir. Tom and I'll get hold of Harry Miles's motor-boat and we'll draw back and have a cruise round."

"Get a ruddy move on then," Pallart told him impatiently.

Winder moved off. He called back.

"No point in you gentlemen staying. You can't do no good. Not unless you ring up the coastguard and say what's happened."

"Come on," Pallart told us. "The quicker we get that coastguard the better. No point in alarming Annie, though."

But the line was dead. He twiddled impatiently and then slammed the receiver back. Annie said she hadn't used it all day, so she couldn't say when it had gone out of order.

Pallart gave me a nod and we went out to the dark again.

"Of all the times for the damn thing to go wrong!" he said.

"I don't think we need worry," I told him. "Winder and Pike will be bound to go to the Point. They'll see the coastguard."

"I'll get along home and telephone from there," he said. "You push on to Drowton. No point in your hanging about."

His car went off first and mine followed. But I did hang about to the extent of waiting at Ninford till he had got through on the telephone. He was much more cheerful then.

"It's all right," he told me. "He's going out now. He's seen the light on Jack's motor-boat."

"What chance would Calne stand in the water?" I wanted to know.

"He's no great swimmer but he ought to keep himself afloat." He gave a grunt. "The tide was coming in. He'd get ashore."

I left it at that, though there was more I could have said. Why, I might have asked him, hadn't Calne let out a series of yells as soon as he hit the water. Then I was probing into that as I drove through the dark towards Drowton, and even when I was back in the hotel again, I wasn't sure. I remembered an occasion when I'd taken a sudden fall into the sea myself and taken a few mouthfuls of water. For quite a few seconds I hadn't been able to get out a sound.

I sat on in the hotel lounge till after eleven and then I rang the coastguard cottage. It was a goodish time before a sleepy voice answered me. The coastguard's wife was saying that her husband was out, and I left it at that. But when I went up to bed I had an alarm-clock which I had borrowed from the hotel and I set it for half-past four.

But though I wanted desperately to sleep, sleep wouldn't come. Then the alarm-clock went off and it was suddenly morning, and I still had the same thoughts that had kept me so long awake. Pallart had come down the stairs a second or two after I had heard that holler. He had been on deck and in the dark, with Calne. What if Calne were dead? What if he'd been murdered? And what if Pallart had been serious after all at the Regency?

CHAPTER V
STRANGE CLIMAX

IT WAS JUST after dawn when I set off, and as I had so much time by the forelock, I was proposing to go first to the coast-guard cottage and, if there was no news there, to return by Ninford and go on to Wandham. Just short of Ninford then, I took the right-hand fork and was almost at once in sight of the Creek. Walker's Ferry, white and flat-topped, was perfectly clear across the water.

That southern side of the Creek seemed singularly bare compared with the Wandham side. Away to my right I could see a farm in the flats but to the left was nothing but a sawmill and a couple of cottages. The timber yard looked extensive and I supposed that boats with a shallow draught could come down the Creek from the Baltic and unload direct. But that morning there seemed no timber in it, and the post-war demand, I was thinking, must have stripped it bare. But trees were piled ready for sawing and there were vast heaps of sawdust towering above the sheds, and it was fine somehow in that clear morning air to sniff the resinous scent of pine-wood.

From the narrow road an unmetalled track led the last hundred yards or so to the coastguard's cottage, and I saw that smoke was coming from the chimney-pot. I was glad of that because I should not have to rouse the household to get news. I left my car and walked along the track and before I neared the cottage I could see that the back door was open. The coast-guard himself appeared as soon as I knocked. He was still wearing thigh-boots and looked tousled and bleary-eyed.

"My name's Travers," I said. "I was on the *Avocet* last night with Mr. Calne. Is there any news?"

"I picked him up this morning," he said.

"Is he all right?"

"He's had a pretty bad time," he said. "If he hadn't come up against a lump of timber, I don't reckon he'd ever have got ashore. I heard him hollering about an hour or so ago over there on the Flat, so I rowed across and fetched him in. Pretty well done up, he was."

"When did he go home?"

"He isn't home," he said. "He's still here. My wife's just attending to that cut on his head. If you like to come in, sir, you can."

He took me through to the parlour and there Calne was. He gave me a feeble sort of grin, and that was the last kind of look I expected, for he was looking mighty queer. A pile of muddy clothes lay on the floor and he was wearing pyjamas, over which was a woman's dressing-gown. The coastguard's wife was putting a strip of surgical plaster on the back of the skull from which the hair had been shaved in a circular patch.

"How're you feeling, Calne?" I asked him.

"Can't grumble," he said. "Can't get the cold out of my bones yet."

I asked the coastguard his name and he said it was Morris. When I asked his wife if the doctor was coming, she said Mr. Calne wouldn't hear of sending for the doctor.

"Not that I can't do as well as the doctor as far as his head goes," she told me. "I've had plenty of experience in the Red Cross. But perhaps you can get him to see the doctor, sir. I tell him he's got to get to bed and have a good rest."

She fastened the bandage round the head and gave herself a nod of approval. It certainly looked a workmanlike job to me. Calne said never a word.

"I'll make some more coffee," Morris said. "You'd like a cup, too, sir?"

I said I certainly would. Mrs. Morris went out, too, and I was alone with Calne.

"What happened last night?" I asked him bluntly.

"Just a ridiculous accident," he said, but he didn't meet my eyes. "Must have slipped on the deck and before I knew what was happening, I'd gone overboard."

"But what about that crack on the skull?"

"I think I must have struck something in the water," he said. "I remember letting out a yell."

He looked too tired to do much talking. Then Morris came back.

"How are you proposing to get Mr. Calne home?" I asked him.

"We thought of ringing the Ferry and having Jack come over with the motor-boat."

"The telephone's working?"

He said he hadn't tried it and I said I doubted if it was. Besides, my car could be brought right up to the door and in ten minutes I could have Calne home. I said he could try the Ferry when we'd gone and warn them we were coming. That was a good idea, he said, so I fetched the car at once while the coffee was brewing. Mrs. Morris was just bringing it in when I got back. It certainly tasted good and so did the cigarette after it.

"Don't you worry about these clothes," Mrs. Morris said. "I'll get them dried out and the mud off them and then I'll send them across."

That coffee had had a lacing of rum and I could feel it still warm in my stomach. Calne said he was feeling much better and he was a bit petulant when Mrs. Morris tried to lend a hand to the car and he made a face when she insisted on wrapping him round in a blanket. I got in a quick word with Morris.

"Where was he, actually, when you picked him up?" I wanted to know.

"Just across there on the Flat," he said. "If he'd only have known the Flat as well as I do, he could have come across on sand and shingle but as it was he came across that far end where it's all mud. Tired him right out, it did, especially after what he'd been through."

"You'd call it a lucky escape?"

"I didn't tell him so," he said, "but it's dam near a miracle. He's no particular swimmer and if that timber hadn't happened to be just where it was, he'd never have made it."

It was bumpy across the sandy track but we made good time on the hard road. As we passed the Old Vicarage I gave a quick look but there was never a sign of life, and I was telling myself I'd call up on my way back. Ninford itself was just beginning to stir and I had to halt the car by the bridge till a straggly line of cows had lazily passed. Then I shot the car on again and on that open road the sun was already warm. Just short of the fork I drew the car up.

"Something wrong?" Calne said. Except when I had asked him if he was comfortable, we hadn't said a word since we left the cottage.

"Not with the car," I said. "But something's wrong with your story."

"What do you mean?"

"If you don't want to talk, or you can't trust me to keep quiet, that'll be different," I said. "But you're not convincing me that you fell overboard. It's a physical impossibility."

"All the same, it happened," he told me curtly.

"That deck was dry as a bone and clean as a new pin," I said. "You couldn't have slipped and there was nothing to trip over. If I'd slipped and caught the rail below my waist, I might conceivably have gone over. You're six inches shorter and it just couldn't have happened."

He was leaning back in the bucket seat, saying nothing.

"Shall I tell you what did happen?"

He still said nothing. All he did was close his eyes as if he wished to God I'd shut up.

"Someone caught you a hell of a crack on the back of the skull," I said. "You were tipped overboard. If you'd been hit a tiny bit harder, you wouldn't have come to just after you hit the water."

He still said nothing.

"Have it your own way," I said resignedly. "That's all I've got to say. If it's any consolation to you, I'm not mentioning it to anyone else. If you want to make it your private headache, that's up to you. I'm not butting in."

My hand went to the gear lever, then drew back.

"I would like you to answer one simple question."

"Depends what it is," he said.

"It's this. Why did Pallart suggest you should take the trip we made yesterday?"

"Why shouldn't he?"

I gave a dry smile. The bluff had worked.

"You've answered my question," I said. "Pallart told me it was *you* who suggested the trip. Think that over, will you, and see if it gets you anywhere."

He was saying no more and I moved the car on. The telephone must be in working order again, I thought, for Jack Winder came to meet us as we neared the Ferry. Annie was at the back door too. Calne made his own way into the house with Annie fussing over him like a hen with one chick. "Telephone all right, Jack?"

"What do you think, sir? The ruddy wire was cut through, right where it goes through to the house!"

"The devil it was," I said. "Who did it? Some mischievous young boys from the village?"

He said he didn't know. But he'd soon had it spliced when he'd located the trouble.

"I don't think I'd mention it," I told him. "Tell Mr. Calne about it and he can do as he likes. And tell your wife to give him a tot of hot milk with a good lacing of whisky or rum, and put plenty of blankets on him. As soon as he's asleep, get the doctor to have a look at him."

But he was insisting on my staying for breakfast. He and his wife were just about to have their meal, he said, and it would be no trouble. Annie came to the kitchen and I told her what I'd told Jack. Already Calne had insisted that he didn't want a doctor, but I told her to do as I said. When they began questioning me about the accident, I claimed to know no more than they. If Calne wanted an accident, an accident it should be.

We had fried fillets of plaice for breakfast and scalding hot tea. I was hungry and made a good meal but Annie was indignant when I tried to force a tip. Just before I left she had a quick peep at Calne and reported that he was already asleep.

"I'll call up at Ninford and give the news to Major Pallart," I said, "then I'll go back to Drowton. About eleven o'clock or so I'll give you a ring and perhaps you'll tell me what the doctor says about Mr. Calne."

*   *   *   *   *

It was still only about a quarter past seven when I drew up outside the Old Vicarage. Leaning over the gate and smoking a cigarette was Georges Loret. When I came up to him he gave me a good-morning in French.

"Look, Georges," I said. "Your English is better than my French. Let's stick to English. Major Pallart up yet?"

"The Major has not returned," he told me, and spread his palms.

"Returned? You mean he's up already and out?"

"Since last night he has not returned," he said.

"Look," I said patiently. "What happened last night? I came back here with Major Pallart at about half-past nine or so. What happened then?"

"First I gave Dr. Kales the message."

"What message?"

It was another five minutes before I had the whole thing pieced together. During the day a telephone message had come for Dr. Kales, and since Susan happened to be down in the village, Georges took it. He remembered what the message was. The caller had simply said, 'Will you tell Dr. Kales as soon as he comes in, that it is a matter of extreme urgency that I should see him in the morning. The name is Montague.' The caller had spelt the name out.

Susan had gone to bed. Half-past nine was her usual time and Friske had cleared away the cold meal before he left. Major Pallart had then looked up trains and found there was a late one at Colchester that would land Dr. Kales in town in the early hours. Richard Brace had by that time gone to bed and Pallart had sent Loret to bed too.

"Is there a time-table about?" I asked Loret.

We went in the house and he found the very time-table that Pallart and Kales had consulted. The train left Colchester at twelve-forty, and Pallart couldn't have been back till one in the morning.

"Did you hear him come back?"

He gave a shrug of the shoulders, then said he must have come back because the car was in the garage. Then he was adding exasperatedly that just as he—Loret—was going to bed, the Major told him not to pay any attention if he heard him moving about in the night, because he'd probably be going to Wandham to hear if there was any news.

"I wonder if I might have a word with Mr. Brace?" I said.

"But he is asleep."

"Then we'll wake him," I said. "Perhaps you'll show me which is his room."

He told me to turn right at the head of the stairs and the room was the first on the right. As I went up I could hear Susan in the kitchen. But I didn't go straight into Brace's room. Loret was watching me from the foot of the stairs and I came down again.

"How did you know Major Pallart wasn't home?"

"Every morning at seven o'clock it is I who bring a cup of tea," he said. "This morning I take it up and there is no one there."

He gave a shrug of the shoulders as if to dissociate himself from the whole affair. I went up the stairs again. I listened at Brace's door, then gently opened it. A cup of tea, undrunk, stood on the table by his bed. I put my finger in it and it was almost cold. Then I shook him gently. I shook him still harder and at last he opened his eyes. He blinked. Then he stared.

"Good lord, sir, I thought it was Georges."

He sat up rubbing his eyes. Then he was asking if there was any news about Calne. I gave him the news. What was puzzling me more, I said, was where his uncle was. Apparently he'd gone out on foot soon after one in the morning and hadn't yet come back.

"I expect he went to see if he could do anything about Mr. Calne," he said. Then he was making a wry face. He caught sight of the tea and had it down in a flash.

"Gosh! I've got a frightful mouth on me this morning," he said. "I didn't drink much either."

"You pulled your weight," I told him dryly. "But about last night. Did you know Dr. Kales was going away?"

"I heard him and my uncle discussing it, then I went to bed."

"Did you hear the car at all?"

"Didn't hear a thing," he said. "As soon as I hit the pillow I was dead to the wide. All that sea air, I expect."

I said I might be seeing him later. There was no sign of Loret when I went downstairs, so I pushed off at once in my car. But I didn't go to Drowton—yet. I went a good mile along the lane by the estuary and left the car and went across to a slight rise of land. I think I was hoping to get a glimpse of Pallart out Walker's Ferry way, but there was no sign of him there. On the deck of the *Avocet* I could see Jack Winder, and a small boat with a mainsail was making for the Point.

I sat down on a sandy tussock and lighted my pipe. But it would be wrong to say that I began putting this and that together and working a theory out. Everything was too simple for that. Once I had trapped Calne into the admission that it had been Pallart who had suggested the sea trip, things were as plain as the fingers of my hand. Calne should have been dead by now. It was his murder that had been planned. And, by that Regency talk, Pallart should be in the clear, for *his* murder, he had said, would be far too clever to implicate himself. He would either have a perfect alibi, or else the murder would never be taken for murder.

Well, the murder might have been taken for an accident, I was telling myself, even if Pallart couldn't claim an alibi. In fact he was far from having an alibi. If murder had been suspected, then he was the perfect suspect. But then there would arise that other point that he had mentioned—the question of motive. Why on earth should Pallart want to kill Calne? Why, and why, I kept repeating to myself. As far as I could see, there wasn't a vestige of motive. Pallart was the last person to wish to murder Calne.

But since Calne was alive, and likely to go on living, there was nothing I could do about it. Calne too was persisting that it had been an accident, even if he guessed the truth, and whatever happened privately between him and Pallart, I should never know a word. It was tantalising nevertheless.

Maybe Calne had seen the man who had struck him. Not as the blow was struck, perhaps, but in that fraction of a second before he lost consciousness.

What was there then for me to do? If Pallart had indeed made an abortive attempt to murder Calne, then Calne was now forewarned, and it would be too dangerous to try again. In other words, if what had happened was no concern of mine, then what was likely to happen was still less my concern, since nothing further could happen at all. But what I would do later that morning, I was telling myself, would be to have a word with Pallart. I'd make the whole thing jocular. Give him a kind of Whartonian dig in the ribs and say, "What was your idea in trying to polish off Calne?" It would be interesting to watch his reactions.

Then as I moved off back to my car, I was being puzzled about Pallart in quite a different way. Where on earth could he have gone to in the dead of night, and on foot? With that game leg of his he couldn't have gone far. And why should he have gone off on foot at all when he had the car? And when had the car come back from Colchester? No one could say. Susan hadn't been asked, but she no doubt had been as soundly asleep as Loret and Brace. It was queer, and then suddenly I didn't see why it should worry me. Pallart would doubtless give some perfectly natural explanation when I saw him later in the morning.

I couldn't wait till eleven o'clock. Curiosity or impatience got the better of me and I rang Walker's Ferry. Jack Winder answered me. He was looking after the house while his wife slipped into Ninford to do some necessary shopping.

"What did the doctor say, Jack?"

"He reckon he've to stay in bed at least two days," Jack said. "He's coming in again first thing in the morning if nothing happens."

"What's he afraid of? Pneumonia?"

"I reckon so, sir. In fact, he told Annie that if Mr. Calne hadn't had such a wonderful constitution, he'd have been down with something already."

"He certainly had a narrow squeak," I said. "But tell me something, Jack. Where were we actually when he went over-board?"

"Where, sir? Well, I reckon if you went about eight hundred yards nor-nor-east from the Flat, you wouldn't be far out."

"Why do you think you and Tom Pike missed him?"

"It weren't none too light for one thing," he told me, "and we hadn't got nothing but an acetylene lamp and that died out on us. Another thing. I reckon we didn't look in the right place. We were working along towards the north shore. Mr. Calne, he was carried right out north of the Flat. And from what I can make out, soon as he managed to get ashore, he collapsed. The doctor reckon he'll be lucky if his heart haven't had a bad strain."

"Thank you, Jack," I said. "I'll be seeing you some time soon."

There was a large map of the Creek hanging in the hotel corridor and I had a look at it. I remembered that when we left the Creek we had kept to the Flat side and had not turned north till some distance ahead. Calne hadn't let us take a turn at the wheel till we had turned north on a comparatively straight course. It had been something to do with the currents and the mud-banks, he had said, and Jack Winder had told us that if any of us had taken what we might have thought the nearest way out from the Creek, we should have had the *Avocet* aground in a couple of jiffs.

But when I marked down the spot where Calne had most likely gone overboard, I was realising what a miracle it was that he had survived. It was true the tide was coming in, but it was a tricky tide and the Flat was invisible in the dark. Only by the grace of God did he hit it at all, and how he managed then to drag himself through and up those mud stretches was altogether beyond me. But Calne had pluck. He'd fight to the last inch, I was telling myself, and then I heard the telephone bell. I didn't have the least idea it might be for me, but it was.

"Hallo?" I said.

"Is that Mr. Travers?"

"Yes," I said. "Who's speaking?"

"This is Detective-Inspector Drane, sir. I'm speaking from the Old Vicarage at Ninford. I'd like you to come along, if you can."

The bottom was suddenly falling out of things, and I didn't know why.

"Why, yes," I said. "I'll come at once. What's happened, Inspector?"

"Just something we'd like to see you about," he told me off-handedly. "We'd like your help, that's all."

"I'll be right there," I told him, and slowly hung the receiver up.

I found myself giving my glasses a polish and wild theories were running through my mind. Then I gave a shrug of the shoulders. Why speculate when in a quarter of an hour I should have all the answers at first hand? But I was in such a state of perturbation that it was not till I was well on the road that I realised that I had forgotten even to put on a hat. And though I'd promised myself not to speculate, one thought would keep obtruding itself on my mind—that something had emerged about that attempt to murder Calne. Maybe Pallart had confessed. Maybe he had committed suicide before he had learned that Calne was after all alive!

There seemed nothing different about the house as I drew near except that two cars were parked in the drive. Then I found the nearer gate locked and when I walked on to the other, a uniformed constable was there. I told him my name and he passed me through. The front door of the house was open and unguarded and as I stepped inside, old Susan was coming from the lounge. She had her apron to her eyes and a tallish man in civilian clothes was leading her gently towards the kitchen. In a minute he was back in the hall.

"You'll be Mr. Travers," he said, and gave me a long, appraising look. "I'm Drane. I telephoned you at Drowton just now. Would you mind coming in here for a minute, Mr. Travers?"

He was opening the door of the dining-room and we went through. The room was spotless and quiet and it held a scent of roses from the table bowl. A window was open and it was deliciously cool.

"Take a seat, Mr. Travers. Smoke by all means if you like."

I took a seat but I didn't smoke. Before I could ask him what it was all about, he was wanting my full name and address and profession. I was keeping Scotland Yard to myself, and I saw him give a little pout of the lips when I described myself as of private means.

"Now, sir," he said briskly. "Would you mind telling me when you last saw Major Pallart?"

I told him but I didn't say a word about the Calne affair.

"And then you went straight to Drowton?"

"Straight to Drowton," I echoed. "I was talking to the landlord of the Ostlers at half-past eleven and then I went to bed. I don't know what you want to know, but I should say that nobody can prove that I stayed in my bed all night."

He gave a little laugh. I was putting him down as a bit of a showman.

"I don't know that we're interested in that, sir." He got to his feet. "I wonder if you'd mind coming in the other room?"

It was the lounge that apparently he meant. He opened the door for me and there were two men in the room. They were talking but they stopped at once as soon as I entered. One was an oldish man who looked like a doctor, and the other was Drane's sergeant. He didn't introduce either to me.

"This is Mr. Travers," he said and was turning towards the long window. A table was there and something covered with an army blanket. Once more I found myself polishing my glasses. He took it for a different kind of nervousness.

"We're not asking you for identification," he told me, "but we'd like you to have a look."

He drew the blanket down. It was Pallart who was lying there, and the body was naked from the waist up. Round the neck was a livid red weal.

CHAPTER VI
THE PRIVATE WANGLE

"So HE WAS strangled," I said. I said it to myself, and aloud. I hardly knew I'd said it at all.

"That's right," Drane said.

"Do you know when?"

"We *shall* know when," he told me enigmatically.

I turned away. The bulging eyes looked horrible. Somehow I had never been able to regard with Wharton's indifference so violent and distorted a death.

I think Drane again misinterpreted the gesture. The sergeant was suddenly at my elbow. The doctor was still at the fireplace, hands tucked under his coat-tails as if it were icy winter and a fire in the grate, and his eyes were curiously on me.

"Might I ask where you found him?" I said.

"I don't know that I ought to tell you that," he said. "But I'll do more. I'll show you the actual spot."

It was the plain-clothes sergeant who led the way out. We turned left and went across the long lawn and turned towards the summerhouse. I followed the sergeant along the path to the side, past where I had stood that night when the unknown snooper had squatted by the window. Then the sergeant drew behind me and Drane took the lead. I felt a squelch beneath my foot. Someone had spilled water there, but as I halted and looked down, Drane was beckoning me impatiently on. We turned left again along the path that ran through the shrubbery.

Drane halted and I saw why. Twigs of laurel were broken and small boughs were pressed back.

"You found him here?" I said.

"That's right," he told me, and his eyes were on me all the time.

"Might I ask when?"

"At about half-past nine this morning."

"And who found him?"

"His nephew—Mr. Brace."

I must have given a Whartonian grunt. As far as I was concerned there was never a spot of daylight. And I was wondering why Drane was so interested in *me*. Did he know what my real job was? And then I wondered who could have told him, for I could have sworn that neither Brace nor old Susan had the least idea. There is a glamour for the layman about Scotland Yard, and yet neither Kales nor Brace had shown the least curiosity. And no one could possibly look less like a policeman than myself.

"Nothing you've noticed . . . or you'd like to say?"

"No," I said, and shook my head.

"This way then, sir."

He didn't go back towards the summerhouse but along the path. Where it emerged from the shrubbery he cut across the lawn. An ambulance was coming in at the gate. We went through to the lounge again and to the side table on the right of the fireplace.

"This glove, sir? Ever seen it before?"

"Good lord, yes!" I said. "It's mine."

"You're sure."

"Of course I'm sure," I told him testily. "Where's the other one?"

"That's what we hoped you might tell us," he said.

I said it might be in the car, though I didn't recall seeing it there. The gloves were old driving ones, and more often than not I didn't use them at all. Then I remembered.

"I must have left them here last night," I said. "I remember I was using them. My hands were a bit cold when I left Wandham."

"Cold?" he said. "It was almost a sultry night."

"Does it matter?" I told him. "I had the gloves on and I seem to remember I had them on when I came in here. The other glove must be about somewhere."

Then I was suddenly giving him a look.

"What's all this about? What's the importance of a glove?"

"It all depends," he said, and his eyes were on me as if he was trying to look clean through me. "This particular glove happened to be found near the body."

My eyes must have bulged, and my fingers went instinctively to my glasses.

"The devil it was!" I said.

The remark must have puzzled him. His lips parted, then closed again, and I could almost feel him hunting for what to say next. Then the doctor was coming in and men were removing the body. The doctor was the last out and, as he closed the door, he was saying he'd be ringing up.

"I suppose you wouldn't like to tell me why you're staying at Drowton?" Drane asked me.

"But why should I?"

He shrugged his shoulders.

"I gathered you had business of some sort at Colchester. In fact I might tell you that Mr. Brace told me as much. He'd heard his uncle say so."

"What the soldier said isn't evidence," I told him, and not I hope, ironically.

"Were we mentioning the word evidence?" he countered, and he was just a bit annoyed. "But would you mind telling me what business you actually had or have at Colchester? This is unofficial and confidential."

"For the moment?"

His grin was none too pleasant.

"If you like it that way—*yes*."

"Then I haven't any business in Colchester," I said. "That was—what shall we say?—a fairy-tale. And I haven't any business in Drowton. I just happen to be staying there. If you like to call it a holiday, that's probably as near as we'll get."

"You've got friends there perhaps?"

"Devil a one," I told him.

There was a tap at the door and the sergeant looked in. "Excuse me a moment," Drane said, and out he went to the hall. I went across to the window and the ambulance had gone. Almost at once Drane was back and the sergeant with him.

"Mr. Travers, I'm going to caution you," he said. "I'm giving you certain information and if you care to make a statement, anything you say may be taken down and used in evidence against you."

It had been as plain as a pikestaff which way things were going. There was a tremendous irony in the situation, and I wasn't thinking of that. I'd been quiet and courteous and informative with Drane, and now he was about to play into my hands.

"I'm perfectly agreeable," I said. "What is it you want to tell me?"

"This," he said, and he couldn't keep back a note of triumph. "You saw where Major Pallart's body was found? And where your glove was found? Would it surprise you to know that a footprint of yours was found within a foot or two, against that summerhouse?"

So the water had been placed there deliberately and I had been shepherded that way to leave a clear print which the sergeant had taken in quick-drying plaster. The print against which they'd checked it had been one I'd left in the soft soil by the summerhouse side-wall that night when I'd waited there and watched.

"I'm not at all surprised there was a footprint of mine there," I said. "You probably know I was dining here two nights ago. Before dinner Major Pallart and I walked round the garden. Mr. Brace may have told you that. We actually went round that summerhouse."

"Wait a moment," Drane said. "This print of yours, and more than one at that, wasn't on the path. It was on the soft ground right up against the side window."

"I'm still not surprised," I said unblushingly. "I looked in that window—or I tried to look in. There were curtains or blinds inside. Pure curiosity. Major Pallart said the place was a white elephant now there was no tennis court, which was why it was kept shut."

Drane and his sergeant exchanged glances.

"As for the glove, that's beyond me," I was going on. "Why anyone should want to incriminate *me* I can't imagine."

"You think that's what it was?"

"Don't you?" I said, and left it at that.

Drane opened his notebook and took a look at the list of questions he'd had in wait for me. He nodded.

"How long have you known Major Pallart?"

"About four days," I said.

There seemed a quick incredulity by the way his eyebrows lifted, so I explained pretty fully, and I said that Mr. Calne could confirm. But there was no mention of that talk we'd had at the Regency, and I was certain enough that Calne wouldn't mention it either. Then I asked if I might have a look at the summerhouse.

"What's the reason?" Drane said, and then there was a tap at the door. A plain-clothes man whom I'd not previously seen took a quick look in and then said Mr. Brace would like to see the Inspector urgently.

I didn't see any particular difference in Brace. He looked a bit dark under the eyes perhaps, and that accentuated the sallowness of his face. He gave me a nod and a tentative smile.

"A bad business all this, Richard," I said.

"Yes," he said, and didn't know where to go on.

"You wanted to see me, sir?" Drane was asking.

Brace was asking if he could possibly get away. He should have left before lunch, but it would do if he could catch the four-fifteen at Colchester. He could explain to his firm and do one or two urgent jobs and then get back to Ninford by the late train if necessary. Drane had a look at his notebook.

"Hawke and Gear, Estate Agents, The Broadway, Feverton," he said. "That's North London. And you'll definitely be back here before the morning?"

Brace said gratefully that he most certainly would.

"Very well, sir," Drane told him. "You're not to leave here till you catch your train."

"Couldn't I go to Wandham to see how Mr. Calne is?"

"I'm afraid not, sir," Drane told him firmly. "There's a telephone here if you want to enquire."

Brace went out. Drane whipped round on the sergeant.

"What was he so keen on going to Wandham for?"

Then he remembered me and knew he'd spoken out of turn.

"Oh yes," he said. "You were asking, sir, about seeing the summerhouse. Any particular reason?"

"Naturally I've got a reason," I said, "even if I'm not prepared at this juncture to tell you just what it is."

Drane shrugged his shoulders.

"Very well, sir. We'll have a quick look."

So in a matter of moments we were on the lawn by the summerhouse and having that look. It was the first time I had had the chance of inspecting one particular window and suddenly I stepped forward and was squatting down. Drane was on my heels in a flash.

"What's the idea?"

"See this bottom right-hand corner?" I said. "A little piece of glass has been nicked clean out. With a diamond, by the look of it. Here's where the diamond slipped."

Drane had a look. He gave a mightily superior smile, and maybe he had a reason.

"All right, sir. Someone cut a corner out of the window. And then what?"

"This," I said, and found a pin under the lapel of my coat. "By manipulating this pin I can gently draw back the blind. I can't see anything at the moment but if it were night and there was a light inside, I could see most of what went on."

He let out a breath as I straightened myself. He gave a grunt, then shook his head impatiently.

"Let's get back to the house," he said, and I knew he was thinking pretty hard as we went back across the lawn. He didn't say a word until we were in the lounge.

"Do you know, sir, I can't make you out. Either you know nothing about this affair or you know a whole lot more than you ought to."

"Before we go into that, let's get back to the summerhouse window," I said. "I don't want you to think I'm being superior when I say I'm an older man than yourself. And I've always been interested in murder cases. That's why I think that when you've found who cut the corner out of that window, you'll be well on the way to knowing who killed Major Pallart."

He had been staring, as well he might.

"You don't tell me, sir, that you suddenly discovered that window." The look was what he meant to be piercing. "Why shouldn't you have cut that hole yourself?"

"If you mean why *couldn't* I have cut the hole, then the answer is that I certainly could have cut it. So could you. But you didn't. Neither did I."

He prowled about the room for a few moments, then anchored himself with his back to me at the window. Suddenly he whipped round.

"I'll get you to stay in the dining-room for just a few minutes," he said. "I don't think I'll keep you long."

So I waited in the dining-room. It was well past lunch time so I stayed my hunger with a pipe. And, self-righteously or not, I was rather pleased with myself. But perhaps I'd better explain just what I mean.

This case, in my unbiased view, was more than a local Detective-Inspector could handle. From what I had seen of Drane I was of the considered opinion that even if I were to tell him every detail of what I knew and what I suspected, he would still be unable to profit sufficiently by the knowledge. He might even bungle things and at the best waste invaluable time.

George Wharton had said—and many a true word is spoken in jest—that if there were a murder, then I, and by that he doubtless meant *we*, should be in a unique position. I thought so now, and it was in the interests of justice that I tried—shall we say?—to think it. Drane and his feelings didn't matter a hoot. The essential thing was that the murderer of Guy Pallart should not escape the law.

Meanwhile, I could tell myself, I'd played scrupulously fair with Drane, and I should hate to be in a position where he would later think that I had been deliberately concealing knowledge and, above all, the knowledge of what my job actually was. But, as I said, I had played fair, especially in the matter of the window. And I was prepared to go on playing fair, provided he played fair with me. And that, it seemed, he hadn't so far done.

But for the fact that I was who I was, I might have been in quite a nasty corner. On the strength of a glove and a footprint, he was making me his principal suspect. And I was telling myself—unreasonably, you may think—that I neither looked nor acted like a murderer. Drane had, in fact, been both too precipitate and not precipitate enough. He had my town address, for instance, and he might by now have got in touch with St. Martin's Chambers, but apparently he hadn't. Unless, as I suddenly thought, he was doing that now.

It was then that he came back, far sooner than I'd expected, and the first look at his face told me that he knew no more about me than when he'd last seen me.

"I don't think there's any need to keep you here," he told me. "Only one thing, sir. We'd like you to stay at the hotel and be on tap, so to speak."

"You'd rather I didn't leave Drowton," I said.

"That's it, sir." Then he added that he didn't know what might crop up.

He went with me to the car where I had a look for my other glove. It wasn't there, which seemed to show, as I told him, that *both* gloves had been left behind the previous night. He didn't seem too interested and off I drove. Then about a mile along the road I saw behind me a motor-bicycle. That was natural enough, but when I slowed, the motor-bicyclist slowed too, and when I shot my car on, he was still lying well placed. Drane, in other words, had a man on my tail, and I wasn't too pleased about that. But I drove on at my usual pace and left the car in the hotel yard.

I had a look at the solenoid and, sure enough, the motor-cyclist drew in at the yard. He hoisted the bicycle to its stand and I went into the hotel the back way. But I didn't go through to the bar. There was another door to the left that led by the lavatory, and when I was sure that Drane's man was inside too, I nipped out again. I loosened the valve of his rear tyre till there was a gentle hiss and then I was in my car and off. I turned sharp right and right again and back towards Ninford. But only the few hundred yards to the Grapes. There I turned into the yard to hide the car and then made my way to the bar.

I had a pint of bitter and a chat with the landlord. When we were on what seemed good enough terms, I asked if I might use his telephone. I also produced a pound note and said I'd have another pint and perhaps he'd have one with me. He could give me the change when the Exchange had told me the cost of the call. Then I rang up the Yard and asked urgently for George Wharton. It was about three to one against his being in, but in he was, and in about a couple of minutes he was on the line.

"Remember Guy Pallart?" I began. "The man who was going to commit a murder."

"What about him?" fired George.

"He's been murdered himself!"

George gave a grunt, and that was all.

"I've got to talk fast, George," I said, "but here's what's been happening. I'll fill in the details when I see you."

I told him about Calne and so to the happenings of the morning. When I came to Drane's suspicions of myself and the man on my tail I was expecting a chuckle and a witticism. George merely gave a prodigious snort.

"What *is* he? A bloody fool, or what?"

I said that maybe he hadn't had too much experience and was just a bit flummoxed.

"What do you want me to do?" George cut in. "Ring up his Chief Constable and say who you are?"

"Not exactly, George," I said, and I was feeling a bit specious as I unfolded the scheme.

"We've got specialised knowledge," I said. "You're the man for the job. Drane can't handle it."

"But he's got to handle it."

"Not necessarily," I said, and I knew George was nibbling at the edge of the worm. "You see the Powers-That-Be and get them convinced that we can act on special information, or what-have-you. Get them to make contact with Drane's Chief Constable. You don't want *me* to tell you what to do."

"What *is* this?" George was asking with ersatz indignation. "A private wangle, or what?"

I ignored that.

"Here's my telephone number at the Ostlers," I said. "I'll be in all day and you can give me a ring. Sorry, but I simply daren't hang on any longer."

I replaced the receiver. Then I rang Enquiries and asked the charge for my call. Five minutes later I was on my way back to the Ostlers, and feeling filled to the eyebrows with beer. Drane's man was standing at the yard entrance but I looked clean through him and when I'd parked the car in the shade, I went on to the hotel. It was almost two o'clock but they found me a tepid lunch.

When I'd finished it, I went along to the telephone booth. Drane's man was inside so I went away. When I came back he was sitting in the public lounge. This time it was Bill Ellice's office that I wanted, and it was five minutes before I was through. Bill wasn't there and his secretary didn't know what had been done about that commission I'd given, except that Bill was working on it.

"Give him this message and make it urgent," I said. "He's bound to be back in time."

"Ready," she said, and I gave her a description of Richard Brace. He was coming to town by the four-fifteen from Colchester, I said, and I wanted him picked up at Liverpool Street and a watch kept on him till he took a train back at night for Colchester. I wanted a highly summarised report of his movements telephoned to me at Drowton in the morning, and, if possible, between eight and half-past. She repeated and said she thought it would be O.K., and with that I went upstairs to my room. There I had a nap—a most unusual thing for me—and it was nearly tea-time when I woke. By the time I'd had a wash and brush-up, tea was on. Drane's man was occupying a strategic position in the hall. I looked clean through him again and went on to the private lounge and tea.

My crosswords took me till well after five o'clock and then I went out in search of an evening paper, and I didn't even trouble to ascertain if Drane's man was on my heels. Then at half-past five a London paper arrived but it was too early an edition to have news of Pallart's murder. So I took a short walk and as I was coming back to the hotel, I caught sight of Drane's man ahead of me. When I went into the hotel he was in the telephone booth again.

The time went slowly by. I went upstairs again, had an unnecessary polish-up for dinner, came down and treated myself to another beer and then went in to my meal. After it I sat yarning with those charming people I've already mentioned and at nine o'clock we listened to the news. The world was in just the same hell of a state as it had been for months, and Pallart's murder, even if it were known, was too insignificant a trifle. After that we had quite an animated discussion on the aphorism that a country gets the government it deserves, and then it was time for my couple to go up to bed. I ordered a whisky and sat doggedly on.

At half-past ten nothing had happened and I went up to bed. I'd hardly got in the room when the hall porter was calling me down to the telephone.

"Hallo?" I said.

"Wharton speaking," came the voice, and that dignified opening told me that George had something to explain away or conceal.

"That matter you were referring to us this morning," he was going on. "We've made contact with the people concerned and we shall probably be taking over. I'd like you to meet me at Ninford at about eleven o'clock Monday morning. The day after tomorrow."

I wanted to say vulgarly, "Come off it, George," or a more tempered, "Good for you, George," but I said neither.

"I'll be there," I said, and before I could get in another word, he had rung off.

I left the booth and made for the stairs. As I glanced back I saw Drane's man making for the telephone. What he'd be doing, I thought, was tracing my call, and if he was successful, then he was due for a shock. But his troubles didn't keep me awake. I slept like a log and when I woke I knew that something more than a new day had dawned. The preliminaries were over and the curtain was up, and life was nothing but anticipation.

PART II
THE WRONG MAN

CHAPTER VII
GETTING TO WORK

WHARTON WAS already at Ninford when I arrived that morning. He can be a fine, dignified, impressive figure when he likes, and that morning he was most urbane. Inspector Drane was going to lend us a hand, he said, and he was sure this business wasn't going to take us too long.

Drane was most apologetic. I was apologetic too, and everything ended as happily as you please.

"What we've got to bear in mind," George said, "is this. Hurry and scurry won't get us anywhere, unless it's in a muddle. There's a score of things we might be doing, but we're not doing them. We're going to sit in the shade of that summerhouse, where we can't be overheard from the house, and Mr. Travers is going to tell us everything he knows. When we know as much as he does, then we can move on from there."

Arthur Friske was hovering round and Drane had him bring chairs to the summerhouse verandah. Another man suddenly appeared; a man of about fifty, clean-shaven and rather sharp-featured.

"Want me to lend you a hand, Arthur?"

"No thank you, Fred," Friske told him. "Nothing to do except these chairs. Unless you like to bring one o' them low tables."

"Who's he?" Wharton asked Drane.

"The gardener, Fred Wilkin," Drane said. "A bit too smart for my liking."

Wharton was pricking up his ears.

"What do you mean?"

"Well, he struck me as being a bit of a sea-lawyer, sir. Thinks he knows all the answers. And a bit of a Nosey Parker."

Wilkin was bringing the table and fussily placing it. He gave a quick look at us from under his eyebrows.

"'Morning, gentlemen. A nice morning. This all right for the chair?"

"Leave it there and we'll see to it," Drane told him snappily, and in a couple of minutes we were comfortably settled. Notebooks were out, though it was Drane who did most writing.

As far as I knew I kept not a single word back. For Drane's benefit I went over the talk at the Regency, the events of the Wednesday night and everything that happened on the cruise.

I suppose the whole thing took me the best part of an hour, and then came the questions.

"The Calne business seems the crux of everything," Wharton said. "But let's get something straight. Just as you were leaving on the Thursday night, Pallart told you that Calne had been ringing up about the cruise, and wanted you to join the party."

"Yes?" I said.

"But Calne told you yesterday morning that it wasn't he who suggested the cruise. Pallart suggested it."

"Right again."

"And Pallart and this Doctor Kales were the only two who had a chance to tip Calne overboard?"

"That's so. Young Brace and I were below. We went below with the chairs and left Pallart and Calne on deck. Then Kales went up with the binoculars. It was after he'd gone up that we heard the holler."

"And this Kales didn't hear the holler?"

"I wouldn't go so far as that," I said. "I don't remember asking him. All I will say is that at no time did he say he *did* hear Calne's holler."

"If you'll pardon me," Drane cut in, "he might have heard a holler and not known what it was. If some people are below deck and some on deck, there's liable to be hollering."

"Not a bad point," said Wharton amiably, and made a quick note in his book. "In a very quiet way we must have a talk with Kales. You say he did actually leave Colchester by that train?"

"No doubt about it," Drane said. "He was in it when the train moved off and he had a ticket for Liverpool Street."

There was a sound by the side of the summerhouse. Wharton frowned, then got to his feet. He could move remarkably quickly when he liked.

"Well, what are *you* doing?" we heard him say.

"Just going to clip this hedge, sir. One of the last things the Major told me to do."

"Respecting the dead master's wishes. That it?"

"Well, something like it, sir."

"Well, perhaps you'll respect them this afternoon," Wharton told him genially. "What time do you go to dinner?"

"Twelve o'clock, sir—usually."

"Well, it's gone that now," Wharton said.

"Well, I'm darned," he said. "Just show you how time does, fly. I never had an idea it was as late as that."

We could hear him moving off. Wharton came back.

"Very touching," he said. "Very touching indeed."

He made a note in his book, then was peering at me over his spectacle tops.

"He isn't a countyman, is he? Mr. Travers," he explained to Drane, "is pretty reliable where dialect is concerned."

"I'd say he's definitely a Londoner," I said. "Whatever words he used, his accent would let him down."

Wharton gave Drane the old Coliseum look—that of the lion who has his eye on a nice fat Christian.

"We're going to keep an eye on Mr. Wilkin. I wouldn't be surprised if he turns out a bit better than a knave. He might be our ace of trumps."

Drane recognised a joke and chuckled suitably. Wharton gave me an incipient glare and wanted to know what he'd been talking about.

"About Calne," I said, "and Pallart lying about the cruise."

"Yes," he said, and gave himself a nod. "I don't know if you're both in agreement, but we shall have to go very warily over the Calne business."

Being in agreement was George's humbug. What he'd made up his mind to do, he'd do and we'd do. But I said I was sure he was right. For one thing we'd get no help from Calne himself.

"Even if it were permissible, you couldn't browbeat a man of Calne's type," I said. "He was struck on the head and I think he knows who did it—"

"Therefore he knows why it was done."

"Maybe," I said. "But if we're dealing with possibilities, then it's not impossible that a mistake was made."

"How do you mean?" Wharton said, and glared.

"Well, the wrong man may have been tipped overboard. I admit that Kales could have been the only one concerned, but he might have intended to kill Pallart and he got Calne instead."

Wharton waved an impatient hand.

"You're getting into far too deep waters. Let's take everything as read and follow it up from that angle first. Calne, I should tell you, isn't allowed to see anyone yet. There might be an exception in your case. Later in the day, perhaps."

That suited me well enough. I was longing to see Calne again and watch his reactions to the Pallart murder.

"Just one last thing," I said. "If it was Pallart who tried to kill Calne, then Calne, now Pallart's dead, may decide to talk a bit more freely."

"Let's hope he does," Wharton said. "It'll save us a hell of a lot of time."

Friske appeared. Wharton was wanted at the telephone. Drane and I sat on. We lighted cigarettes and Drane said it ought to be an education to work with anyone like Superintendent Wharton. I said it was, and I didn't add that Drane might be a bit over-educated by the time he had completed a course with Wharton. But I did add a word of advice. Wharton was often inclined to be secretive and keep his subordinates in the dark. That, I said, was because he liked to be sure of his ground. I was just adding that his bark was worse than his bite when George appeared. He was coming towards us at a goodish rate.

"A spanner in the works already," he told us. He dropped heavily into the chair, adjusted his spectacles and gave Drane a look. "What was the earliest time for Pallart to have been killed?"

"One o'clock," Drane said, but the tiniest bit nervously.

Something in Wharton's look made him pause.

"Wait a minute, though. He took Kales to the station to catch the twelve-forty. He might have been killed on the way home."

Wharton nodded. I could discern a specialised form of that Coliseum look.

"Pallart didn't go to the station," he said. *"He was dead at eleven o'clock."*

Drane's eyes bulged.

"There isn't a shadow of doubt about it," Wharton was going on. "Your own man and our man are in agreement. Your man took too much account of rigor mortis. That gave the time as round about one o'clock. But you can be wrong about rigor mortis and you can fake it, but you can't fake a stomach content. Mr. Travers knows what Pallart had for dinner at Dovercourt, and when he had it."

"Then who took Kales to the station?" asked Drane.

"Why worry?" Wharton told him amiably. "We shall know. It's more than enough at the moment to know that Pallart didn't. If we hadn't been aware of that, we'd have been on the wrong track and probably for good and all."

"Mind if I mention something?" I said. "Let's take this house on the Friday night, at ten o'clock, which was the time when I left. Loret went straight to bed. Is that right, Drane?"

"Quite right. Brace confirmed it."

"And Brace went straight to bed?"

"That's right. Loret confirmed it."

"How?" cut in Wharton.

"Because Loret made him some hot milk toddy," Drane said, "and gave it to him in his room on his way to his own bed."

"Then Kales was left with Pallart," I said. "Friske cleared away the supper that wasn't wanted and he went—when?"

"He says at ten o'clock."

"He was probably in a hurry," I said. "His wife would be expecting him home before then. Susan Beavers is a sound sleeper?"

"Sleeps like a log and snores like blazes," Drane said. "Loret once had the bedroom next to hers but he had to move it to one further along. The only thing is that, like all old people, she wakes up early. Generally as soon as it's light and then she says she doesn't go off again."

"Very well," I said. "It's likely that the whole house was asleep at ten-fifteen except for Pallart and Kales. Why shouldn't Pallart, for some reason or other, have taken Kales to the station then?"

Wharton stole some of my thunder.

"I see what you're getting at. Someone had to take Kales to Colchester and someone brought the car back. If it wasn't Pallart's car, then it was a hired car, and that'll be easy to trace. But assume Pallart did take Kales to Colchester and got back here in time to be murdered." He peered at us over his spectacle tops and wagged a cautionary finger. "Why should Kales he taken to Colchester two hours before his train left?"

"And what did he do with himself during the two hours?" added Drane.

"There're two answers," I said. "Pallart had an urgent appointment at eleven o'clock with the man who murdered him. That's why he got Kales away."

"What man?"

"Don't crowd me, George," I said. "I haven't got second-sight. But at a guess I'd say the appointment was with that German prisoner whom I saw on the Wednesday night."

George moistened his lips and blew out his moustache. "That's an idea," he said, and then he was glaring again. "But what's the other answer?"

"Kales," I said. "Interview Kales and we may know everything. Even if he can't give all the answers, or the right ones, he can tell us what Pallart told *him*."

George looked at his watch and got to his feet.

"Time we had a bite of something. No reason why we shouldn't eat and talk at the same time."

*   *   *   *   *

George's headquarters was temporarily at the Wheatsheaf, and it was there that lunch had been arranged for the three of us. George was in quite a good humour and I knew why. The lunch looked good and when George feeds at Government expense, he likes the Government to do him well. You'd have thought by the lavish way he ordered beer that he was paying for it himself.

"This Kales," he said. "A quiet, studious sort of chap according to Travers. But what was the point of contact between him and Pallart?"

"Ask me another," I said. "Pallart was something of a dark horse. He liked to give an appearance of cynicism or flippancy but my idea is that he was a very shrewd fellow indeed. He might have had plenty of interests that nobody suspected."

I'd been wondering how to divulge what Bill Ellice had told me over the telephone the previous morning.

"For instance," I went hastily on, "as soon as I saw something serious about that talk at the Regency, I got a friend of mine to make a few judicious enquiries—"

"Bill Ellice?" George asked bluntly. After all, Drane didn't know who Ellice was.

"Yes," I said. "Pallart was a prisoner for five years and I wanted to know what his prison life had been like. Ellice's information hasn't been cross-checked but he's learned from an unimpeachable source that Pallart was just a good fellow-prisoner, if you know what I mean. He had only one hobby, and he took it up in 1942 when some French officers were in the same Camp. He studied French and got really good at it. He had books sent him from home. He was still hard at it when he was freed."

"Where's that get us?" Wharton asked. "Didn't most officers take up the study of something or other? Some even sat for English examinations through the post."

"You didn't know Pallart," I said. "He was the open air type—"

"I know he was a good cricketer," Drane said. "I'd seen his name before the war. He played for the Club and Ground."

"He was good at tennis and a good swimmer," I said. "You'd never think of him as studious. Yet he began specialising in French, and he stuck to it. I admit he had a game leg, but that doesn't account for it." I realised I was getting a bit from the point. "All I'm trying to prove is that he wasn't a county lounge-lizard. He had brains. And Kales spoke French like a native. That may have been the point of contact."

"Curious what you were saying about Kales," Wharton told Drane. "Not a mention of him among Pallart's papers. No address, no telephone number, no nothing."

"Surely that shows they were pretty close friends," I said. "One keeps the address and telephone number only of an acquaintance. You know those of your friends by heart."

"Well, we'll soon have our hands on Kales," George said. "I've set the ball rolling with the Home Office and we ought to be hearing something soon. And now what about that young Brace? Would you mind going over that bit about him and his uncle? That private talk you and Pallart had?"

I repeated it quickly. Dance bands, crooners and jazz generally were an infuriation to Pallart. They were the lowest form of a vulgarity of which it was in the worst possible taste even to speak. If Brace didn't stick to the profession he had now chosen, or one of which his uncle approved, then Brace, as far as Pallart was concerned, would be washed completely out. Brace knew it, and had had his final warning.

"Which brings me to something else," I said quickly. "I haven't had a chance to mention it before. But I happened to be present when Brace was asking Drane for permission to go to town on urgent business. I wondered what that business was, so I got hold of Bill Ellice again."

"I checked up," Drane said. "I got hold of his firm and spoke to one of the principals." He whipped out his notebook. "A youngish fellow by the sound of him. A Mr. Charles Hawke, of Hawke and Gear, Estate Agents. He said there *was* urgent business for Brace to attend to, but he said he'd see that he was able to be back here if we wanted him."

"Everything's above board so far," I said. "Brace parked his bag at Liverpool Street and went straight to his firm. He didn't stay more than a quarter of an hour. Then he collected his bag and went to his flat. A nice little flat just off Jermyn Street. It costs him three-fifty a year, furnished."

George actually stopped chewing.

"Throwing his weight about, isn't he? And weren't you saying something, Drane, about his trying to hot-stuff you about his allowance?"

"He told me an absolute lie," Drane said, "though I haven't had the chance to confront him with it yet. He said his uncle allowed him two hundred and fifty a year, I checked as well as I could by counterfoils and made it a hundred and fifty. I rang the bank and they confirmed it *was* a hundred and fifty, payable monthly."

"And what's he get from his firm?"

"A hundred and fifty, according to that Mr. Hawke. He's learning the job and it's what Hawke called a nominal salary. Hawke spoke very well of him, by the way."

"Two hundred-and-fifties don't make three-fifty," George said. "Was that what his uncle meant when he told you, Travers, that he'd discovered something?"

"Most likely," I said. "Brace explained it away by a big win over a horse."

"Well, I ran my rule over him," George said, "and I think that young fellow's got something on his mind. It might be good policy to keep him hanging about."

"You haven't heard the rest of his movements on Saturday," I reminded him. "And something else seems unusual. Wouldn't his firm be closed on a Saturday evening? Unless he had a key of his own, he'd find the place shut."

"Apparently they were expecting him," Drane said. "That Mr. Hawke knew he couldn't get to town before early evening."

"We'll leave it," I said. "But you may remember he told you that he had some urgent jobs to do. Yet he was only at Feverton for a quarter of an hour. My idea is that the whole thing was an excuse to get to town."

"But Mr. Hawke told me personally that Brace was wanted at the firm for something urgent."

"Well, there we are," I said. "I've got a hunch that there was something remarkably fishy about Brace's having to go to town on a Saturday evening. But to go on from when he went to his flat. He was there till about half-past seven. When he came down he was wearing a dinner-jacket suit. Then Ellice's man lost him."

"Lost him?" George glared as if I'd been responsible myself.

"Yes," I said. "Brace must have ordered a taxi by telephone and he simply walked downstairs and into the taxi and was gone before Ellice's man could do anything about it. Brace came back at nine-forty, changed his clothes and then took the Underground for Liverpool Street. If you ask me what he did during his absence from the flat, I'd say he either stood some girl a dinner or had one by himself."

"Next time we turn him loose we'll see he doesn't give us the slip," George said, and pushed his plate aside. Drane and I had finished eating long since. George groomed his hanging garden of a moustache and wondered when the pot of tea was coming in. Drane dutifully pushed the bell.

"There's one thing you and Drane may have discussed," I said, "and if so, I'd like to hear your views about it. What was Pallart doing with that German prisoner in the secrecy of that summerhouse?"

George made a wry face. Drane was looking down his nose. I had a sudden horrible realisation.

"My God! You don't mean that Pallart was a sexual pervert?"

"The obvious explanation, isn't it?" George said.

"But Pallart wasn't that sort."

"What do you mean—that sort?"

"He wasn't the type. I never heard him make a dirty joke or mention sex in any way. We all agreed he was an outdoor man. A sportsman."

"So were one or two others I could mention, and international figures at that." He sniffed. "But your ideas are all muddled. First you say you never heard Pallart mention sex and you claim that that makes him normal. That's what makes him abnormal."

"Then what about the snooper?"

George gave me a pitying look.

"Didn't we discover him this morning?"

"You mean Wilkin, the gardener?"

"Isn't it plain as the nose on your face?"

The pot of tea came in and George promptly began pouring out.

"What was Wilkin's idea?" I said. "Blackmail?"

"That, or sheer curiosity."

"If it *was* Wilkin—"

"Who else could have tampered with that window?" cut in Drane.

"Of course," I said. "Let's say it *was* Wilkin. What I was going to add was that it wasn't the first time he'd snooped. On that Wednesday night he'd been on the lookout for Pallart's car. As soon as Pallart and the German were in the summerhouse, Wilkin came across the lawn like a streak."

I remembered something else.

"By the way, I've never had a look inside that summerhouse."

"We're going back there now," George said, and added piously while he poured himself a second cup, that we couldn't stay talking all day.

"There's a special job for you this afternoon," he told me, and he began briefing me between gulps at the tea. He'd got in touch with Morton and Hall well, the Pallart family solicitors, and had learned the main provisions of the will. I was to see the solicitors personally and collect a confidential draft.

"That's only a blind," George told me. "The real job's right up your alley. Get people to talk and learn all you can about Pallart. Not," he added unctuously, "that I need to tell you your job."

He finished his cup, hesitated about having a third, and then got to his feet. We piled into my car and in a couple of minutes were on the summerhouse verandah. George produced a Yale key and inside we went.

The place smelt musty.

"Might as well have some daylight in," he told us, and was adding that someone had made a pretty thorough job of the black-out. I watched the room slowly come into view.

"Practically no dust," I said.

"Wilkin said he had orders about a month ago to give the place a thorough cleaning," Drane said. "He said it had been shut up all the war and was all cobwebs and filth."

"Probably that was what aroused his curiosity," I said. "Why he had to clean out the place, and then it was locked up and never used."

There was a trestle table on end against the back wall, and oddments of chairs. A sack hanging on a hook had a tennis net in it, and there was a marker, and a box containing a croquet set.

"What's the coil of rope for?" I was wondering.

There looked about ten foot of it, and it was also on a peg on the south wall. I said it looked remarkably new.

"It wasn't a piece of this that Pallart was strangled with?" I asked.

"It was something much finer than this," George said. "And the strangler took it away with him."

My thoughts shifted on.

"I suppose it was that game leg of his that stopped Pallart from putting up a fight."

"He was cracked on the skull first and strangled after," George said casually. I felt a sudden irritation at having been kept in the dark about that. Then I realised that for once George wasn't being secretive. He just hadn't had the occasion to tell me before.

"That chair looks rather out of place, doesn't it?" I said. "Surely far too good to be kept in here?"

It was a Tudor chair of heavy oak, with the usual carved back and square, uncarved stretchers, and it stood almost in the centre of the room.

"Is it genuine?" George said.

"Collector's condition," I told him. "A very nice piece indeed."

It was like George to ask what it was worth. I told him I wasn't *au fait* with modern prices, but I'd cheerfully give fifty guineas for it myself.

"Perhaps it didn't suit the rest of the furniture in the house," Drane said.

"Maybe not," I said, but it was queer that that chair should be there. And there was no point in telling Drane that he was talking through his hat. In the hall of the house was a carved chest with which that chair would have gone to perfection. What I'd do, I told myself, was have a word with Susan. She'd know how long the chair had been in the summerhouse, and who put it there and why.

Another couple of minutes and I was on the way to Colchester. I was to be no more than half an hour with the solicitors, and had I but known it, I was to be told all that was needful for the Case. The sifting of talk and rumour and gossip and what is supposed to be evidence is always a tricky business. What seems important may have no value whatever, and an apparent triviality may be an essential clue. That afternoon I was to have that essential clue in my fingers, and it slipped clean through.

Not that I'm blaming myself unduly. George Wharton and Drane were told all that I heard, and neither saw the significance of one vital thing.

CHAPTER VIII
MIRROR FOR PALLART

GEORGE HAD rung through and I was expected. Without any preliminaries at all, I was shown into the room of Henry Hall well. He was a man of over seventy, still hale and upright. He had a fine, old-world courtesy, and I won his heart by guessing that the rose he had in his button-hole had come from his own garden.

He gave me a sealed envelope for Wharton, and apologised for insistence on secrecy. But obviously he wasn't expecting me to rise from my chair and depart before we'd had a friendly chat.

"A great shock to me," he said. "I knew Guy Pallart as a boy and it was almost like the death of one of my own. You knew him well?"

"Not too well," I said. "He was a member of a club of mine— the Regency—and I met him there."

"That's strange," he said, and smiled. "We must be fellow members. I put Guy up for the Regency quite recently. I was only too glad to. I thought it would give him a new interest in life."

"I saw him very little," I said, "but I liked him quite a lot. He came of good stock?"

"The very best. And he was a credit to it." He gave a little apologetic clearing of the throat. "I hope you catch his murderer. Some burglarious scoundrel, I expect, whom he happened to surprise."

"That's one of the lines we're working on," I said unblushingly. "But about the will. I'll certainly hand this envelope to Superintendent Wharton, but would you care to give me a rough outline meanwhile?"

He said he'd be delighted and as soon as he began, I knew that the conditions were unusual. First there were pensions, handsome ones, for Susan Beavers and Arthur Friske, and a gift of £500 to Loret 'whether or not still in my employ'. The testator expressed the fervent hope that Susan would stay on as housekeeper during her life, and that Friske and his wife would move in also, Friske acting as gardener and general factotum.

That much foreshadowed that the house would not be occupied by whoever the new owner happened to be. Brace was that owner, but on conditions, and a trust had been created to administer the estate and to decide about Brace himself. If at the time of the testator's death he should be earning his living in some honourable profession, then the interest on the estate should be his, and the use of the house. If after five years he was still in the same profession—always at the discretion of the trustees—everything should be his in his own right and he would then assume the additional name of Pallart. There was also a renewed wish for the employment of Friske and his wife, and of Susan if still alive. If Brace did not fulfil the conditions, the house was to become the property of the British Legion as a convalescent home and the estate—some £60,000 gross—would provide for upkeep.

"Isn't that word *honourable* somewhat tricky?" I asked.

"It is," he said. "But the testator insisted on the wording. Later he wrote me a letter which might be produced as evidence in the event of the will being contested. It specifically rules out"—he gave a little cough as if the very words were distasteful—"such things as dance bands."

"He felt pretty strongly?"

"My dear sir, but of course. It was a shock to him and to us all. His sister's son; the only one left of the family, leading a life like that! And after the money that had been spent on him."

"Guy Pallart must have been a generous man," I said, if only to get the conversation to something new.

"Generous to a fault."

"I'd like to have known him before the war."

"I'm glad you said that," he told me. "Five years of captivity made a tremendous difference. And there was his lameness."

"What would you consider his finest quality?" The question may seem stilted but I could see that if the subject was Pallart, Hallwell would go on talking for hours.

"He had many fine qualities," he said reflectively. "He was passionately loyal. Yes," he said and rubbed his lean chin, "perhaps that was his finest quality. Obstinate, of course. Once he made his mind up there was no moving him. His father intended him for the Church, but he held his ground. He wanted to go into the Army, and his father had to give way."

"He was clever?"

He frowned slightly. I knew I hadn't used just the right word.

"He had a fine brain," he said. "Queer in some ways. Take that obstinacy, for example. But a very fine brain."

"And you noticed a difference after his return?"

"An enormous difference. He was infinitely older. He seemed to me to have queer moods. One minute almost childishly—what shall I say—well, irresponsible is perhaps the word. Then he'd retire into himself, so to speak. He'd seem cynical and embittered. It took me some time to discover why. I should have known, of course."

I raised enquiring eyebrows.

"The death of his fiancée," he said. "And the fact that he heard of it in Germany, in that Camp. What could he do but brood."

"A charming girl was she?"

"Perfectly charming," he said. "Marie Courtold. Her father was British consul in Algiers at the time of his death. Her mother—she was French—died just after the death of the daughter. I'm not exaggerating when I say the death of her only child broke her heart.

"Everything was made more tragic," he was going on, "by the fact that Marie Courtold and Guy Pallart should have been married on his last leave before Dunkirk. The two were passionately in love, but Marie had some job or other at the Foreign Office and her leave had to be cancelled, and so the wedding was put off till Guy's next leave. That leave never came."

"When did she die?" I asked him.

"In 1944," he said, and shook a sad head. "It's only lately that we've been told how. She was doing some special work in France—Normandy I think, or was it Paris?—and fell into the hands of the Gestapo. I believe she was tortured—poor girl!—and finally shot."

"How perfectly damnable!"

"It doesn't bear thinking of," he said. "But there we are. It was no wonder he was an embittered man. He'd never have married after it. He assured me of that the very last time I saw him."

"It's curious," I said, "but I never noticed that embittered side of him. The flippancy and perhaps the cynicism—yes."

"He was beginning to get over it," he said. "I noticed quite a change for the better the last few months. I thought he'd found some new interest in life. He was much more like his old self."

He was getting to his feet then and apologising for keeping me so long.

"Something I was meaning to ask you," I said. "Did you ever run across David Calne? He was a friend of Guy's."

"David Calne?" he frowned. "I can't say I remember the name. Not that I know all Guy's friends."

"David Calne hires Walker's Ferry," I said.

"Walker's Ferry?" he said. "Of course, yes. Calne, you said."

"David Calne."

"Of course," he said again. "I remember now. We drew up the agreement." He smiled regretfully. "At my age we begin to forget things, especially names. But I should have remembered the name. I remonstrated personally with Major Pallart about the amount of rent."

"Too stiff?" I asked, and smiled.

"Not at all," he said. "This is highly confidential, of course, but the rent Major Pallart was proposing was absurd in the view of my clerk and he referred the matter to me. Between ourselves, fifty pounds a year, even unfurnished, is ridiculous. Still"—he waved a dissociating hand—"he refused to treat the matter seriously. He said this Mr. Calne was a friend of his and lion didn't eat lion, or words to that effect. I suppose he was right. He didn't really need the money."

It was touch and go whether or not I was outstaying my welcome but I did venture to ask Hallwell if he'd dined at the Old Vicarage in the last few weeks. He said he had—about three weeks ago.

"That French chef of his knows his job," I said.

"Between ourselves," he said, and gave me a rather quizzical look, "I've been wondering if I could get hold of him myself. You'll pardon anything so blatant, so soon after poor Guy's death."

"It's not blatant at all," I said. "It's foresight. Susan's a great character?"

"A fine, trustworthy woman," he said. "I've known her almost as long as I've known anything. If ever I live to be her age, I hope I shall be as active."

"And as mentally alert."

"Exactly," he said, and gave himself a nod.

I held out a hand and said how grateful I was. The pleasure had been his, he said, and he hoped he'd see me again. He went out with me to the car, and I told him that as soon as we'd anything whatever to report, I'd give him the news confidentially. He waved a final goodbye as the car moved off.

I didn't push the car on; in fact, I dawdled, for I was trying to assess the value of what I had learned. By the time I was nearing

Ninford, it seemed that the one unusual and unexpected thing had been that matter of Walker's Ferry. It confirmed, it is true, that Pallart and Calne must have become pretty close friends in the comparatively short time they had known each other, but what it didn't explain was the total lack of agreement between what Hallwell had told me, and what Calne had told me. According to the lawyer, Guy Pallart was generous to a fault, and the fact that he had charged fifty pounds a year for what would have fetched three times that sum was very definite proof. But Calne had said that Pallart was rather close in money matters, and had instanced the fact that he had charged him a rather exorbitant rent. Why should Calne have told me that deliberate lie?—for that was what it was. Try as I might I could find no answer and the more inexplicable it became, the more importance did it assume.

As I drove in, I caught sight of Richard Brace in a deckchair on the summerhouse verandah, and he waved back in response to my cheery salute. I was thinking he was a lucky fellow. Jacob served seven years for Leah, but Brace was getting a much better bargain. He had only to put in another five years with his present firm and he'd get a house and an income that even Comrade Dalton couldn't wholly confiscate.

The lounge door was open and Wharton and Drane were working there. A telephone extension had been run through while I was away, and George said that among other things they'd been working on that telephone call that the chef had taken for Kales. Exchange was emphatic that no distance call had been received on the Friday, and the call must therefore have been a local one on which they had no check.

"What's it mean?" I said. "That Kales was lured away?"

"That's what we were just wondering," Wharton said, and was running a quick eye through the contents of the sealed envelope. I wandered out to the cloak-room and had a freshen-up, and just as I got back to the lounge, Susan was looking in. She seemed to me to be looking older, but she was straight as ever, and her scarcely wrinkled face still had that wonderful rosy colouring.

"That would be wonderful, Mrs. Beavers," Wharton told her. "But only if it's not going to give you any trouble."

"No trouble at all, sir," she told him, and I thought what a fine, natural dignity she had. And the tea must have been practically ready, for in a couple of minutes she was coming in with a tray. Wharton sprang forward at once, before Brace or I could move. He always did have a great way with women.

"No, sir, don't you bother," Susan told him, and clung to the tray. "You put that table where you want it and I'll see to the rest."

I caught her eye and it seemed to me for a moment as if she must give one of those little laughs of hers.

"There you are, sir," she said. "You just ring the bell when it's finished and I'll see the tray's taken away."

George was almost drooling as he looked at the plate of cakes.

"These are yours, Mrs. Beavers?"

She smiled as she told him that Loret had made them.

"Not that I ain't a good pastry-maker," she told him with a little toss of the head.

"I'll wager you are," Wharton said, and added a whimsicality of his own. "You're like my mother. You belong to the time when women were really taught to cook."

Then he was peering archly at her over his spectacle tops.

"We mustn't forget to congratulate Mrs. Beavers."

For a minute we heard Wharton at his condoling and then congratulatory best. Susan's eyes blinked, but she didn't cry.

"I don't want the money, sir," she said. "I'd give every single penny I have or am likely to have, if only he was back here again."

"I know you would," Wharton told her. "Still, it was what he wished. And don't you bother about the tray. Send Loret in for it. There's one or two things I want to see him about."

Wharton presided at the tray. There were exactly six cakes, and that gave Drane and me a fair share. I began a recital of what had happened that afternoon, and I pointed out the queer discrepancy in the matter of the rent of Walker's Ferry.

"I want you to see Calne this evening," Wharton said. "Round about six o'clock ought to fit in pretty well. Drane's starting the hunt for that blond German prisoner. He thinks, and so do I, that he's one of the prisoners allowed to live out. There's a big camp at Tuddley, near Drowton, where they keep the records."

Drane was going to use his own people and lay hands as soon as possible on that German, George went on. Pallart had originally intended to be home at about nine o'clock on the Friday night, but that dinner at Dovercourt had upset the schedule, and if he'd had an appointment with that German, then the German would have been waiting in or near the summerhouse. And that was where Pallart had been struck down and then strangled.

I was thinking that George must have something up his sleeve which he wasn't as yet prepared to disclose, for what he had said about the German cut clean across what we had agreed about Kales. If the German was waiting and Pallart knew it, then Pallart must have gone to the summerhouse as soon as Loret and Brace had gone to bed, and that would be when the German—according to Wharton's new theory—must have killed him. Then who took Kales to Colchester? Kales couldn't have driven himself, unless the car had come back from Colchester of its own accord.

Drane was leaving and I happened to be making a note or two when I saw something underlined in my book.

"There's something I've made a note to ask you, George," I said. "When you were speaking of rigor mortis and how it could be faked, were you thinking of anything specially connected with Pallart's body and the time of his death?"

"As a matter of fact I was," George said. "I didn't put it more clearly because I didn't want to hurt Drane's feelings. But his own man—remember that bonfire case? I—let him be influenced by what he'd heard. There'd been some loose talk about Pallart going to Colchester and not getting back here till one in the morning. That's why he was relying on rigor mortis. He still swears that rigor mortis showed the time of death as round about one o'clock."

"Was there any faking on somebody's part?"

George shrugged his shoulders as he went over to the bell. "It was a warm night but it needn't have been so warm in any one particular spot. There's no guarantee that Pallart was killed where his body was found. A dozen different things might have to be taken into account."

He didn't say what they were, for Loret was at the door. "Come in, M. Loret," Wharton called. "Come and sit down. We'll speak English if you don't mind, though I speak a bit of French myself."

George was being modest. George's mother had been French, and it had been his knowledge of French that had put him on the first rung of the ladder. George could even swear fluently in French—an ultimate accomplishment in any language. Now he passed his cigarette case and mentioned that M. Loret had already talked with Drane. Then he got his pipe going.

"How did you and Major Pallart get acquainted?" was his first question.

"Ah!" said Loret. "It was in Paris, ago six months. I work then at Chez Victor, rue Maillot. You know it? It is a street that gives on the Boulevard Haussmann. You write it down—yes?"

Wharton smiled wryly. He'd had his notebook open and his pencil in hand.

"Major Pallart he come many times to the restaurant and then he talk to me. Everything between us is sympathetic. I fight for the Resistance and am a prisoner and escape, and he is a prisoner. I specialise in learning the English and he specialise in learning the French. You write it down—no?"

Wharton chuckled. Loret's very earnestness was amusing, and so was his abundant gesture.

"And what happened then?" Wharton asked.

"He say if I am chef for him in England he will pay well. There will not be much labour and I shall be comfortable. So he obtain the English permit and I come."

"You are glad you came?"

"But naturally. I have the English money, which is good. I have the English food which is also good—"

"Then you're damn lucky," said Wharton *sotto voce*.

"And also I am comfortable. Everybody is very nice." Then he was cringing his shoulders. "But now it is not nice. M. Pallart was my friend. You catch his assassin—yes?"

His black eyes were grimly on Wharton's.

"We hope to catch him," Wharton said. "That's why we're asking you to help. Now tell us just what happened when Major Pallart and Mr. Brace got back here on Friday night."

What he told us varied scarcely a word from the report of Drane's which Wharton now had in his hand. The party had got back at a quarter to ten. Loret had spent a half-hour at the Wheatsheaf and then had awaited the party's return. Then he had asked if anything was wanted. Brace said he felt very thirsty and Major Pallart told Loret to make him a hot milk with a dash of rum and a pinch of spice. Dr. Kales had one too. Pallart had a whisky. Pallart said Loret wasn't wanted any more so he went to bed and took Brace's drink with him. Brace was already undressed. Loret reckoned he himself was asleep almost at once, though he couldn't answer for Brace whose room was in the front of the house. Loret heard no conversation between Pallart and Kales, and he didn't hear the car go or come back.

"Well, I don't think we need keep you any more," Wharton said. "You might ask Friske to come in, if he's about."

"I send him at once," Loret said, and bowed himself out with the tray.

"I like that chap," George said, and gave a chuckle. "But I'll bet he could be a pretty tough customer. Did you see how he glared at me when he was talking about Pallart's assassin?"

"You're checking up on his story?"

"Most decidedly I am," George said, and then Arthur Friske came in. Wharton hailed him just as heartily, had him seated and passed the cigarette case.

"A bad business this, about Major Pallart."

"You're right, sir," Friske said dourly. "If I got my hands on the one who did it, sir, he wouldn't kill no one else."

"I don't think he would," Wharton said. Then he was congratulating him on his legacy and Friske was making much the same comment as old Susan.

"You and your wife will come here?" Wharton asked, and Friske said if that had been the Major's wish then they certainly would. So to Drane's notes which Wharton took from his case.

Again there was no variation. Friske had had nothing to do after his return but clear away the unneeded meal. He had actually been home in his house very shortly after ten o'clock and asleep by half-past.

"Suppose I told you that your car never went to Colchester that night," Wharton said. "What would you say?"

It took him a moment or two to get some idea of what Wharton was driving at.

"I'd say you were wrong, sir. The car either went to Colchester or somewhere the same distance. There was a gallon of petrol down on the gauge. And there was some dust on the body."

"Good for you," Wharton said, and peered at me. "I don't think we need keep Mr. Friske from his tea? But you might send Wilkin in, if you can find him."

Friske grunted.

"I doubt if I will, sir."

"Why not?"

"He's a clock watcher, sir. Never knew him stay over his time. Generally he try to go before, especially if he thinks no one knows."

"Well, have a look for him," Wharton said.

"Wilkin's not popular," I remarked tritely to George. "I wonder what connection there was between him and Calne? Calne recommended him to Pallart."

"Something you might try and find out tonight," George said. Then he was pricking an ear.

"I'll tell him myself," we could hear Susan saying, and in a moment or two she was in the room. She'd seen Wilkin go about a quarter of an hour before. The look on her face showed what she thought of Wilkin.

"He just didn't belong here," was what she told Wharton. "Sometimes he fair used to give me the creeps. Like that Boris Karloff on the pictures."

"How do you mean?"

"Well, he'd sort of suddenly be somewhere just when you didn't expect him. Too smarmy too for my liking. I like them as speak their minds."

"By the way, Susan," I said, "did you ever see Miss Courtold? The lady Major Pallart was engaged to?"

"That I did, sir," she said, and shook her old head. "The nicest young lady there ever was. Like two love-birds she and Mr. Guy were."

Suddenly a corner of the white apron was going to her eyes.

"I'm sorry, Susan," I said, and got to my feet. "I shouldn't have reminded you of all that."

"I'm all right, sir," she said. She almost snapped the words at me. "Only sometimes it don't seem as if it's time. At my time o' life you don't get over things so easy as you did."

"I know," I said, and then tried to put a surprise into my tone. "I knew there was something I'd been meaning to ask you. What's that lovely oak chair doing in the summerhouse?"

She gaped at me.

"Well," she said. "So that's where it is!"

Then she was giving a little chuckle.

"And me thinking Mr. Guy had taken it off and sold it or give it to someone. Just show what an old fool I am."

The look of surprise came back again. How on earth had the chair got in the summerhouse?

"That's what we thought you might tell us," I said.

But she could tell us nothing. Naturally she'd missed the chair and she'd asked Pallart where it had gone. He'd simply said he wanted it for something. That was about a week ago. She'd asked him later when it was coming back. Its absence spoiled the look of the hall and his father had thought a lot of that chair. All he'd done was put her off. He'd been in one of his mischievous moods, she said.

At the door she turned.

"Could you tell me when the funeral's going to be, sir?"

"On Wednesday. Probably at two o'clock," Wharton told her gently.

She gave a little bow and that was all. We both sat looking at the door through which she'd gone.

"A great old lady," Wharton said, and let out a breath. Then he got to his feet. "Well, I've got work to do. Time you were pushing off to Wandham."

CHAPTER IX
TOO MANY CLUES

SOMETHING unusual seemed to be going on in that small enclosure of ground which was the kitchen garden of Walker's Ferry, for as soon as I took the right-hand fork I could see what looked like two corks bobbing on dry land. As I neared I could see that the two corks were two heads, and finally they resolved themselves into the heads—plus arms—of Jack Winder and Tom Pike who were making some sort of deep ditch.

"Going pretty deep for worms, aren't you?" I said.

That amused them.

"'Tain't worms," Jack said. "This bit o' garden lay so dam low you can't get nothing early to grow in it. That's why we're making this here drain. We have to keep deep so's to get a fall to the Creek."

"I thought land drains were fairly shallow," I said.

"So they are, sir," Tom Pike told me. "This here's the main drain what'll take all the shaller ones away. We can make them at any time."

Jack said Annie was in so I left my car where it was and walked on to the house. The garage door was open and I could see Calne's car. It was a huge, broad-beamed American car that must have cost a packet. I should have liked to look at it, but Annie must have heard the men and me talking for she was at the door.

"Come to see Mr. Calne, sir?" she said. "You'll find him in his office. I told him I'd seen you."

Calne was mounting some photographs and he seemed glad to see me. He said he was feeling fit as a flea.

"What does the doctor say?"

"He's a blasted fuss-pot," he said. "Says I've got to go steady for a time. All that nonsense about a strained heart."

"You should know," I said, and was taking the cigarette he offered me. He was drawing a chair in for me but I managed that for myself.

"You're still in Drowton?"

"Yes, and no," I said. "I'm really working in Ninford. Poor Guy Pallart, you know. Scotland Yard has taken over."

"Shocking business," he said. "I can't believe it even now. Who do you think did it? Some burglar bloke or something?"

"That's one of the ideas we're working on," I said. "But it's a bit too early yet."

Then I let out a sigh.

"It's the damnable irony of the whole thing that gets me."

"How do you mean?"

"That talk at the Regency," I said. "Pallart was talking about murdering someone, and it's he who goes and gets murdered."

He clicked his tongue exasperatedly.

"I told you that was all damn nonsense. He was simply posing for your benefit. I oughtn't to say it, but he always loved an audience."

"Even if he *was* talking hot air, it's still ironical," I said, "when you consider what's happened. It's even more so when you think that you might have gone the very same way the very same night."

He said nothing to that. He might not even have heard.

"Listen, Calne," I said. "Why stick to that ridiculous accident business? Guy Pallart's dead. He tried to kill you that night, didn't he?"

He still said nothing but I could see him frown annoyedly.

"He's dead," I said. "What he did need never be known. There'll be no aspersion on his memory."

"I thought we'd settled all that," he told me, and a shade too quietly. Then he was shrugging his shoulders. "If I say something—"

He broke off and he was shaking his head.

"Yes," I said.

"Anything to bring this business to an end," he said. "Let's be hypothetical. Let's suppose for the sake of keeping you quiet that it wasn't an accident. Suppose I was struck over the head, as you said. Then it wasn't Guy Pallart who struck me."

"Why? Still, of course, keeping to the purely hypothetical."

"Because that game leg of his would have made his steps distinctive. If you're as lame as he was, you couldn't disguise the fact."

"It was Kales then?"

"Forget it," he said, and there was an edge in his tone. "If it's all the same to you, we'll forget the whole thing."

"Sorry," I said. "But there's just one thing I would like to mention if only because it's been worrying me. This telephone wire of yours. Why was it cut?"

"God knows," he said. "Probably by some village boy or other. Sheer mischief."

"But a boy would have cut it in the dark. He wouldn't have risked being seen doing a serious piece of mischief like that in daylight."

"Who says it was done in daylight?"

"I do. I think it was cut by somebody just before we left on that Friday morning. Look at it this way," I explained. "Annie doesn't use the telephone. She hasn't any need to. If anybody wanted to ring you here during the day, then the line would be out of order, but Annie wouldn't know that anything was wrong. Then when we got here on the Friday night we went straight to the house, and there was the telephone out of order. That's why I say the wire had been cut all day."

"But why?"

"Some idea of Walker's Ferry not being able to ring the coastguard's cottage and report a man overboard," I shrugged my shoulders. "Sorry to bring all that up again."

There was a tap at the door and Annie came in.

"Excuse me interrupting you, sir, but that man Wilkin is here."

"Wilkin?"

"Yes, sir. The man who came about the gardening job."

"Damn Wilkin," he told her exasperatedly. "What the devil does he want now?"

"Says he wants to see you, sir. He won't keep you a minute."

"Tell him I'm busy." A moment and he was changing his mind. "No, tell him to wait."

"That fellow's getting a pest," he told me as soon as Annie had gone. "He was a mess orderly at the depot when I rejoined my regiment. A real scrounger type. I don't know how, but he found out I was living here and he turned up one day asking if I could find him a job in the garden. I told him there wasn't enough garden to employ a man, and then I remembered that Guy Pallart wanted a gardener, so I put him on to him. Now I suppose he wants to leave again."

"I don't think he's very popular at the Old Vicarage," I said.

"I'm not surprised," he said. "He turned up here to thank me for getting him the job and on the strength of that kept turning up every now and again. Jack says he's nothing but a ruddy Nosey Parker."

"I must say I don't like the look of him myself," I said, and was getting to my feet. "Time I was pushing off. Superintendent Wharton, who's in charge of things, is expecting me back. I believe, by the way, that he's got wind of that accident of yours, so if he turns up, you'll know who he is."

"But why should he turn up here?"

"Ask *him*," I said. "I'm only a little cog in the machinery. But possibly he may be thinking that any information whatever about Guy Pallart might be a bit of help."

"If he likes to waste his time, that's his business," he said. "But something I particularly wanted to ask. When's the funeral?"

I told him and he said he'd be there. He was coming out with me to the car but I insisted that he wasn't to bother. When I got outside I saw Wilkin standing by the trench but there didn't seem to be any talking. At Wandham too, Wilkin didn't seem particularly popular.

It was only just after half-past six when I got back to Ninford. Wharton was sitting at the telephone extension table, making notes. No sooner did I see him than I realised that I'd forgotten to bring up the subject of the rent of Walker's Ferry with David Calne. Wharton was pushing the notes aside.

"Get anything?"

"Yes," I said. "Calne told me in so many words that it wasn't an accident, and he as good as swore that Pallart didn't hit him on the head."

I elaborated slightly. Wharton said Calne must have heard the quick steps of the man who struck him, and the man must therefore have been Kales.

"But why?" he said, and pursed his lips and blew out that heavy moustache. "Pallart said he was going to murder someone. Did he hire this Kales to do the job for him?"

"If it comes to that, why should Pallart want to kill Calne? And why should Kales consent to do it?"

"Leave it," he told me testily, but he made a note in his book all the same.

"Wilkin was at the Ferry," I said, and repeated what Calne had told me.

"Thinking of leaving here, is he?" Wharton said amusedly. "Well, we'll see. First thing in the morning we'll have a little chat with Master Wilkin. That reminds me. Dinner's at seven o'clock here, did you say? Just time for a word with young Brace."

I pushed the bell, thanking heaven that George hadn't remembered the matter of the rent of Walker's Ferry. Brace had evidently been warned, for it was he who came in. Wharton couldn't have been more genial. Brace couldn't have been more ill at ease. One thing too that I noticed about him was that he was letting the hair grow on his upper lip.

"I hear we have to congratulate you," Wharton said. "You look like being a very lucky young man."

For some reason Brace wasn't looking too pleased. If any-thing he was a shade more anxious.

Wharton told him the terms of his uncle's will. Brace's face went a flaring red and I wondered why.

"You're a fortunate fellow," Wharton said. "Five years will be gone in no time, and then you come into this charming house and a good income, and a fine old name."

Brace shuffled in his chair and said he supposed he *was* lucky. Wharton tried a joke.

"Which reminds me. Mr. Brace here, is right in the line of business and he might feel like doing us a favour. What about a nice little furnished flat?"

"That's really not my department," Brace said woodenly. "All I do is go round looking at likely properties. That's why I have to be out so much."

"And not a bad job either," Wharton said. But he wasn't any too pleased. George hates his jokes to fall flat. I too was thinking that Brace was taking himself far too seriously.

"Well, we'll leave your prospects and come to something else," George said, and ran a quick eye over what was evidently Drane's report on his interview with Brace. "The Friday night when you got back here after the cruise. Tell us in your own words everything that happened."

Yet once more everything was as Drane had reported it. Brace said he didn't do a lot of drinking and at Dovercourt he'd drunk more than usual, and when he got home he was feeling both very sleepy and uncommonly thirsty. Perhaps the day's fresh air had had something to do with the sleepiness too. He'd asked Loret for hot milk but Major Pallart had told Loret to make it a toddy. Dr. Kales had said he would have one too. Loret had brought that toddy into Brace's room just when he, Brace, was getting into bed. As soon as Brace's head hit the pillow, he must have been asleep.

"And you heard nothing all night? No sound of the car? No one moving about?"

"Not a thing," Brace said. "I've never slept so soundly in my life." He gave something like a smile. "When Loret woke me in the morning I simply turned over and went to sleep again before he was out of the room. I was asleep when Mr. Travers came in."

Wharton said we'd go up and have a quick look at the bedrooms. I knew he'd seen them before, for he turned right at the stairs and paused at the first door on the right.

"This is your room, isn't it?"

Brace said it was. Wharton opened the door for a moment.

"And your uncle's room?"

"Back this way," Brace said. "The corresponding room the other side of the landing."

Wharton took a quick look inside.

"And Dr. Kales's room."

"This one next to it."

That room had had its bed stripped and had a general air of emptiness. All three rooms were the best in the house: large and airy and overlooking the front lawn.

"And Loret's room?" asked Wharton.

"This way," Brace said, and we went back past his own room again.

"And this room?" Wharton asked, already opening the door of the fourth bedroom on the right of the long corridor.

"Not being used, I think," Brace said, and he was right. The mattress was rolled up on the bed and the furniture was covered with dust-sheets.

A corridor turned left and a landing appeared, with a flight of stairs, uncarpeted, that led down to the kitchen. There were three bedrooms in that wing. Susan's was on the right and its windows looked over the shrubbery and the summerhouse. Then came an empty room, and then Loret's room. It overlooked the yard and the kitchen gardens. I was amused to see that he had rigged up a dart-board on the far wall for private practice. No wonder the habitués of the Wheatsheaf said he threw a remarkably good dart!

"That's all, I think," Wharton said, and down we went again. Brace was thinking the interview was over, but Wharton waved him back to his old seat.

"Now," he said, and gave a magisterial look at the notes. Then he peered at Brace.

"Let's get down to hard facts. Your uncle was murdered, and murder's a pretty damnable thing."

He was peering fixedly at Brace. Brace murmured that he supposed it was.

"Any evidence whatever might be of help," Wharton went on. "You might know something which seems to you to be unimportant. Perhaps it is and perhaps it isn't. That'll be for us to judge, and whatever it is we'll be grateful. Now then. On that Friday night did you or did you not at any time whatsoever hear anything which either then or now might have struck you as unusual?"

Brace frowned in thought.

"Well—no."

But there was something on his mind. I cut hastily in.

"It doesn't matter how trivial it may seem. If there was anything at all, just mention it."

"Well," he said, "it wasn't here at all. It was on the way home in the car."

"Yes?" said Wharton, and waited.

"Well, Friske was driving and I sat with him in front. My uncle and Dr. Kales sat behind and as soon as we moved off, they started talking in French. Sort of quietly."

"But you heard something?"

"Well, yes. I suppose I did."

"You speak French? Or understand it?"

"Well, yes. I do and I don't. I mean, I understand it better than I speak it." He smiled a bit sheepishly. "French was one of the few things I took an interest in at school."

"I get you," Wharton said crisply. "And what did you hear said? No English, mind you. You give us the French as near as you can."

Brace smiled sheepishly again.

"Damn the accent!" Wharton said testily. "Tell us what you heard."

"Well, my uncle said, *'Qu'est-ce que tu as fait?'* or *'Qu'as tu fait?'* I don't remember which now, but that's what it amounted to."

"He said that to Kales?"

"Yes, and then there was something I didn't catch. I know there was the word *fou* and *insensé.*"

Wharton gave me a look.

"I see. Your uncle wanted to know what he'd been mad enough to do. Was that it?"

"Well, it sounded like it."

"And what next?"

"Well," Dr. Kales said, "*Mais je n'ai rien fait. Je vous l'assure.*"

"In what tone did he say it?"

"Well, it was louder than they'd been speaking at first."

"I see. And what then?"

"Well, I think I craned my neck round, and they stopped talking."

"Oh, my God!" said Wharton despairingly. "You mean they didn't say anything else till you got home?"

"Well, it's only a minute or so from Wandham," Brace said. "But when we did get home—it was just as I'd got out of the car—my uncle asked if I spoke French. I told him I didn't—only the sort you learned at school."

"Why'd you tell him that?"

"Well, I didn't want him to think I'd been listening. I mean, it was hardly the thing."

There was a tap at the door and Susan looked in.

"I'm sorry, sir—"

"That's all right," Wharton told her. "We're just going."

"I was only going to tell Master Richard that dinner will be ready almost at once," she said. "It isn't right to cook good food and then have it spoilt."

"He'll be there," Wharton assured her, and got to his feet as the door closed.

"Just one word, Mr. Brace. What you've told us is to go no farther. Mention a single word of what you've told us to a living soul and I won't answer for the consequences. Is that understood?"

Brace said it was. Wharton relaxed. He patted him paternally on the shoulder.

"Now go and enjoy your dinner. I wish I was joining you myself."

Brace hurried out. The look on his face showed that the last company that he'd long for at dinner would be George Wharton's.

*   *   *   *   *

We got into my car and till we got to the Wheatsheaf George never said a word. As we went through the bar he ordered a couple of pints to be sent through to the dining-room, and then we went upstairs for a wash. I was brushing my hair in his room when he came back from the lavatory.

"One thing we've done nothing about," I said, squinting down at myself in the glass, "and that's that glove of mine that was planted near Pallart's body."

He grunted and said our meal was probably getting cold. But it was a cold meal in any case, and he needn't have worried. And when he'd had a long pull at his tankard, he looked more cheerful.

"This Case is the very devil," he said. "Young Brace wasn't making anything up. Pallart *did* think Kales had given Calne that crack on the skull."

"Or else Pallart was trying to clear himself."

"One thing at a time," he told me snappily. "Kales said even more emphatically that he hadn't done anything, so where's that get us?"

"In some ways, just where we want to be," I said. "Remember this. Even when we got to the Ferry we didn't know what had happened. If we thought anything at all, it was that Calne had had an accident and had fallen overboard. Very well, then. If Pallart asked Kales what he'd been mad enough to do, then Pallart must have known what had been done! And if Kales replied at once—without expressing any ignorance, mind you—that he hadn't done anything, then Kales must have known what had happened, too!"

"You're right," George said. "And that means that one of them did try to murder Calne."

"And since Calne as good as told me this evening that it wasn't Pallart who did it, then it must have been Kales."

"That's logical enough," George said, and clicked his tongue exasperatedly. "The devil of it is, it only lands us in a bigger hole. Why the devil should Kales want to kill Calne?"

"It's even worse than that," I said. "Why should Pallart *know* that Kales should want to kill Calne?"

"Damn the whole thing!" exploded Wharton. "Leave it alone for a bit. You can't go playing chess all day as I've been doing and expect to think. Wait till the morning and think about it then. Some idea or other is bound to turn up."

"And we may have news of Kales."

"We ought to have heard something from the Home Office before now," George said. "The first thing in the morning I'll ring them up."

After our meal we went into the bar. I was in no hurry to get back to Drowton and it was much more fun watching George playing darts. Then at about half-past eight Loret came in, and was vociferously welcomed. George had won his first game and the locals were anxious to set Loret against him. Loret and his partner wiped the floor with George's side. Then George made Loret's eyes pop by going into French so colloquial that I could follow hardly a word. The locals were highly impressed.

Then Wilkin came in. He looked cheerfully round.

"Evening, gentlemen all."

The greeting of the room was somewhat indistinct. Wilkin asked for a pint of mild and old.

"Sorry, but no more old and mild," the landlord told him, and that was odd, for he'd only just poured a pint of the same mixture for George and his partner.

"Bitter do you?" the landlord said. "Only spare you a half-pint. Must look after our regulars first, same as I told you Friday."

Wilkin looked down his nose but took the half-pint. Then he had a look round and remarked that no one was playing darts. If he'd had an idea of issuing a challenge, he was promptly forestalled and a foursome was made up as if by magic.

"That's Wilkin, gardener at the Old Vicarage, isn't it?" I whispered to an old chap on the settle beside me. "He doesn't seem very popular."

"He ain't a mucher," I was told, and it was a fine old word I hadn't heard for years. "Only gardener I knew what have to go to work on a motor-bike."

"Where's he live, then?"

"Just down the road," he said. "Lodge with old Mrs. Snow."

Wilkin watched the darts for a minute or two, then gave a 'good night, all,' and went out.

"Got no mild and old for *him*," the landlord told the room. "The Peace and Plenty's his house."

George drained his tankard and gave the room a good night. I followed him through to the dining-room to say good night myself. It was high time I was moving on to Drowton.

"I've been thinking," George said. "That's why we got beaten at that game of darts. I couldn't keep my mind on the game."

"It's about young Brace," he said. "There's something wrong about that young man, or my name's Robinson. Notice when I was telling him about the will? You'd have thought I was telling him the bank was bust, or something, and his money was all gone, instead of the other way about."

"He's got a first-class motive for killing his uncle," I said. "And he hasn't got much of an alibi."

"I don't think it's that," George said. "It's something to do with that job of his. Why did he have to drag in that bit about having to be out a lot? That didn't strike me as natural."

I said I didn't know. As a matter of fact I was thinking that George hadn't yet forgiven the ignoring of what should have been taken as a joke.

"Look here," George suddenly said. "It wouldn't be much of a waste of time if it turns out that we're barking up the wrong tree. You go up to town tomorrow morning first thing and see what you can find out. Feverton will be dead on your way."

"What sort of inquiry? Official or otherwise?"

"Tactful. Very tactful," George said. He didn't quite know himself just what he meant by that except that he was passing me the baby. "Don't see any of the principals." He gave an impatient snort. "You've got brains, haven't you? Find out what he does in the firm, and all about him. That ought to be right up your alley."

CHAPTER X
A BIT OF BAD LUCK

As GEORGE had said, that suburb which I have called Feverton lay particularly handy. I had merely to cut through to Epping and the Forest and at Waltham I was almost there. I crossed the arterial road and in a mile was in the outskirts. There were traffic lights just past the police-station and the turn to the right was obviously the Broadway. I moved the car slowly along and drew in at a handy gap by the kerb.

It was just after ten o'clock and I found the office of Hawke and Gear a half-minute's walk away. And there, as I had known all along, my troubles began. There was the firm of Estate Agents, but how was I to get to work? I couldn't walk in unofficially and ask for a report on Richard Brace; all I could think of, in fact, was to keep the office under my eye and try to get into touch with one of the employees, and that might mean a wait till lunch-time. So to kill time I found a restaurant and had a cup of coffee. Then I took my car on and round and drew it up almost opposite the office on the other side of the road. It was half-past ten and I wondered if I should ring Bill Ellice and get him to send along a man for relief and help. It was then that I saw a man leaving the office.

He was hatless, and that seemed to make him an employee of the firm. Luckily for me he hadn't gone more than ten yards when he met someone he knew, and the two stood talking. That gave me a good view of him. He looked about forty and a superior kind of clerk.

I crossed the road and waited. Then he waved a farewell hand to his companion; I moved to meet him.

"Excuse me, but are you connected with Hawke and Gear, the Estate Agents?"

"I am, sir," he told me genially.

"Then perhaps you'll be good enough to help me," I said. "Do you know Mr. Brace? Richard Brace?"

"Brace?" he said. "I'm afraid I don't."

"But he works for your firm."

He smiled.

"There's no Mr. Brace working for our firm, sir."

"That's strange," I said. "Have you been working for them long?"

"For twenty-five years," he told me, and his smile was slightly ironical.

"It's inexplicable," I said. "He told me to meet him here at ten o'clock. I wasn't to go in but he'd come out and meet me here."

"You must have made a mistake in the name," he said. "There's another Estate Agent's just down the road. I should try them."

He moved on and I watched him enter a restaurant a good hundred yards along the street. Suddenly my mind was made up. Everything was so amazing that I didn't give a cuss for Wharton's instructions about not interviewing principals. What I'd do was to see that Charles Hawke to whom Drane had spoken, and already I found myself at the door.

A youngish woman gave me a smile. I asked if I might see Mr. Hawke.

"Mr. Charles Hawke or Mr. James Hawke?"

"Mr. Charles Hawke."

"Would you give me your name, please?"

"Holloway. George Holloway."

"Would you mind waiting just a minute, Mr. Holloway, and I'll see if Mr. Hawke is engaged."

Inside two minutes she was ushering me into a cosy little office. A beautifully-dressed, good-looking young man rose from his chair at the desk and gave me the most engaging of smiles.

"Good morning, Mr. Holloway. Delightful morning, isn't it."

I didn't talk about the weather. While I told him my name wasn't Holloway, I was showing my Warrant Card. He was far less assured as he gave it me back.

"From Scotland Yard?"

"Yes," I said. "Ring them if you want a further check."

"But of course not," he said, and was looking a bit anxious all the same.

I told him I had come from Ninford and recalled Inspector Drane. I said we had to make routine checks for official purposes on everyone even remotely connected with the Ninford murder. That was where he cut in. Up till then he'd looked more uneasy than ever.

"But Mr. Brace is *at* Ninford. Can't you get any information from him direct?"

"That wouldn't be a check," I said, and then I told him of my encounter with that man of his outside. For a moment he looked in a state of absolute panic. Then he helped himself to a cigarette from the box on the table and he didn't pass the box to me.

"That's easily explained," he said. "Murlow wouldn't know anything about Mr. Brace. Mr. Brace is one of our unofficial scouts who look out for properties. We have to keep that sort of thing secret. Too much competition, you know, and the state of the market."

"You mean that you can't trust a man like Murlow?"

"Well,"—he smiled feebly—"we can and we can't, if you follow me. We'd rather that as few people as possible knew what properties are likely to come into the market. In this office that particular branch of the business is my special concern. I run it my own way."

"That's all right," I said. "The trouble is that Scotland Yard is allergic to contradictions. And am I to take it that the information you gave to Inspector Drane is correct in every detail?"

"I think so."

"Thinking isn't good enough," I told him tartly. I didn't like him, or his patter, or his sleek black hair. "You assure me that the information was correct?"

"I certainly do."

"That's all I need trouble you about," I said, and turned to go. But he was round that desk like a flash.

"You'll find this the handier way out," he said, and opened a side door. "Just turn right and you're back in the Broadway."

I turned right and I *wasn't* in the Broadway. I walked back again and turned left and then left again, and I was in the Broadway. And there I stood for a good minute, polishing my glasses.

And just as I hooked them on again, I caught sight of Murlow entering the office again. Then I knew why young Hawke had shown me through that side door. He had been playing for time till Murlow got back from his coffee.

And when I asked myself what was wrong, I didn't take long to find an answer. Some sort of black marketeering was going on in houses. Maybe cash deals were taking place and never appeared on the books of the firm. The man Murlow must be in the game too, but whether or not he was, I had to get hold of Wharton. So I nipped across to the car and damned if the solenoid didn't begin its temperamental tricks. By the time I'd undone the bonnet and tapped it, time had been lost. Then the traffic lights were against me and when I turned I found the street had No Parking signs. But there was a side road at the back of the police-station and I overshot it before I noticed it. Then I had to go on for quite a way till I could turn.

In the station I showed my credentials and gave the Ninford number. The station-sergeant was quite an old stager, and while we waited for Wharton to come on the line, he asked how the Ninford case was coming along.

"How's the Old General these days?" he wanted to know. That was George's nickname at the Yard.

We had quite a chat for a minute or two, even if it wasn't a pleasant one. I was too anxious to get George on the line, and then the buzzer went. The sergeant grunted as he replaced the receiver.

"Number's engaged, sir."

I don't know what I said. It would have taken a good deal to shock that sergeant in any case. About three minutes went by and he was buzzing through again. And grunting again.

"Still engaged, sir."

There was more than a chance that George was having a protracted argument with the Home Office or the Special Branch, and it was more sensible in any case to relax. The sergeant and I had a cigarette and yarned a bit more—chiefly about George— and then at last the line was clear.

"That you, George?"

George it was.

"Something pretty queer going on," I said. "But would you tell me first who was having a long talk on your telephone just now? Was it you?"

"It was Brace," he said, and his voice lowered. "A call came for him and he took it himself. He's only just finished."

"Oh my hat!" I said. "That's torn it properly."

"What do you mean?"

"Can't explain now," I said. "It'd take too long. I'll be back as soon as I can make it. Meanwhile keep an eye on Brace. Don't let him do any telephoning. Keep him in the house, even if you have to tie him down."

As soon as I was clear of the suburbs I moved the car along and I was telling myself that I'd had an unlucky deal. Only two minutes sooner at the police-station and I'd have got in ahead of Charles Hawke. Now he'd had the best part of a nine minute call in which to prime Brace. If there was black-market work going on, then Hawke daren't risk any enquiry by us and the Commissioners of Inland Revenue. If Brace was engaged in such work, then his profession certainly couldn't be called 'honourable' and it was a debatable point whether or not he'd qualify for the Pallart estate.

It was still short of midday when I got to the Old Vicarage, which meant that I'd moved pretty fast. Wharton was on the summerhouse verandah and he actually came to meet me. The look in his eye said that if anything was wrong, then I was the sole begetter of the disaster. Ten minutes later he knew as much as I did. And before we could discuss the matter, Friske was calling that I was wanted on the telephone. Who should it be but the man Murlow.

"Are you the gentleman, sir, who spoke to me this morning about a Mr. Brace?"

"I am," I said.

"Then I thought I'd better explain," he said. "Our Mr. Hawke says he's explained already, but I thought I'd better explain about myself. You there?"

I said I was.

"Well, you'll understand how it is from what Mr. Hawke was telling you," he went on. "After I left you I *did* remember something about a Mr. Brace, but it's all hush-hush, so to speak. Even if I'd remembered when I was speaking to you sir, I wouldn't have let on; you being a perfect stranger, if you know what I mean."

"That's all right," I told him, as genially as I could make it. "And thank you very much for letting me know."

I had taken the call in the lounge and George was at my elbow.

"The pitch is queered, George," I said. "Everything's now right and tight—or so they think."

"Let's get along to the Wheatsheaf," he said. "I've got to do some thinking. That black-market idea of yours doesn't seem to fit in. There's more to it than that, or my name's Robinson."

Now the horse had gone he shut the stable door by putting a utility man of Drane's at the telephone. Messages might be taken but no one was to use the telephone, and there was to be a copy of all messages received.

"Why doesn't the black-market idea fit in?" I asked as we walked down the hill.

"I didn't say it didn't," he told me. "I said I didn't like it. Work it out for yourself."

But he had to do the working out for me. It was a question of what was at stake, he said. Young Brace stood to get a fine property and at least forty thousand pounds. Long before his uncle's death he had been warned of the consequences of disgracing the family name. I said I knew all that, and why didn't the black-market idea fit in? George looked too exasperated for words.

"Drop the whole thing," he told me. "It's still the best policy to let Brace think he's in the clear. After the funeral he can go where the hell he likes and he'll have someone on his tail. He won't be able to bat an eyelid without us knowing it."

I might have said a lot but I didn't: that even if there were a man on Brace's tail, for instance, Brace would merely go to Feverton and how could that help? We couldn't install a microphone in Charles Hawke's office. Or the two could conduct business over the telephone. But we said no more about Brace and at lunch George was telling me about his own troubles.

Kales was the mystery. There was no record whatever of anyone of his name.

"That's right," George said, when I began asking questions. "No record whatever. As far as my Department is concerned, he just doesn't exist. I've talked with Friske and Susan and Brace, and Pallart never gave any information whatever about who he really was, or his origins or anything. All we know, and from you, is that he's a Czech physicist."

"We don't exactly know it from me," I pointed out. "We know it, for what it's worth, from what he and Pallart told me."

"Well, I'm having no hanky-panky, and I'm wasting no time," George said grimly. "You're going to get out a detailed description and there'll be a wireless appeal."

He didn't seem as if he wanted to take the Kales business any further, so I asked him if he'd seen Wilkin. He cheered up at once and actually gave that belly rumble of his which is meant to be a chuckle.

"I had the pleasure of twisting his tail," he said. "Funny how it happened. I was just about to send for him when Susan said he wanted to see me. I said send him in, and that's when the fun began."

Wilkin had come with all obsequiousness, cap in hand and flicking a respectful finger to his forelock. He'd heard about the will and it was striking him that Susan Beavers would now be in charge, and he'd never liked working under women, if the Superintendent knew what he meant. In other words he wanted to give his notice, but what he didn't know was to whom to give it.

Wharton said the best thing to do was to send a written notice to the solicitors, and asked when he'd last been paid and what were the terms of his agreement with his late employer. Wilkin said he'd been paid the previous Friday and was supposed to give a fortnight's notice. Wharton said the solicitors would doubtless overlook the broken week and the notice would become effective on the Friday week.

"And what if I have another job to go to?" asked Wilkin.

"That's not the point," Wharton said. "You're bound in law to work out your time."

"No law ain't going to stop me taking a job," Wilkin told him belligerently. "I know all about the law. The law's made for the privileged classes."

I could just see George taking that lying down. But according to George, Wilkin became positively abusive, and finally he was ordered to get to hell out of the room and on with his work.

"As soon as he'd gone I began to think it over," George said. "Do you know it almost looked as if he'd asked to see me just to make a row. Then I rumbled him. What do you think his idea was?"

"Trying to work his ticket?"

"That's it," George said. "He had the idea that I was in charge. What he wanted was for me to give him his cards. Money didn't worry him. He'd been paid last Friday."

"Wonder who's employing him," I said. "I've a good mind to ring up Calne."

I was well ahead of George, as usual, with my meal and when I'd finished I did ring up Calne. But there was no reply.

"The worst telephone system in the world," the landlord told me. "Who were you trying to get, sir?"

I told him and he said his boy could slip along on his bike. There'd be plenty of time before school. So I wrote a quick note and told the boy he was to give it to nobody but Mr. Calne. If Mr. Calne wasn't there, he was to bring the note back.

George had finished his meal, and his first cup of tea. I asked him about Wilkin's alibi.

"He hasn't got one," George said. "He lodges with an old lady in one of those cottages by the bridge. Most of his evenings he used to spend out—at the pubs, so he told Drane—and he used to go to bed soon after ten. The old lady always went about half-past nine."

"What about the Friday night?"

"He says he was at the Peace and Plenty. Drane enquired and was told he left there soon after dusk. Then he says he looked in here, and so he did, but not till half-past nine and he only stayed long enough to drink one half-pint. Then he says he went to bed soon after ten as usual."

It didn't take us long to agree that Wilkin's evening bad been spent with a view to the return of Pallart's car. No doubt he'd questioned Friske and learned that the party was expected back at about nine, so he left the Peace and Plenty and made his way to the house. Nothing happened and he walked back to the village and waited near the Wheatsheaf. Pallart's car would pass the pub and it was as good a place to watch from as any. He nipped in later and had a drink, with his ears doubtless pricked for the sound of the car. Probably he waited outside till the car did pass. What happened then couldn't be proved.

"Why all this snooping?" I said. "What was his idea?"

"Blackmail," George told me. "If what we suspect was going on in that summerhouse, he'd have Pallart under his thumb."

"It's not inconceivable," I said, "that Wilkin saw Pallart killed. He may even have done it himself."

"No motive," George said. "At least we haven't run up against a motive."

He made a note and said he'd have enquiries started at the Depot where he'd been a mess orderly. Then the landlord's boy came back with the letter. I read it and handed it to George.

Walker's Ferry,
Sept. 14th.

DEAR TRAVERS,

Sorry you had all the bother of a note but this telephone has gone phut again. It should be right by tomorrow.

No, I certainly have not offered Wilkin a job. He told me he was leaving the Old Vicarage. Apparently he doesn't get on any too well with Susan, and he asked if I knew of anything. I said I didn't.

The man's a pest and the sooner he leaves the district, the better I shall be pleased.

I may see you at the funeral.

Yours, D.C.

The note was handed back without comment, and almost at once he was busy outlining the programme for the next twenty-four hours. That afternoon Pallart's body was being brought back in readiness for the funeral, and George was proposing that we should remain at the Wheatsheaf. Drane was due at about two o'clock to report and hear the news.

"After that you might as well push off," George told me. "I'm having a look at the scene of that accident of your friend Calne. I've fixed up with the coastguard to take me out. I may see Calne later—just a friendly visit—or I may not. Then I'm running up to town to report and I shan't be back till tomorrow evening after the funeral. If I'm wanted you can get me through the Yard. All I want you to do is to turn up at about three o'clock tomorrow for the reading of the will. I've arranged that with Mr. Hallwell. Watch reactions and see if you get any ideas."

Drane turned up on time, and he was none too pleased. "These Saxons, or whatever they call these blond Germans, seem to be about half the collection they've got in these parts," he told us. "It's slow work. We're concentrating on the prisoners living out, but I'm none too optimistic."

I suddenly thought of something. My fingers went to my glasses, and fell again. I must have looked a bit sheepish for George, who knew the symptoms, was asking what the matter was.

"Your enquiries are based on that camp near Drowton?" I asked Drane.

"That's it," he said. "We have to make a beginning somewhere and clear one thing up at a time."

"Then I'm sorry," I said, "but I've remembered something. I may have mentioned it before and I may not. Probably not. Remember the Wednesday night when I heard Pallart's car return? It came *this* way. Therefore he couldn't very well have brought that prisoner from Drowton. It looks more like Colchester."

George glared, and no more. He wasn't letting me down in front of Drane.

"Colchester," Drane said. "There's a big camp at Overy."

He too seemed to be remembering something. He felt in his breast pocket and brought out some papers.

"Two prisoners are missing from Overy. That's right. Hans Messner, missing for ten days now, and an Ernst Ungler."

He stared.

"Ungler's been missing since Thursday morning! He wasn't in the camp when morning roll was taken."

"Sounds interesting," Wharton said, and then his face fell. "That doesn't fit in, though, with our theory. Ungler's an escaped prisoner. We want a man who's been here probably two or three times."

He gave me a look as if I were the cause of the muddle, and then was telling Drane he might do worse than make an enquiry at Overy.

We were playing scrupulously fair with Drane, and I'm not being cheaply cynical when I say it wouldn't have paid us to be anything else. That was why we gave him an account of things as they stood up to date. He had only one comment to make, and that surprised me.

"That chef's getting £500," he said. "Seems pretty handsome for the time he's been here."

"I think Pallart had a very high regard for him," I said. "I think they were definitely friends, irrespective of their stations."

"The whole will seems funny to me," Drane said, and he paused. "I expect I'm wrong, though, or you'd have noticed it yourself, Mr. Travers."

"What's funny about it?" Wharton asked. "Speak your mind, Drane. We're all in this together. Doesn't matter whose toes get trodden on."

"Well the whole will doesn't seem right somehow," Drane said. "Unless, that is, you regard it as a temporary will. Take Mrs. Beavers. She couldn't be expected to live for very long now, and if she died, he'd have to make a new will. Then there's that bit about Loret. If I heard Mr. Travers rightly, the words were *whether or not still in my employ*. What did he want to put them in for?"

Wharton was frowning. He didn't see what Drane was driving at, and neither did I.

"To put it in a nutshell," Drane went on, "it looks to me as if Major Pallart had an idea he might die at any time."

"Yes," said Wharton slowly. It was a good point and now I saw it. "What's the date of the will, Mr. Travers?"

"About three months back," I said.

"Yes," said Wharton again. "I think you've got something there, Drane. He thought he might meet with sudden death."

He nodded to himself and scowled away in thought.

"I think we've got something. Just what use to make of it is quite a different thing. Perhaps we'd all better think it out by ourselves and then pool any ideas."

He made a note in his book and asked if there was anything else. There wasn't, and the meeting duly adjourned. I walked back up the hill to my car.

As I came into Drowton I drew up at the cinema and had a look at the programme with a view to the first or second house. The picture was one which I'd made a note to see, and the first house—there were matinées on Wednesdays and Saturdays only—would be over in time for the hotel dinner. That was how I came to run into Jack and Annie Winder.

It was after tea as I was making for the cinema and they were just leaving a shop.

"What are you two doing here?" I said. "Going to the pictures?"

"Not today, sir," Jack said. "If we go to the pictures, we go Saturdays. We just come in to do a bit of shopping and when we've had a bit of tea, we're going back. Mr. Calne's gone to Colchester so he reckoned we might as well have the afternoon and evening off."

Annie Winder said she had an old aunt in Ninford and she'd be spending the evening with her while Jack paid one of his rare visits to the Wheatsheaf.

"I thought I'd never seen you at the Wheatsheaf," I told Jack.

"I drop in sometimes," Jack said. "Everyone knows me there. I can generally slip a good hiding into their dart players."

"What about Loret?"

"Loret?" he said. "Oh, you mean Frenchy." He smiled. "I'm not counting him, sir. He isn't what you might call Ninford."

"Tell Mr. Travers about next week," Annie said.

"Next week we're going up to Norfolk," Jack said. "Tying up in the river by Blakeney Point. The guvnor's got permission to do something or other at that big bird sanctuary, as they call it."

"You two are due for a fine holiday," I told them. "I wouldn't mind a spell of that myself."

"We're right looking forward to it," Annie said. "That'll be the first time we've really been away."

As I moved on to the cinema, it struck me that if Wharton was calling at Walker's Ferry that late afternoon, he'd find Calne out. The last thing in the world I could possibly have thought of, was that Jack Winder was never going to see Blakeney Point.

CHAPTER XI
LINKS IN THE CHAIN

THAT WEDNESDAY was a day of odds and ends: a day of apparently unconnected happenings. Not a single one could have been thought of as vital, and yet each was a link in the chain.

It was about a quarter to three when I neared the Old Vicarage, and I drew my car up a hundred yards short of it, and waited. Half the county seemed to have been at the funeral, judging by the number of cars that were still left, but they slowly went and by three o'clock there were none parked in front of the house. There was only one car in the drive and that was Hallwell's.

"A very impressive funeral," he told me. "The family had many friends."

He introduced me to a member of the County Committee of the British Legion who would be present at the reading of the will as a possibly interested party. That reading didn't take long, since there was no one there but the beneficiaries. Old Susan was still wearing a kind of black bonnet which she must have donned for the funeral, and it made her rosy face look pinched and hid her lovely white hair. Loret looked strange in a dark lounge suit. Friske's wife was a pleasant-looking young country woman. Brace was wearing his grey suit with a black tie. Friske had on a black armlet.

I watched Brace. As soon as his name was mentioned, his forehead went to his cupped hand, and I couldn't see his face. As far as watching reactions was concerned, it was a wasted half-hour. And when the reading was over, Hallwell solemnly shook hands with the room, myself included, and he and the British Legion man left in his car.

It was Loret, of all people, who stayed behind to speak to me. I congratulated him on his legacy and hoped the Powers-That-Be, as George calls them, would let him take his money out of the country. That is, if he was thinking now of going back to France.

"In a few days I return," he told me. "For the moment I take a holiday. The good Suzanne, she wish that I take my time."

"Why not stay in England?" I said, thinking of Hallwell's hint to me.

He couldn't bear it, he said, now that Major Pallart had gone. England would never be the same.

"Almost I could cry," he told me, and his palms shook with emotion as he gesticulated. "I ask you, monsieur, why should he give me so much money? Always I am paid well and everything is so comfortable that there is nothing that I can spend."

"He liked you, Georges," I said, "just as you liked him. The five hundred pounds was only his way of telling you so."

"I return to France," he said, as if announcing a something irrevocable. "With the money I shall establish a restaurant of myself."

"Fine," I said, and I took out a visiting card and gave it to him. "That's my address. As soon as you get your restaurant established, let me know and I'll try to take a short holiday in Paris and my wife and I will come and see you."

His face beamed.

"That, monsieur, will be a day of pleasure." He shrugged his shoulders. "It will be a sadness to leave Ninford, all the same. Everyone is very nice."

"No more darts?" I said, and smiled. And I remembered something. "Did you play last night?"

"One game, monsieur." The shrug of the shoulders was accompanied by a smile. "That time I am beat."

"Jack Winder?" I said, and it took him a moment to recognise the name.

"Jack," he said. "Everyone calls him Jack. He is very good, that Jack."

"So I gathered," I said, and was adding that I should be seeing him again before he went away. Then when he'd gone I went out to the hall. Brace was hanging about and I thought he wanted to speak to me.

"I'm going back to town now, Mr. Travers," he said. "Friske is driving me to Colchester to catch the five-thirty."

"Superintendent Wharton doesn't want you here any longer then?"

"He knows I'm going," he said, a bit uneasily.

I was thinking two things. Brace was uncommonly anxious to get away if he was leaving now to catch the five-thirty. And since Wharton knew he was going, he doubtless knew too the time of the train and Brace would have a man on his tail. But I decided to keep Brace for a minute or two. There was something that to my knowledge hadn't been quite cleared up.

"Just come in for a moment," I said, and turned back to the lounge. "I want to talk to you like a Dutch uncle. Take a seat. Have a cigarette."

There followed a Whartonian preamble. Young men, as I knew from experience, did foolish things. They weren't always—I was going to say *truthful* but I made it *explicit* instead. And people like Brace, I said, forgot that Scotland Yard had means of finding most things out.

"That flat of yours in town," I said. "It costs you three-fifty a year, and on top of that you've got to live. You get a hundred and fifty from your firm and your uncle allowed you a further hundred and fifty. How do you account for the discrepancy?"

His face coloured and I could almost see his brain at work. He looked down, flicked the ash from the cigarette, and then had his answer.

"The hundred and fifty from my uncle was only the official allowance," he said. "The last time I saw him in town he gave me fifty pounds—in cash. He was always asking me how I was fixed and giving me money like that. In the course of a year it came to a good deal. And, of course, I do a bit of composing in my spare time. I've written a couple of songs that brought in quite a bit."

I said he must send me copies, and he said he would. That seemed about all, so we shook hands and I wished him luck. As soon as he'd gone, Susan looked in. She still had that bonnet thing on.

"You'd like a cup of tea, sir?"

"I'd like one of *your* cups of tea," I said. "You shall make tea for me in heaven, Susan."

Her black eyes twinkled and for a moment she looked somehow like a robin. Then she remembered what day it had been, and she was prim and dignified again.

"I'll bring one in, sir," she told me, and gave her little bow.

In two minutes she was bringing in a dainty tray and there were two of Loret's French pastries.

"You'll excuse me, sir, if I mention it," she said as she set down the tray, "but were you going back to Drowton? If you were, would it be troubling you too much to bring me a bottle of peroxide? We don't seem to have none in the house."

"I certainly will," I said. "What size?"

She said the medium size would do. I was wondering if I should congratulate her again on her good fortune, and then I decided I would not. I had only to mention Guy Pallart on that day and in a moment she might be in tears.

"You're a person of great importance now, Susan," was what I did say.

"What? Having this house to run, sir?" She gave a toss of the head. "I ain't no stranger to that, sir. Even when the Canon was alive, everything used to be left to me."

"And it couldn't have been left in better hands," I said.

"There's nothing to do if you go the right way to work," she told me. "These here modern gals, as they call themselves, aren't worth two pins. It's their mothers to blame more than them. That's what I always say."

Then she was remembering something.

"That Wilkin, sir. What do you think he did?"

I said I couldn't imagine.

"Never went and showed up this morning—this day of all days. And never had the decency to show himself at the funeral. Helped himself to a holiday."

"Superintendent Wharton will be asking him about that," I said. "And thank you for the tea, Susan, before I forget it."

"You're kindly welcome, sir," she told me, and I suddenly stared.

"Susan, you're not Essex. You're Suffolk!"

"I don't know how you knew that, sir," she said, "but I *am* Suffolk. I married Beavers at Stowmarket and come to live here, and here I've been ever since."

"Stowmarket," I said, and smiled. "Do you know Savenham?"

"I was born within three miles of it. At Needham Market."

"And I was born at Savenham," I said. "That makes us almost relations."

She remembered my father well, and all at once it was like a family reunion. Curious wasn't it? If Susan hadn't used that fine old phrase of being *kindly welcome*, there'd never have grown up between us that quick intimacy. And I should never have learned about her hair.

The previous afternoon Wharton had gone to the coast-guard's cottage in the car which Drane's Chief Constable had placed at his disposal. I had only the vaguest idea what was in his mind, but he was perfectly frank for once when he gave me an account of the afternoon.

George likes the elimination process. His first aim is always to compile a list of possible suspects, and then eliminate them one by one. But before a single suspect is so eliminated, or wiped clean off his list, he has to feel even more than sure of that suspect's innocence. He hadn't been sure about Brace, for instance, whatever his probable alibi, and that was why he had sent me to Feverton.

At the stage in the Case at which we had arrived, his favourite suspects were, in order: The German prisoner, Brace, Wilkin and Kales, and enquiries were still going on about each. But there was another man—Calne. I had insisted that Calne could not possibly have been in the water at a certain spot and then have contrived to get to Ninford within an hour to kill Pallart before eleven, even if Calne had a vestige of motive. Wharton accepted my statement—with reservations. He knew, for instance, that I was no authority on tides and currents and had no local knowledge of the Creek. Calne's 'accident' was a mystery, and George likes unsolved mysteries as little as I do. And this mystery, and those concerned in it, had at least a superficial connection with the Case. In other words, Wharton wanted to reduce his list of suspects by eliminating Calne, but he was going to be uncommonly sure before he did so.

George was surprised when he got to the cottage. It was the land to the right of the road that was marshy. By the cottage and along the shore it was sandy and stiff with tussocky mounds. He was just as surprised when he and the coastguard reached the Flat in the motor-boat. It was only the north, or Estuary, end that was mud. The rest was shingle and sand, held together by tussocks of the same coarse grass.

The boat moved on to the approximate spot where Calne had gone overboard. The whole trip was highly confidential but even then George had to be wary about the questions he asked.

"What sort of swimmer are you?" he asked the coastguard.

"Fairish," he was told.

"Better than Mr. Calne?"

The coastguard smiled.

"Well, I reckon I am, sir. He's no particular swimmer. I know that for a fact."

"Think back to last Friday night," Wharton said. "You know the tide and currents and everything. It's you who have an accident and fall overboard. We'll even imagine your head isn't hurt. How long would it take you to get ashore?"

"I doubt if I'd have made it at all," he said. "If I had got ashore I'd have been like Mr. Calne. Too exhausted to do a thing."

"And suppose you'd had the good luck to come across a bit of timber?"

"I'd have managed all right then," he was told. "The only thing is I'd have been much slower. If you've got one hand resting on the plank or whatever it is, you can only swim with your legs. It might have taken me an hour and more to reach the Flat, and then I'd have been pretty well worn out."

"Would any sort of timber help?"

"Even an oar would help," the coastguard said. "It's amazing what'll keep the human body afloat. You can even keep yourself afloat if you know the way."

They went back to the cottage and the coastguard's wife offered Wharton tea. While waiting for it he had a look at the garden. By the shed was a sawing-horse and some odd pieces of driftwood and timber. The coastguard said he picked up a goodish bit in the course of a summer, and he sawed it in his spare time ready for the winter.

"That looks a good stout bit," Wharton said. "Big enough for a nice little gate-post."

The coastguard looked a bit sheepish. Wharton gave him a dig in the ribs and mentioned the word *scrounging*.

"It is and it isn't, sir. If everyone had their rights, I suppose it belongs to the timber yard down there."

"That's their mark on the butt?"

"You're not supposed to see that, sir. I'll have to saw that end off soon as you've gone. But that's the piece of timber, sir, that saved Mr. Calne's life. I recovered it off the Flat where it had washed up."

"Well, you can rely on me to keep it quiet," Wharton told him jocularly. "And if you catch me out doing a bit of scrounging, you'll know what to do."

After tea Wharton came back through Ninford and on to Wandham. No one was at home at the Ferry so he went back to the fork, intending to enquire at the village. Then he went back to the Ferry instead. The garage doors were shut and Calne's car was not there. So he helped himself to a good look round and was sorry there was no gangway so that he could go over the *Avocet*, for she was lying about twenty feet out in the deep water. All the same he felt he had had a pretty fair afternoon. Calne was definitely off the list, though it still remained a mystery who had struck him. The blow on the head had been a wicked one, the coastguard's wife had said. The hair was all matted with blood and she had had difficulty in shaving it off.

Wharton was driving to Colchester. When he reached town there was another suspect to remove from the list, and this time not a serious one. Everything Georges Loret had related about himself was true. He was a chef by profession, and had held the rank of captain in the Resistance Movement. There he had a very fine record, especially in certain operations around Bayeux. After the Allied landing he had taken part in the fighting in Paris. Later he had worked at Chez Victor, and had left to work for Pallart.

My description of Kales had already been telephoned through and George so expedited matters in town that the following morning the police message was broadcast. It was of the usual type, that the police were anxious to get in touch with a Dr. Kales, presumed to be a Czech refugee, and then followed the description in some detail. I had heard that broadcast myself at nine the next morning, and I thought it pretty effective.

After a little chat with Susan Beavers I went on to the Wheatsheaf, and I'd been there about an hour—always expecting George to arrive—when Drane rang me. He had tried the Old Vicarage first.

His news was that Ernst Ungler *was* a blond. His hair, in fact, was the palest of yellows. What Drane wanted was the best description I could give of the man I'd seen. I said I'd seen him for the merest flick of a light through a doorway, and all I could add was that the man had been fairly slim, and if anything below medium height. I distinctly recalled the two dark shapes of him and Pallart as they neared me across the lawn and how Pallart, who was tallish, had rather towered above him.

"Hold on, sir, will you?" Drane said. He was ringing from the camp at Overy, by the way.

When he was back on the line, he was quite excited. The little I'd given fitted Ungler exactly. He added that Ungler would also fit into a certain theory after all. His wasn't really an escape—it was a species of absence without leave. He was a German prisoner taken by lorry each morning to a certain nursery garden where he worked. As he was of good bearing and conduct and anti-Nazi, he came under the new privilege of being allowed out of camp for walks in his leisure, or even to visit the houses of acquaintances he might have made. He might have taken advantage of such privileges to have been taken by Pallart to the Old Vicarage. Moreover, Pallart could take him back to the camp by car by the time Ungler was supposed to return.

When he added that Ungler spoke a certain amount of English, I was asking if that wouldn't make his capture more difficult.

"Don't you worry, sir," Drane said confidently. "The Commandant here thinks we'll get him in a day or so. The average time they stay loose is only about a week, so he tells me."

I asked if he'd be coming to Ninford and he said he wouldn't be able to make it till the morning. Almost before I'd time to hang up the receiver, George was arriving.

George said he'd had tea on the train but could do with another cup. While he was having it we brought each other up to date. He was interested in the news about Ungler, but when I told him that Wilkin had been absent all day, he gave a pretty grim smile. It changed to a glare.

"What about his lodgings? Is he still there?"

I couldn't say I'd had no time to enquire for I'd been kicking my heels in the Wheatsheaf for an hour. George muttered something about nothing going right if he was a moment away. I left him to his tea and made my way to Wilkin's lodgings. An elderly woman came to the door.

"Is Mr. Wilkin in?"

"He's gone," she said. "Been gone since yesterday evening."

As George would have put it, you could have knocked me down with a steam-roller.

"Mind if I come in a minute?" I said, and she drew back and let me in.

There was no doubt about it. Wilkin had packed up and gone. All I could gather was that he'd told his landlady that he wasn't going to be humbugged about by no women, and Ninford wasn't the only place where there was work. He'd volunteered to pay her for the whole week, and just after dusk he'd gone off on his motor-bike with his bag strapped on the carrier.

"Which way did he go?"

"Colchester way," she said. "He said he'd be sending me his address as soon as he got one."

"What sort of motor-bike was it?"

She knew nothing about motor-bikes, she said, so I thanked her and moved further along the village. At the one little filling-station they ought to know something about Wilkin's motor-bike, and they did.

"It was a little old-fashioned two-stroke, sir," the ironmonger-cum-petrol-agent told me. "Name all worn off but I think it was an old Martindale. Not a bad engine though."

"That's the kind of machine you get on and paddle gently away," I said.

"That's it, sir. Don't make a lot of noise. Keep up a regular thirty or so miles an hour and do about a hundred to the gallon. The plugs want cleaning regular, though."

I went back to the Wheatsheaf expecting an explosion. All I received was a look of grief. George hauled out his thick notebook. In town he'd got in touch with Wilkin's war-time Depot, and he had the number. Off he lumbered to the telephone. When he came back the evening meal was coming in.

"It may take some time for the call to come through," was all he said, but before he'd scarcely settled to his cold mutton and salad, the bell rang.

"That's no use to me," I heard him roar. "Get me someone who knows something. The Adjutant, or whoever's in charge of the Records. You'll ring me again? You'd better take care you do."

The meal proceeded. It ended and the usual pot of tea arrived. George was on his second cup when the bell went again. I listened at the door.

The conversation, at least for a minute or two, was touchingly polite. Then George began working up to a crescendo.

"But you were telephoned from Scotland Yard? What the devil do you fellows do with your time? . . . No, I certainly won't wait to be rung again. I'm keeping this line open if I stay here till midnight. And you'll foot the bill."

Apparently the other end had retired. George let out a snort and I moved away from the door. A moment and there came a kick at it. George was still holding the receiver at the full length of the flex and reaching out with his foot to attract my attention.

"What about Wilkin's ration and identity cards?"

I could have said, "Well, what about them?" Instead, I gave a nod and went by him and out by the side door to the street. Once more the elderly woman came to the door.

"Sorry to trouble you again," I said, "but was Wilkin's ration book in order?"

She said it was. And he had had to produce his identity card when he registered at Ninford. I hurried back to the Wheatsheaf.

"That's all right then," said George mildly. He was now sitting in a chair and he had his pipe going. One hand held the receiver to his ear, and I felt an impish desire to ask him if I should tell him a bedtime story.

"For one moment I wondered if he'd come here under a false name," he said. He caught my look. "I know that Mr. Calne knew him, but he might have had a false name at the Depot."

He showed no particular desire for my company so I brought him the third and last cup of tea and retired to the dining-room. Inside ten minutes I heard his voice.

"Oh, you have, have you? Well, let's have them . . . Yes, I'm taking them down."

There were a series of grunts as the talk proceeded. Then came something different.

"What! What's that you say?"

Another grunt or two.

"You're absolutely sure? . . . You don't know the firm? . . . I see. Well, send a written confirmation to me, care of Scotland . . . Yes. And thank you very much . . . Goodbye."

In he came like a whirlwind.

"What do you think? What was Frederick Albert Wilkin doing before he volunteered for the Army?"

I shrugged my shoulders. George's huge shoulders hunched, his head bent forward and his look was a glare.

"He was an agent employed by a firm of detectives!"

It was I who suggested ringing Bill Ellice. Bill's office was open till a very late hour and if he wasn't there, we still might get him at his private address. He happened to be there.

He said he knew a Fred Wilkin, and Wharton was promptly asking for a description. It tallied.

"He worked for Hedge and Frankfort up till just before the war," Bill said. "They gave him the push and he came to ask me for a job. I took the precaution of getting hold of Tom Hedge because Wilkin had the reputation of being a pretty smart man and I guessed there must be something behind it. So there was. Wilkin had been trying to blackmail one of Tom's clients."

"Wilkin got jugged?"

"No, no," Bill said. "That would have done the firm no good. Wilkin was told by Tom Hedge just where he stood and suitably warned, and given the push."

"I see. And you've heard nothing of him since?"

"Not a thing," Bill said. "I hadn't even thought about him till I heard you mention his name just now."

There followed a hectic hour. George got the Chief Constable's office and at last Drane was on the line. Drane was given a description of the motor-bike and told to pick up the trail. I gathered that Wilkin was now Priority Number One.

I had slipped down to the filling-station again to try to get the number of Wilkin's motor-bike, but I got only the registration letters, which were local, though the man was sure the number had ended with a 3. George told me to ask in the bar, and the number turned out to be 533. George was now talking to the Yard, and within ten minutes they had a description of Wilkin and his motor-bike ready for the *Police Gazette*.

George came back to the dining-room and let out a breath. If Wilkin wasn't in our hands inside a couple of days, then his name was Robinson.

It was after ten o'clock and I asked what about the morning.

"At the Vicarage," he said. "Somewhere about nine. Don't worry if I'm a bit late."

He said he felt like a whisky. The landlord brought two doubles, and when we'd finished them, I said I'd be getting along. Then the telephone went again. The Yard was back on the line.

This time it was Brace. He had gone straight to his flat and hadn't left it, but as soon as he had reached Liverpool Street he had telephoned from a call-box.

"Keep going," George said. "If anything happens in the morning, ring me at once."

That was that, and I said a last good night. As I drove past the Old Vicarage, I saw never a sign of light or life. That night I slept like a log and I woke to what I knew might be another busy day. What I couldn't foresee was that it was to be as eventful a one as I'd ever known.

PART III
TORTUOUS CHASE

CHAPTER XII
SENSATION IN COURT

I BOUGHT Susan's bottle of peroxide and knew I should never reach Ninford till well after nine. But I needn't have worried. George wasn't there, and as I'd taken the precaution of bringing with me my two newspapers, I took my ease in the shade of the summer-house verandah and did my crosswords. It was a drowsy autumn morning; a day to lounge away with a pipe and a book.

Just after ten o'clock George turned up.

"I don't know that there's very much we can do," he said. "Every possible thing's been set going. All you and I can do is wait."

He stretched out his legs and had a good look at the morning. Then he said he might possibly go to Overy and get some possible new slant on Ungler. The men Ungler had worked with might know a good deal about him.

That burst of energy over, he got his pipe going, then had a look at my newspapers. It was a quarter to eleven when Friske called him to the telephone. And it was then that I remembered I hadn't given Susan her peroxide. I told myself I'd wait till Wharton was back before I stirred.

The minutes went by and there was no sign of George, but when I strolled near the lounge window, I could hear him still talking. Twenty minutes had gone before he came back.

"Where ought Brace to have gone first thing this morning?" was what he was asking me.

"To Feverton," I said, and then was adding a rider. "I forgot, though. If he's a freelance, he might have gone anywhere. He's supposed to be scouting round for houses."

"In Portland Place?"

I stared.

"That's where he's gone," George said. "To the B.B.C."

I stared again. Then I had an idea.

"He told me he'd written some songs. Maybe he's gone to try to get them broadcast. To do some plugging, I think, is the term."

"Well, we're going to town," George said. "You'd better drive us in that hell-wagon of yours. We might have to stay the night."

He said he'd slip down to the Wheatsheaf and collect some things and cancel meals. We could call at the Ostlers on our way through Drowton. And even before he'd gone I knew he'd discovered far more than he'd divulged to me. The Yard had reported Brace's movements, but that didn't need twenty minutes of telephoning.

I went to the car and collected Susan's bottle of peroxide. She didn't seem to be about, so I gave a call. Her answering call came from above, so I made my way upstairs. She was stripping the bedroom that had been occupied by Brace and she thanked me as she took the bottle and asked how much it was.

"And now I haven't any money on me," she said exasperatedly. "I'll go down and get it."

"Nonsense!" I said. "What's a bottle of peroxide between friends."

Then I noticed something peculiar about her.

"What's that thing over your hair for, Susan?"

"Oh that," she said, and gave me a quick look. "Just to keep the dust out."

I gave what I thought was a roguish smile.

"Susan, you're hiding something. You kept that bonnet on all yesterday. What's the matter with your hair?"

Her little black eyes shot me another look, as if she was wondering whether I knew.

"I just had a little accident, that's all. It ain't nothing really."

"But you've such lovely hair," I said. "And it's thick too. What happened to it, Susan?"

"Oh dear," she said, and her eyes twinkled. "I see I'll never get no peace till I tell you. But you won't laugh?"

"Heaven forbid!" I said solemnly.

"Well, it was like this," she began, and then she closed the bedroom door and began all over again. "It was like this. I did want to have my hair sort of special for the funeral. I thought I might do something about them yellow streaks. Lamb's tails we used to call them when I was a girl at school. So I put some of the stuff what I had on a brush and started to rub it in. I thought it was some sort of tonic. And look what it was!"

She was unfastening the wrap and there on the silver hair was a blob of black and streaks that radiated out.

"It weren't tonic at all. It must have been some sort of dye!"

I don't know why but we suddenly had a fit of laughing. Maybe it was her look that set me off—the horror and then the mischievous twinkle. But we laughed and laughed.

"Well, well," she said at last. "'T'ain't nothing particular to worry about. I reckon that peroxide'll get it off. Next Wednesday I can go to the hairdresser's."

"But how on earth did you come to make such a mistake?" I said.

She said it was on account of the bottle being foreign, and because she was an old fool. She said she'd show me, and we went along to her room. And I soon saw why she'd made the mistake. The label was French and there were two pictures on it that must have misled. One was of a handsome Frenchman with a superb head of black hair and beard to match—the other was of a woman combing a mass of shining black tresses.

"It was that Dr. Kales that really put me up to it," she said. "He had beautiful shiny hair."

"Yes, but where did you buy the bottle?" I said. "Surely they should have explained about it in the shop? What did you ask for?"

She clicked her tongue impatiently.

"Haven't I told you I didn't buy it? It was that Dr. Kales. When he went away and I was cleaning out his room, I found it back of one of the drawers. Thinks I to myself, 'If he write about it I'll have to send it on. All the same there won't be no harm me trying just a drop or two that he won't miss.'"

She gave me a look of mock apprehension. Once more I wanted to laugh. But I didn't. My fingers rose, and fell again. Also I remembered Wharton.

"Well, good luck to the peroxide treatment," I said. "Superintendent Wharton's probably waiting for me, or I'd wait and see what it does."

I gave a smile and a nod and hurried off along the corridor. Through the open door of a bedroom I saw Wharton standing by the car. When I reached him he gave an impatient snort and was taking his seat. I got the car moving.

"George," I said, "I think I've discovered something."

"Oh?" he said, and waited.

"It's that German prisoner," I said. "He doesn't exist, so to speak. Neither does Kales. What I mean is, they're one and the same person!"

When George rides with me, he keeps me throttled back. When he drives himself, his two hands clutch the steering wheel like grim death, and only once—when his brake slipped on a downhill gradient—has he ever exceeded thirty an hour. When I once twitted him about it, he gave me the best of all possible retorts.

"I'm still alive, ain't I?"

But as I began telling him the queer story of the house-keeper's hair, he was wholly unaware that I was doing fifty.

"I think you're right," he told me at last. "That blond hair you saw was dyed that same night and Kales took the bottle to his room in case it might need touching up the next morning."

"Let me see," he was going on. "Loret would go to bed. Susan *was* in bed, and Brace didn't arrive till the next day. Pallart could take Kales—or Ungler or whatever you call him— to the house and next morning everyone would suppose Pallart had brought him late the previous night from Colchester station. If you'd stayed on that Wednesday night, I'll bet you'd have seen Pallart go off again in the car and then come back for pretence."

He gave himself a confirmatory nod or two, and then was asking how the discovery was going to help us. But then we were streaking into Drowton and it was not till we had left the town again that he put the same question.

"It's going to make all the difference in the world," I said. "At least it will when we've settled just why Ungler had to become Kales."

It was unfortunate that at that moment I accelerated to sixty to pass on a perfectly straight stretch of road a huge van that had been keeping us back on the bends. George clutched the side of the car and wanted to know what the hell I was doing.

"How many times have I told you you can't drive and talk. You drive the car and I'll do the talking."

He didn't say another ten words till we were nearing Epping.

"Stop at the police-station here. I've got some telephoning to do. And you might as well get yourself a cup of coffee. Don't know how long I shall be."

Once more he was about twenty minutes. I wanted to know which way he'd like me to enter London.

"Make straight for Portland Place," he said. "No need to hurry. We're meeting someone there at one o'clock."

I came in by Finsbury Park and went straight across at Camden Town. It was five minutes to one when we drew up outside Broadcasting House. I waited while George made enquiries, and in a couple of minutes we were being shown into quite a comfortable office. A youngish man in bow tie, black coat and striped black trousers got to his feet. A minute later Wharton was setting the ball rolling.

"Scotland Yard has rung you about a material witness in an important case—a Mr. Richard Brace. This is highly confidential information. Anything you tell us will be treated in the same way. Now then. Just what was Mr. Brace doing here this morning?"

But red tape wasn't to be cut so easily. Wharton was told that the question was most unusual and concerned the sanctitude of contracts. Wharton's eyebrows lifted, and he gave me the archest of looks.

"So Mr. Brace has a contract! We're getting on."

That was the way things proceeded till we had what we wanted. Brace had a contract for twelve consecutive weekly appearances and the same number of re-broadcasts. I don't remember the exact jargon but that's what it means.

"I'm not interested in the figures," Wharton said, "but was it what you'd call a good contract?"

"Quite a good one," the other told him. "He's one of our most popular features. I must insist however about secrecy in all this. If it ever emerged—"

"Pardon me," I cut in. "When the contract was drawn up, was it Brace who insisted on any secrecy? What I mean is that I've gathered that there's some sort of mystery about him. And I've never seen his name in the *Radio Times*."

Then more came out. Brace *had* insisted on his name being kept a very close secret, and for reasons which Wharton and I well knew. But his reasons were the value of the mystery element. To the public he was not a name but—

"Let me guess," I said quickly. "He was the Voice In The Night."

There was a moment's consternation. I said there'd been no leakage though I preferred not to say how I knew. And that was about all, except that we heard that Brace had made a couple of Music Hall appearances, had already made some records and looked like having a lucrative future if he kept his head. Wharton was getting to his feet.

"Can we spare another ten minutes?" I asked him. "If so we might hear one of Brace's records. And I'd rather like the two last issues of the *Radio Times*."

There was no difficulty about the records and in a couple of minutes we were listening to Richard Brace. I thought him a flagrant imitation of the Whispering Baritone of the old Savoy Hill days, for his voice was little more than a friendly huskiness. But he did have a sense of rhythm and style. I could see him being mightily popular with that vast audience that one thinks of as the Workers' Playtime class of wireless addict.

Before I moved the car on again I had a look at an issue of the *Radio Times*, and then George was wanting to know how I had guessed about that Voice In The Night.

"It was something to do with that Thursday night when I dined at the Old Vicarage," I said. "Brace put the wireless on and infuriated his uncle. I think I told you about that. Then Susan tried to divert the shock by pretending it was she who had asked Brace to turn it on. But it must have been Brace. He couldn't resist basking in his own personality. It must have given him quite an ironic pleasure. It was a re-broadcast of course. And this *Radio Times* shows where he was when Bill Ellice's man lost him on the Saturday night. He was one of the turns in Music Hall."

"Well, we know where his money comes from," Wharton said. "All we've got to do now is clear up the Feverton end. I think Brace will talk."

I asked where to, and he said to the Yard. Brace ought to be waiting. Our old friend Sergeant Jewle had been told to collect him from his flat.

Brace and Jewle were sitting outside Wharton's room, and Brace was looking as if he had hellish toothache and Wharton was a butcher of a dentist.

"Bring him in," Wharton said as we passed, and in the two came. Wharton took his time over adjusting his spectacles, and his tone was as mild as milk. All he wanted to know was whether Brace preferred to tell the truth, the whole truth and nothing but the truth, or be taken along to Feverton to the senior member of the firm of Estate Agents. In less than no time Brace was telling the truth.

Everything was due to his late uncle's absurd prejudices, he said. That was why everything had had to be so secret. Charles Hawke, with whom he had been at school, was a friend of his and it had been Hawke who had really thought out the scheme. Brace, for purposes of any inquiries by his uncle, would be learning the business of the estate agency, and if he was described as a freelance, then he would be conveniently out if the uncle rang or called. As for a chance letter, Hawke had told the letter clerk that any letters to Brace—a possible client of the firm—were always to be handed to him direct.

"Well," said Wharton, and peered at me over the spectacle tops. "I've always heard that if honest men devoted as much talent and time to their energies as the rogues, they'd all be millionaires. Our friend here makes me believe it."

"But there was nothing really dishonest about it," protested Brace.

"No?" said Wharton, and his tone was a bit sharp. "Let's suppose a thing or two. Suppose you got your friend Charles Hawke to induce his father to take you into the firm. You could even afford to pay a big premium—we'll call it that—on condition that there was continuity. On condition, that is, that the job was pre-dated. Then when inquiries were made by the trustees or executors into your uncle's will, you'd qualify for the income from the estate." He wagged a minatory finger. "And you sit there and tell me there was nothing dishonest! Why did you ring Charles Hawke? Why did you rush off to see him on Saturday night? Why did he ring you after Mr. Travers had seen him?"

Brace shifted uneasily on his seat and mumbled that it wasn't that at all.

"Let's do some more supposing," Wharton went on, and now his voice had a solemnity, or was it a horror?

"Your uncle had warned you of certain consequences and you'd persisted in telling him lies. If he discovered those lies, and it looked as if he might, then you stood to lose far more than you'd gain by all that Voice In The Night sort of stuff."

Brace's face went a sudden red.

"I didn't want his money. I could make enough of my own."

"Then why did you go on lying to him?" He gave me a triumphant look. "And you went on taking his money."

In his grunt was a sneer.

"Let's go on supposing. Supposing it had struck you that if your uncle was dead—"

"I didn't kill him. I couldn't have killed him. You know that."

"That's just what we don't know," Wharton told him smoothly. "You went to your bedroom. Loret and Susan were asleep. What was to stop you coming down again?"

"I didn't come down. Everyone knows I was dropping asleep on my feet before I even went up."

"Why are you connected with the B.B.C.?" Wharton said. "Because you're something of an actor. You have to be to get those songs of yours across."

He got to his feet.

"I'm not accusing you of killing your uncle. That isn't the way we have here. All the same, if you did happen to kill him—"

"But I didn't!" The voice was almost a shriek.

"If you did happen to kill him," went on Wharton imperturbably, "nothing is surer than that we'll find out. Meanwhile you'll stay at your flat, and you'll be under supervision, so to speak. If you've anything else to tell us in due course, you've only to let me know."

A wave of the hand and Jewle was taking Brace out. Wharton hooked off the spectacles and stowed them away in the antiquated case.

"What did you make of him?"

"He's a nasty specimen," I said, "but he hasn't the guts for murder."

"It was a nasty murder," Wharton said. "Even a coward can crack a man on the skull in the dark."

He got to his feet.

"Better see about a meal. I don't know about you, but I'm devilish hungry."

It was then past two o'clock, and it was a quarter to three when we got back. We hadn't mentioned the Case during our meal, and now George stoked his pipe again and I gathered that we were settling to work.

"Let's go into that Kales business," he said. "We'll say that theory of ours is correct. Ungler *is* Kales and Kales is Ungler. Now then. Why should Pallart—"

And that was as far as he got. The buzzer went and he muttered exasperatedly as he picked up the receiver.

"A who?" he said, and "Put him through."

He drew a pad towards him and picked up a pencil.

"Yes?" he said, and "Yes" again. Then there was a "What!" that made me jump.

"Wait a minute," he was saying impatiently. "Let me get it down. The Tonbridge Hotel, Tufnell Street, Holborn. . . . Yes, go right on."

He listened for a couple of minutes and gave no more than a grunt or two.

"And they're still there? . . . Right. Tell them I'll be along straightaway."

He hung up, and by the way he was looking at me, I knew he was wondering how to get the full effect out of some climax.

"It's Kales," he said. "We know where he is! He's at a hotel and the manager heard the broadcast and got suspicious. He telephoned here and a couple of men are watching the entrances."

Then he was on his feet.

"Well, what are you waiting for? We haven't got all night."

Even when I got in the back of the police car, too many things were happening for me and I was feeling a bit muzzy. George sat quiet in his own corner as we went along the Strand and up Kingsway. At the lights we went right and made a couple more turns. The driver slowed.

"Stop at the hotel, sir, or where?"

"A bit short of it," Wharton told him, and almost at once the car was drawing up. Wharton got out. A plain-clothes man folded the newspaper he had been reading and came up.

"Nothing happened?" Wharton asked him.

"Nothing at all, sir. Far as we know he's still there."

The manager was waiting by the hotel desk. It wasn't a shabby hotel and it wasn't palatial. It simply looked as if it had known better days, and still wasn't doing so bad. Wharton came straight to the point.

"He's still upstairs?"

The manager said he was.

"What made you recognise him?"

"I think it was that little nick at the side of his nose. And how nervous he was."

"What's his room?"

It was number thirty-five, on the second floor. Wharton took the master-key and looked round for a lift. But there wasn't a lift and we went up the stairs, the plain-clothes man at our heels. We went up and up to the last landing. Rooms 24-36 were to the right. Wharton ticked them off and halted at the corridor end. He motioned the man to stand by the door, then suddenly had the key in the lock. The door opened and in he went. I was there, too, and I had my back to the closed door.

It was a smallish room with a single bed. A wireless set was built into the wall by the bedside table, and there was a chair, a wash-basin and the usual fumed-oak wardrobe. Kales was on the bed, and sound asleep. Our feet had made no sound on the carpet, and he didn't even stir. For a moment I wondered if he were dead.

Wharton was looking down at him. Then his hand went out and he was shaking the sleeper. Kales rolled over and opened his eyes. They blinked and suddenly he was really aware of Wharton. In that still sleepy moment Wharton was no more than a stranger; a burly, not unfriendly looking man in a grey suit and old-fashioned trilby hat.

Then I must have moved for his eyes caught me. They recognised me, and the look on his face was a queer mixture. In a flash he knew it was some friendly visit, and as quickly he knew it was not. He made a quick movement but Wharton had him by the shoulder.

"You're the man who calls himself Dr. Kales?"

He didn't wait for an answer. He was twisting Kales round and peering at his face.

"This is him all right," he told me. "Perhaps Dr. Kales wouldn't mind taking that chair and we'll have a nice little comfortable talk."

CHAPTER XIII
ERNST UNGLER

KALES TALKED. He wasn't scared so much as wary, and I was thinking that a man who'd been captured in battle wouldn't need to be scared at a recapture by civilians. That is, if his conscience was clear.

I have said that he spoke very good English. It was mainly his intonation that betrayed him as a foreigner, and then only rarely. He sat on the one chair and Wharton and I were on the bed. Wharton's man now stood inside the door.

"You are Ernst Ungler?" was Wharton's first question.

"Yes," he said, as simply and directly as that. I almost gaped. Wharton was taken aback, too.

"Then how did you come to be friendly with a man like Major Pallart?"

"It was in 1940 when he was captured," Ungler said. "It was south of Laon and I was with the 42nd Infantry to whom his Division surrendered. They were cut off and it was hopeless."

His eyes wrinkled and he was looking across the room as if to recall the scene.

"The prisoners were in trucks and wagons," he went on, "and they were crowded like animals." He shrugged his shoulders. "It had to be so. And it was hot. There was no time to sort the wounded from the unwounded, and if a man could move he was put into the trucks. That was when I first saw Major Pallart. He had collapsed from his wound and the heat, and it was I who filled his water-bottle and saw he was comfortable. When we reached Namur I spoke to one of our doctors and he was taken from the train. He has told me since that that was what saved his life. When he was on the stretcher he asked my name and I told him. He said he would remember."

Wharton gave a grunt.

"I see. And a very touching story it is. Well, go on. What happened next?"

"It was in England," he said, "about three months ago. I was walking by myself near Overy when a car passed me. Then it stopped and a man got out. He looked hard at me and asked if I was Ernst Ungler. Then we recognised each other. He asked if there was anything I needed and he would have given me money. I said there was nothing I needed unless it was to return to my home in Karlsbad. Then he arranged that I should meet him the following week."

"And you did meet him?" I asked.

"He waited till the road was deserted," he said, "and then he took me in his car to where I do not know, but there was a wood where we were not seen in the car. That was when he planned my escape."

"Yes, yes?" said Wharton impatiently.

There was a kind of inexorability about the story and the unruffled way that Ungler told it. He had told Pallart all about himself, how he was a Sudeten German with a Czech mother—maiden name of Kales—and how he had been educated at Prague and had then become a teacher of languages at Karlsbad. Pallart had taken voluminous notes and that was all that had been done that night. The next meeting was arranged for a fortnight later.

Things had moved in that fortnight. Pallart said he had been making inquiries and he hoped to get the necessary papers made out in the name of Mikail Kales. He also took Ungler's measurements, and he said that Ungler mustn't get anxious if there was a delay. But every Wednesday Ungler was to take the same walk and Pallart hoped soon to have news. But meanwhile Ungler had been transferred to the nursery-garden job and it was difficult to take that walk. Pallart had twice come to see him, and six weeks had gone by before the two were able to talk again. Pallart said he would have the papers ready in a fortnight at least and a meeting was arranged. This time it was to be the escape meeting. If Ungler couldn't leave camp in the ordinary way, then he was to get out by some other means.

And so to the Wednesday night, when everything in Ungler's story tallied with what I had seen. In the summerhouse Ungler changed into the suit and underclothes which Pallart had ready, and there was also a case with more clothes and necessaries.

"Is this the case?" asked Wharton, stirring with his feet the almost new leather case by the wash-basin.

Ungler said it was, and he went on to describe in some detail what had happened that night. His hair was carefully dyed and he took the bottle to his room so that any retouching could be made in the morning. Finally they went to the house where a cold meal had been left. Most of the night was spent in rehearsing the role which Ungler now had to play. Pallart said, too, that he would have to stay a few days in Ninford and meet people, and so test out the disguise and be more assured of his part. And that, Ungler said with a shrug of his shoulders, was all.

"It isn't all," Wharton told him. "It's just the beginning. What about Pallart's death?"

That had been terrible, Ungler said. When he had read it in the newspaper, he had found it impossible to believe. If he had been a woman, he would have cried, so much did the tragedy cut him to the heart. And he had also begun to be afraid. There were things he might tell the police, and yet he daren't risk going to the police.

"What things?" Wharton said, and leaned forward.

Something about a man whom Pallart was seeing the night he was killed, Ungler said, and went on to explain. It had been arranged, for example, that Pallart should drive him to Colchester in time to catch a late train to town. That had been arranged because the man named Montagu had ready the papers, and, since Pallart did not want to be connected more than absolutely necessary with the business, Montagu was bringing the papers to that very hotel. All that had been previously arranged.

Everyone was in bed but Ungler and Pallart. It was about a quarter-past ten, and Pallart left the lounge to do something or other and Ungler was left alone. Soon afterwards Pallart came back and he was in a state of perturbation. He now had an engagement, he said. He'd just heard that a man wanted to see him on urgent business at eleven o'clock, and would Ungler mind hanging about at Colchester. It was something that had to be done and they went off in the car at once. They discussed final arrangements on the way; how, for instance, Pallart would come up to town in a day or two to decide the next moves. At Colchester, well short of the station, Ungler left the car, and that was the last time he saw Pallart alive. He himself came to London next morning and saw the man who gave him the papers.

"That night when you were alone in the lounge and Pallart was out," said Wharton. "Did you hear the telephone go?"

Ungler had heard nothing; nothing at least that he could recall.

"What did you mean when you said Pallart was perturbed?"

Ungler said his mood had changed. He seemed very nervous and the nervousness communicated itself to Ungler himself. Pallart didn't notice that.

"And what did you do with yourself at Colchester?"

Ungler said he had sat on a public bench under some trees, and he had dozed off part of the time. The day at sea had made him tremendously sleepy.

"I know the spot," I said. "And did anyone speak to you there?"

Ungler said it was dark under the trees, which was why he had welcomed the spot. Though it was a fine, warm night, hardly anyone was about.

Wharton began looking through Ungler's belongings in the bag. They were fine quality things—the kind that Pallart would buy. Then he asked for Ungler's forged papers. They seemed remarkably well done, for his eyebrows raised as he took a look at them. Then he put them in his pocket.

"Pack up anything else you have," he told Ungler. He nodded to the man. "When he's ready, bring him along to the Yard."

Wharton and I went out to the corridor and a few yards from the door.

"You were bursting to ask a question or two," he told me. "Plenty of time for that at the Yard. The atmosphere'll be a bit more intimidating there. Also I must get hold of Overy to fix up an escort and hear just what was on his papers when he was captured. That yarn of his has to be carefully checked. What did you think of it, by the way?"

I said I was damned if I knew. It had either been marvellously well rehearsed, or else it was simple truth.

"That's a hell of a lot of help," he told me with a snort. "But here he comes."

Ungler drew abreast. Wharton halted him.

"When were you captured?"

"In 1945, soon after the English landings," Ungler said.

"Where?"

"Near Caen."

Wharton waved him on.

"Superior sort of chap," he said to me. "Doesn't behave like a German, not that that's any guide."

We fell in behind. Another car was now by the entrance, and Ungler and Wharton's man got in. The car moved off.

"I don't think there'll be anything doing for you before another hour," George said. "I'll move along, and you might get yourself a cup of tea."

We went off to his car. I went back to the hotel. There was some part of Ungler's story which it seemed I might verify, even if I couldn't disprove.

"You been here long?" I asked the manager.

"Twenty years," he said.

"A long time," I said, and he said it was. When he first came there, it had still been a fine old family hotel with an excellent list of country patrons. Now the tide of fashion had moved more west.

"Did you ever have staying here anyone of the name of Pallart?"

"Pallart?" he said, and smiled. "A Canon Pallart and his wife always stayed here. The last time he came—that was during the war—he told me his wife was dead." He gave a reminiscent shake of the head. "All our old clientele were faithful to this hotel. But they're dying out now."

There was my confirmation. Pallart must have sent Ungler to the Tonbridge. The coincidence would have been far too great for Ungler to have chosen it for himself. Then as I was walking away it struck me that Pallart himself might have stayed at that hotel as a boy and young man. That made me think of something else. The old Canon loyal to the hotel. Loyalty was a Pallart characteristic. Hall well had stressed Guy Pallart's loyalty. Pallart had been loyal to Ungler. Another proof, or so it at that moment seemed, that Ungler's romantic story had been true.

* * * * *

I told Wharton all that in his room at the Yard just before Ungler was brought in. He made no comment except to say that he still preferred to keep an open mind.

Ungler came in again and he seemed not the least disquieted. When he heard Wharton's questions he answered with only the necessary pause for thought, and then—or so it seemed to me—only that his English should be perfect.

"Why had you no papers when you were captured?" Wharton began.

Ungler said it was the order of his Company Commander. There were S.S. men among them and it was feared that discrimination might be shown.

"You were S.S. or Gestapo. Which?"

Ungler said imperturbably that he was neither. He was an interpreter, attached to Brigade Headquarters, and he had happened to be at Company Headquarters when cut off by the English.

Wharton switched the attack when he'd added that the absence of papers had been remarkably convenient.

"Is it permitted to point out that at the time of my capture I had no thoughts of Major Pallart?" Ungler said shrewdly.

Wharton ignored that, if only because there was no answer. He switched the attack, as I said.

"Doesn't it strike you as an amazing coincidence that you should meet Major Pallart? England's a biggish place and East Anglia is what I'd call comparatively remote. Only one Englishman you might want to meet and—lo and behold he turns up!"

Ungler frowned at that *lo and behold*, but he couldn't help knowing what Wharton meant.

"But it was not unusual," he said. "Major Pallart told me that he had begun to make enquiries about me as soon as he got back from captivity himself. He said he had ways and means. He had got as far as knowing I was somewhere in Suffolk when I met him that night."

Wharton merely gave me a look over his spectacle tops. I took over.

"The afternoon of the cruise that we took with Mr. David Calne," I said. "You remember the events of that day?"

"Perfectly well," he said.

Then I was telling him what I had overheard as I came up the gangway.

"Major Pallart asked if you had recognised someone, and you said you had. He asked if you were sure, and you said you were absolutely sure. Who was that person whom you recognised?"

He frowned in thought. He asked me to repeat the time and exact circumstances. Then at last he smiled. It had been an experience of his own that he had been relating to Pallart: the story of a German deserter whom he had spotted: a German who had been acting as spy for the French.

"One other question," I said. "We move on to when we all left Walker's Ferry that night. You and Major Pallart were talking in French. He accused you of being concerned in the accident which had happened to Mr. Calne. Isn't that so?"

Ungler looked amazed.

"Mr. Brace heard him so accuse you," I said. "He said you'd been mad to hit Mr. Calne on the head, and you protested that you hadn't. Then Mr. Brace happened to look round, and Major Pallart nudged you not to talk so loudly."

Ungler shrugged his shoulders. Nothing of the sort had happened and he recalled no word of such a conversation. Yet it seemed to me that all the time that Ungler was protesting his brain was working hard to find—and as if by chance—some explanation. I waited, but the explanation didn't come.

"Just one more question," I said. "There was a message telephoned to you by this man Montague. Loret, the chef, took the message. It came from town?"

Ungler presumed so.

"Then it may surprise you to learn that Exchange was sure no message *had* come from town."

"But it must have done!" he said, and stared.

"Leave it," I said. "But why wasn't this message for Major Pallart? He was dealing with Montague."

He said Pallart didn't want his name to be overheard under any circumstances. The risks were too great. I could only shrug my shoulders and hand him back to Wharton.

As George told me afterwards, the rules concerning the taking of evidence didn't apply to an alien or prisoner of war like Ungler. Not that there was any third degree. Wharton was far too wily for that, and he had to have in mind the possible chance that Ungler might be a witness in court—if we got our man. But for two solid hours he worked in his own way on Ungler. I was so tired myself that I'm pretty sure I'd have owned up to most things if only I could have been free of that eternal voice.

Everything was gone over again in laborious detail from the beginning. He sneered, he threatened, he cajoled, he tried to bribe by promises of this and that and there wasn't a trick of the trade that didn't at last emerge from his sleeve. But he couldn't shake Ungler. He could sneer at the touching humanity when a German filled a water-bottle; he could probe and bully for twenty minutes on the question of Pallart's nervousness; he could call the meeting of Ungler and Pallart an obvious pack of lies, and Ungler took it all with the same imperturbability and explained each point with the same patience. Then at last Wharton got to his feet. He said nothing for a long minute, and it was like the All Clear after a bad blitz.

"You'll be going to a Detention Camp," he told Ungler quietly. "If you like to withdraw anything while you're there, or make a different statement, you've only to apply to your new Commandant."

Jewle took Ungler out. Ungler gave me a timid, friendly smile as he passed. The door closed and Wharton sank into his chair and let out a breath.

"Damned if I know what to think," he said. "All sorts of things seem to fit in—and yet I don't know. I've got a hunch the whole thing's fishy."

"What other things fit in?"

"He had seventy pounds on him in cash," Wharton said. "He says Pallart gave it him."

Then he was waving a furiously impatient hand.

"What's it matter what fits in? The whole thing stands or falls by that gratitude yarn. If it's a lie, then why did Pallart do what he did for Ungler?"

I said I didn't know. But I did mention again that matter of Pallart's loyalty.

"Loyalty, my foot!" He clicked his tongue. "I don't know, but sometimes you can't see further than your nose end."

"And what aren't I seeing?" I asked him.

"Loyalty!" he said again. "Pallart loyal to Ungler. What about the other way round? Ungler loyal to Pallart! Keeping his mouth shut and making up all that yarn just to shield Pallart! He's had days to think out the story, hasn't he? No wonder he had it all pat."

"Shield Pallart from what?" I insisted.

He looked at me. His hands rose despairingly, then fell.

"Forget about it. How should I know what he's shielding him from? If I knew that, the Case would be over."

He went on muttering for a moment or two then let out another breath.

"You'd better be pushing along. I shall probably be here an hour or two yet."

I asked what about the morning, and he said I'd better be at the Yard with the car at ten o'clock. I went to my flat and made myself some sort of a bed. I had a service meal and fumed in early after a very stiff whisky. I thought I shouldn't sleep, but I did. I woke early, it is true, but I didn't want to get to sleep again. I don't think I could have slept again if I had tried, and it would have been the thought of Ungler that would have kept me awake. German or not, I couldn't help liking the man. What was worse, from the point of view of the Case, I was almost entirely believing him.

Soon after ten o'clock Wharton was ready and we set off for Ninford.

"No hurry," Wharton told me. "You keep moving, and that's all. Then we can do some talking before we get there."

His manner was quite genial and maybe he'd discovered overnight how to suffer fools gladly. I asked him if he was keeping the Calne affair absolutely apart from the main case. He said he didn't get me.

"If we're to confine ourselves to Pallart's murder," I said, "then it doesn't matter two hoots about those two questions I put to Ungler last night."

George said he wasn't prepared to go as far as that. Calne had nothing to do with the killing of Pallart, but he still had a hunch that Pallart and Ungler had had something to do with the attempted murder of Calne. I didn't say so, but I could see everything beginning to get tangled up again.

"Very well," I said. "We come to the question of motive. Calne as good as told me that it wasn't Pallart who struck him. Therefore it must have been Ungler. There's no other possible person. Winder was at the wheel and Pike in the little engine-room or the cubby-hole near it. Brace and Friske and I were below deck. That leaves Ungler. Why should he want to kill Calne?"

"Wait a minute," he said, and I thought he meant me to halt the car. But it was an idea that had come. For quite a minute or two he was egg-bound. Then he was shaking his head.

"Can't be anything in it," he said. "It's too vague."

"What's too vague?"

"Something I was thinking."

I didn't press him and he did some more thinking. Then all at once he was asking a question.

"Rather a lot of French about all this case, isn't there?"

"I don't know," I said. "I suppose there is, in a way. But it crops up quite naturally."

"All right," he said. "You tell me what it is, and how it crops up naturally."

"Very well," I said. "If you don't try to rush me, I will." In a couple of minutes I was ready for him.

"Guy Pallart was engaged to a girl whose mother was French," I said. "She'd be bilingual, so naturally he'd wish to speak the language too. That was why he specialised on the language in his prison camp. Perhaps, too, he thought it might lead to some

Staff appointment that would keep him in the Army, in spite of his game leg. When he found that Ungler spoke almost perfect French, he always spoke French with him. That would give him practice. It was also natural that Pallart should take a trip to Paris, and that he should get friendly with Loret. Pallart was a natural thoroughbred. He didn't need to be a snob. If he could bring Loret to Ninford, then also he'd have someone always there on whom he could practise his French."

"That the lot?"

"For the moment," I said. "Why? Anything wrong with it?"

"That question of Pallart's girl," he said. "I can understand him wanting to learn French so as to speak it with her. She'd be wanting holidays in France, for instance. She might want to spend the winters in Algiers. But when she died—a terrific shock to Pallart, I gather—why did he still go on with it? It isn't human nature. He should have hated everything French, for the simple reason that it would keep reminding him of the girl he should have married."

I said he wasn't entitled to speak for all humanity. He couldn't measure everyone by the same foot rule. Then I had a happy thought and reminded him of *Great Expectations* and how some people might make memory an obsession. Like the woman of the cob-webbed, sunless room, Pallart might have been obsessed with the idea of surrounding himself—though in a saner way—with everything that might remind him of the dead Marie Courtold.

"You're a bit too nimble-witted for me," he said, and he said it so genially that I wondered what had come over him. But he was making a note in his book, and I knew that what I had said, however little to the point, had given him some new idea. And, strangely enough, he didn't revert to the Case till we were some miles farther along the road. When he did hark back to what we'd been discussing, I still had only the most tenuous idea how his brain had been working.

"Where did that Marie Courtold die?" was the question he suddenly put.

"I think it was in Paris," I said. "Either there or in Normandy. I wouldn't be sure. Hallwell might be able to tell you exactly."

"Ungler was captured in Normandy."

"And why not?" I said. "Surely you're not finding a coincidence there?"

"No," he said. "Perhaps not." And once more he left it at that.

I should have contributed something there. It stuck out a mile but I just didn't happen to see it. But it was vaguely in my mind before it disappeared, and maybe because I had more to think about than Wharton. The road, for instance, and the petrol tanker that I was anxious to pass. Then when I had passed it, Wharton was saying something that took me utterly by surprise.

"Something else about Ungler. Why shouldn't Pallart have been dead before he left?"

"You mean, he killed Pallart?"

"Yes," said George slowly. "If we could find a motive. Or somebody else may have killed him—Brace, for instance—and Ungler found the body."

"Then who drove Ungler to Colchester?"

"No one," Wharton said. *"He might have walked."*

"You're right," I said. "That case of his wasn't heavy. He could have done it easily, even if he hadn't left Ninford till eleven o'clock."

The missing gallon of petrol might have been drawn off, I said, but that wouldn't take long. There were two or three spare petrol tins in the garage.

Then I thought of something else. It wasn't that point I'd missed before, but something new.

"A very peculiar point in the relationships between Pallart and Ungler has just struck me, George. Get back to that conversation I overheard when I was coming up the gangway that Friday. It doesn't matter a hoot what Ungler was telling Pallart: whether it was about a German deserter or about Santa Claus. It's what was said that matters."

"You mean the *tutoyer* business?"

I stared.

"You noticed it?"

"Didn't you?" he said.

"I suppose I did," I said. "But I only just this minute saw the significance. With Pallart it was *tu*. With Ungler it was *vous*. That couldn't have been politeness. Therefore Pallart must have regarded Ungler as a social inferior, and the two were supposed to be more than friends. If Ungler's story was true, Pallart owed him his life, and knew it."

"But there's something even more important that arises out of it," George said. "Take that second conversation that Brace heard in the car. Brace might have made it up, but he didn't. And this is why. Ungler again used the *vous* and Pallart the *tu*. If Brace had made it up he'd have made them both use the *vous*."

"Therefore Brace heard what he said he heard. Which means that Pallart was furious with Ungler because he thought Ungler had had something to do with the supposed accident."

"Exactly," said George. "And now you know why I'd like to have another word with Calne."

We were running into Drowton and when we left the town again, George didn't revert to the subject of Ungler. It was Wilkin whom he mentioned, and in connection with David Calne.

"Calne didn't *get* Wilkin his job at the Old Vicarage," I said. "Pallart happened to be in need of a gardener and Calne mentioned Wilkin and sent Wilkin to see him."

"And what about the snooping? You still think Wilkin was working on his own?"

"Don't you?" I said. "He'd tried to blackmail before. And who could have employed him? Certainly not Calne. Calne had no possible motive for spying on Pallart."

"Maybe you're right," George said. "But one other thing, and about our friend Ungler. Pallart suggested that cruise to Calne. Didn't it seem a bit of a risk to take Ungler?"

"Not at all," I said. "Pallart wanted Ungler to get used to people and lose his nervousness. The more people he met, including myself, the better. I think that's why I was asked to dinner on the Thursday. It may have been one of the reasons why Brace was brought down."

We were passing the Old Vicarage and I caught sight of Loret as we passed. He was wearing his best suit and strolling on the lawn, and I think he was smoking a cigarette. George must have seen him better than I, for he had craned his head round.

"Loret's still having a holiday," he said. "Wonder when he's going away?"

We drew up at the Wheatsheaf. Lunch was almost ready and we had a beer apiece while we waited. We left the case to itself till the meal was over and George had emptied the tea-pot. Then he stoked his pipe and asked what about getting along to see Calne.

CHAPTER XIV
TENSION

I DREW the car up and we got out. Jack Winder was at work on the kitchen garden and he was so absorbed in his job that he didn't hear the faint sound of the car. He looked to be laying the shallow drains that would fall into the central sump which the ditch would take to the Creek. A little stack of field drain-pipes stood by the garden.

He looked startled when he did see us. Then he stuck the draining spade in the soil and came to meet us, wiping his boots on the grass of the path.

"You've got down to subsoil," I said.

"Only about two spits for the shallow drains," he said. "The big 'un went down to six just afore we got to the Creek. But I'm glad to see you, sir."

I introduced Wharton officially.

"You'd be the gentleman who's looking into that Major Pallart business," Jack said, and then looked at me. "I never was more glad to see anybody, sir. Annie and me are worried out of our lives. Perhaps you'll tell us what we ought to do. It's about the guvnor."

"Why, what's the matter?"

"He disappeared from the house last night, sir, and no one know anything about him."

Wharton and I looked at each other.

"Perhaps you two gentlemen will come to the house," Jack said. "Annie's worried out of her life. Nothing like this has ever happened before."

Annie certainly looked relieved to see us.

"Tell us all about it," Wharton said.

"Better go in to the office," Jack told us, and led the way.

"Now," he said, "the last time we saw Mr. Calne was when Annie took away the coffee things and that was about eight o'clock."

"Exactly eight," Annie said. "I remember I looked at the clock."

"What was he doing when you left him?" Wharton asked.

She waved a hand and we could see. On a folding table were photographs of bird life, and Calne had been pasting them on stout paper. One of the photographs was of gulls in flight and another of smaller sea-birds on the mud of the Creek at low tide, for the coastguard cottage was visible in the distance. They were superbly done.

"The guvnor was writing a book," Jack said, "and some of these here photos was going in it."

Annie went on with the story. When it was dark she had drawn the curtains, chiefly to keep out the midges, and she had done some knitting. She had also remarked how quiet everything seemed.

"These blinds were drawn?" Wharton asked.

Jack said they were. Sometimes Mr. Calne drew them and sometimes he didn't. It was Jack's job to take a last look round. Calne went to bed soon after ten o'clock—and when he looked in about the usual time, the light was on and the blinds were roughly drawn, but there was no sign of Calne. So he tapped at the bedroom door to say he was going to bed, and the bedroom was empty. He then went to bed, leaving the lights on in the office, for the only conclusion to draw was that Calne had gone out by the front door.

"We'd probably have heard him if he's used the back," Jack said. "Not that we can hear a deal. The kitchen come between our room and this and we'd had the wireless on low most of the night."

"And this morning?"

"Everything as usual," Jack said, "except that we didn't hear him moving about. I had a look at the boat first, then the garden. He've lent Tom and me a hand there lately. Getting them drains in. But he weren't there, so I peeped in here. The lights was still on and his bed weren't touched!"

"What'd you do then?"

"First I went down to the village, but no one hadn't seen him there. The car hadn't gone, and Annie said he hadn't put on a hat nor nothing. I didn't like it, I tell you. Then just afore lunch I rang up the bank at Colchester. That was the only place I could think on. They reckoned he hadn't been there. He'd been in only a day or two afore, they said, and got some money."

"That was the afternoon when you called and he was out," I said to Wharton. "I met you and Annie in Drowton, Jack. Mr. Calne had told you he was going to Colchester."

That was confirmed. Wharton said nothing. He stood there frowning in thought, then moved across to the fine old mahogany bureau that stood by the window.

"I want you and your wife to be witnesses," he told Jack. "Watch what I do. I'm doing it in what I think Mr. Calne's own interests."

His fingers were at the bureau flap. It opened. He looked surprised.

"He hardly ever locked it, sir," Annie told him. "That was one of the things we liked about Mr. Calne. He always trusted us. He'd leave most things lying about and never troubled to lock them up. Except, of course, his photos. He wouldn't even let me dust them or his papers."

Wharton lowered the flap. He looked in the drawers and found a cheque book.

"A hundred pounds cash," he said. "Any idea where he kept it?"

Annie showed him the secret drawer. It wasn't secret to her and Jack, she said, because Mr. Calne would use it when they were there.

It was a widish drawer concealed at the back of one of the short ones. Wharton drew it out with a glove on and I saw it was close packed with notes. Nearly all were five-pound notes.

"Why five-pound notes?" Wharton was asking himself aloud.

"We were paid five pounds a week all found, including insurance," Jack said. "That's why they were handy."

Wharton counted them and made the total ninety-five pounds.

"A lot of money to have in the house," he said.

"Don't forget we was going away next week," Jack pointed out. Wharton said he'd forgotten that.

That was apparently all he wished to do, for he closed the bureau flap. Then he went out of the front door and we followed him. There was nothing to see except the broad concrete strip between the house and the private quay. The *Avocet* still lay just off shore.

"You looked in the boat?" Wharton asked.

"Almost the first thing I did," Jack said. "Went through every nook and cranny, I did. But he hadn't been there."

"Mind if I have a look?"

Jack got ready the small boat at once and Wharton and I stepped in. A special wooden ladder with tilted treads was hooked amidships and we were soon aboard. In ten minutes we had finished the search. Wharton had a look round the empty deck, and every now and again would peer over the sides.

"He couldn't have fallen over here and drownded himself," Jack told him bluntly. "I tell you he couldn't even have been here. I'd have seen his steps down there on the shore."

We got into the boat again. As Jack picked up the oars I noticed something.

"What's that ring for?" I asked. "It's nothing to do with Mr. Calne, of course."

It was a stoutish metal ring just below the rail, and welded apparently into the plates of the boat.

"If you look, there's three on 'em," Jack said, and I saw he was right. One was forrard and the other was near the stern. "What you must remember, sir, is that this was one of them experimentals. Originally, till Mr. Calne had her altered, she was intended to carry an auxiliary main-mast. Them rings would be so as a sheet could be made fast if there was heavy weather. They're welded in and that's why Mr. Calne didn't have 'em taken out. I think they look rather natty."

We got back to the quay. Annie was waiting for us.

"What do you think can have happened to him?" she asked Wharton anxiously.

"Frankly, I don't know," Wharton told her.

"You don't think he's—" She broke off as if frightened.

"He's what?"

"Like that Major Pallart?"

Wharton smiled.

"Don't get any ideas like that in your head. He'll turn up. Telephone all right?"

"Was this morning," Jack said.

"Mr. Calne his old self again after his accident?"

"He did complain of headaches," Annie said.

"He was all right," Jack said impatiently. "He lent Tom and me a hand with the filling in. He wouldn't have done that if he hadn't been his old self again."

This time we went round the house by Calne's quarters and so to the back. It was a procession with Wharton leading and the rest of us at his heels. He looked at the ground and he looked round him, but he didn't say a thing till we were at the back door.

"Well, we must leave it as it is," he said cheerfully. "No need to worry, Mrs. Winder. He'll turn up. But I'd like you to do this for me. As soon as he does turn up, ring me at Ninford Wheatsheaf. If I don't hear something from you by the morning, I may ring you myself or come along."

A couple of minutes and we were slowly driving back to Ninford.

"I don't like it," Wharton said.

"Neither do I," I told him.

He said nothing for a moment or two, then was wondering if there was any smuggling by way of the Creek.

"Drane could tell us," I said. "But what's the idea?"

He said it was only an idea. When I asked him if he hadn't believed what the Winders had told us, he looked indignant. I still insisted that Jack Winder was the last person in the world to be suspected of doing away with Calne.

"Smuggling's in the blood, like poaching," he told me enigmatically.

"Even if Calne had discovered that Winder was implicated in any smuggling racket, Winder needn't have murdered him," I said. "I know Calne took life a bit seriously, but he wouldn't have dreamt of giving Jack away to the authorities. Calne just wasn't built that way, and he thought a good deal of Jack and Annie."

"Who said anything about murder?"

I shrugged my shoulders. When George is in one of those contrary moods, the only thing is to leave him alone. In any case we were in Ninford. Standing outside the Wheatsheaf was Drane.

We were talking till tea and it was not till almost time for the evening meal that Drane finally left. He hadn't picked up the trail of Wilkin and, now that Ungler was in the bag, he was to concentrate on Wilkin and nothing else. He was also to be prepared to take over the matter of Calne if Wharton and I had to return to town.

The more we thought about Calne, the less we knew. The whole thing was inexplicable, for he'd simply disappeared into thin air. He was in that office of his, and then he wasn't. The Winders hadn't heard the telephone, and even in their sitting-room they usually heard it. And Calne couldn't have gone far, for he hadn't put on a hat, and Annie Winder had said he rarely went out without a hat. And she had never known him to leave his work of an evening to take a stroll before bed. His work to him was recreation as well; it was everything in life that really mattered. Another thing Annie told us when we rang her up was that Calne always had a whisky at about a quarter to ten. That night he had evidently gone out before that time, for the whisky was still in the corner cupboard and no glass had been used. She also told us, after consulting with Jack, that a window towards the Creek had been open, though the curtain was drawn.

Drane's idea was that someone must have come round by the side of the house, moved the curtain aside and spoken to Calne through the window. Calne had gone out to join this mysterious individual, and what then happened one couldn't say. It was only after we'd gone over things again and again that we came out into the open. Calne, it seemed fairly certain, had either met with an accident or had gone the way of Pallart. As for the accident, we even discarded that.

But there was nothing we could do about it, at least for another few hours. Drane left, as I said, and Wharton and I had a wash. The evening meal came in and I wasn't hungry. Wharton ate far less than usual too. Concentrated brain-work, as he said, was the one thing that could put him off his feed. But he enjoyed his three cups of tea.

"Well, I ought to write some notes," he said, when he'd got his pipe going. "Don't feel like it, though."

Then he was cocking an ear.

"A lot of noise in there tonight?"

Something seemed to be going on in the bar and we looked in. Loret was there and it turned out that it was his farewell to Ninford. In the morning he was going to town and he was expecting to cross to France the same evening or the following day. The drinks were on him, and Wharton, with a show of reluctance, had a pint. I had one too.

It was early for darts but a rather uninteresting game was going on, and Loret sat on the settle with Wharton and me. Wharton was asking him about his legacy. The two were speaking in French and I was making heavy going of a translation. I did gather that Loret had been to Colchester that morning to see Hallwell, and that was why he was all togged out. Hallwell was handling his affairs on behalf of the three trustees and apparently Loret could take his money to France if it were changed into francs on this side. That, Loret said, was a pity. Wharton guilelessly asked why.

"In the black market I make a thousand francs; I make more perhaps than a thousand francs for the English pound. *Ici ce n'est-pas un échange. C'est un vol.*"

Wharton roared. Loret had looked so earnest in his plea that he was being robbed, that George simply had to laugh. In his private capacity George is like most of us—he rather likes a cheerful rogue. George didn't catch the wink that Loret gave me.

The talk turned to the restaurant business. Loret said I had promised to look him up in Paris and now he was issuing a fervent invitation to George. But the game had come to an end and Loret was wanted. They tried to get George in a four, but George was sportsman enough to hold back. It was Ninford's celebration of farewell or whatever they called it, and he'd be a looker on. Later, perhaps, he might have a game but for the present he'd much rather look on.

So I said goodbye to Loret and good night to the room and George. The last thing I did that night was to ring Walker's Ferry. Annie told me there was still no news.

There had been two tremendous days, and I woke up the next morning wondering what that particular day would have in store for me. Later there was to be that sombre, horrific climax, but from that morning when I woke speculating on the events of the day, nothing whatever was to happen. From that moment on, believe it or not as the phrase has it, the case was slowly to peter out. Two days went by and there was nothing whatever about David Calne. If his 'accident' had been an attempt to kill him, then his death—if dead he was—was a mystery altogether beyond us, for the only two concerned in the 'accident' were out beyond all question. Pallart was dead and Ungler safe in a detention camp.

Wharton went to see Ungler but could make not even a dent in his cast-iron story. Drane laboriously made enquiries along the road from Ninford to Colchester and even had a police enquiry in the local paper, but no one came forward who had seen Ungler carrying a bag towards or in Colchester on that Saturday night. What further could we do?

Then there was Wilkin. Another broadcast appeal was sent out and it produced nothing. Wilkin had vanished into thin air just as Calne had vanished. Wharton had more enquiries made at the Depot. He even found Wilkin's last civilian address in London, but nothing whatever was learned. Again I can only ask what else we could do.

We went back to town to make enquiries there about Calne. We saw his sister and men who had been friendly with him at the Regency, and we were as wise as before. We went to Colchester and stayed there two days while enquiries were made about Calne's last visit. We found he had left the bank just short of closing time in the afternoon and then had had tea at an hotel. He had dined at the same hotel and had let it emerge to the hall porter that he had spent the time between tea and dinner at a cinema. After the dinner, just before dusk, he had driven off in his car, and, presumably, for Walker's Ferry. The Winders had found him having his usual evening drink on returning from Ninford.

We saw Hall well again while we were there, and shifted our ground to Pallart. The lawyer could add little to what he had told me. We went to Ninford and questioned Susan, and the only new thing we got—if new it was—was a confirmation of what Hallwell had told me, that Pallart had been gloomy and depressed immediately after his liberation. Then it had seemed as if he had thrown off much of the depression and had gone frequently to town and had stayed for some time in Paris. Even later than that he had seemed to throw off the depression altogether, as if life had a new interest. Most noticeable was that cynical, irresponsible humour.

But none of that was any help and we moved back to London again. Wharton tried the War Office, and all he learned about Pallart was what this story had already told. And while he was at it, as he said, he tackled them about David Calne. That, he soon gathered, was not so easy. One of the few amusing things about Intelligence is that it will persist in confusing intelligence with secretiveness. But we did have an interview with what George calls one of the Big Bugs of M.I.5.

"Calne's was one of the really risky jobs," this Big Bug said. "Some people were dropped in France to organise sabotage. Some to get information across about what the Germans were doing. Some had to fight with the *maquis,* but all of them, as you see, were on what we might call the right side of the line. They were working with the French and against the Germans. Calne was one of the few who worked with the Germans."

"A real old-time spy, in other words," Wharton said.

"More than that," the other told him. "He didn't have to pretend to be a German. He was a renegade Frenchman, in the eyes of both sides. Mind you, he did get what information he could to the local Resistance people, but his main task was to get it to us. It was the Bosche who had to trust him, and, if necessary, protect him—against the Resistance, that is."

"A tough job," I said.

"Oh, it was tough," he told me wryly. "Make no bones about that. Calne—this is strictly between ourselves—cracked up well before 1945 and we had to get him out. As soon as he was fit again, he wanted to get back but it was too late then. We were in France ourselves."

"Where did he operate?" Wharton asked.

"In Normandy principally."

Wharton gave me a look.

"I mentioned that," he said, "because most of our contacts in this case have been to do with Normandy. It seemed unusual."

"Not at all," he was told. "Flying bomb sites, hush-hush sites and the lord-knows-what had to be investigated and information got through to us. And it was in Normandy we were going to land."

That was the gist of what we learned, and, as Wharton said, it helped precious little with the case. But it did lead to some sort of connection with Calne's disappearance. That breakdown of his might have made that 'accidental' crack on the skull much more than it might have appeared to that local doctor who saw him at Walker's Ferry. Besides, Annie Winder had told us that Calne had complained of headaches.

So the Calne story was released more fully to the Press, and most of them played it from the angle of amnesia. There were the usual crop of false alarms that took Wharton and Drane and myself all over the place, but there was still no news of the real Calne. Meanwhile two things had been done.

Brace had been let loose for one thing, and the main channel of the Creek had been dragged.

The weather had now changed as it can so bewilderingly do in September. In the earlier days of the case it had been high summer, followed by the first nostalgic signs of autumn. Now for a few days it was late autumn, with dreary rains and cloudy skies and a chill that was more like late October. But it was not the weather that was the main cause of the depression that had slowly begun to grip me.

It wasn't even a depression; it was more of a tension. The other day I lost a fountain pen. At one moment it had been on my bureau and the next moment it wasn't there, and I had a momentary bewilderment. But I moved various papers, shook them out or looked beneath them, and every moment I knew I should find my pen. I opened every drawer and looked through it, and then I moved the bureau back from the wall and looked to see if by chance the pen had fallen to the floor and rolled beneath. I hunted, in fact, in every conceivable place, and there was no sign of the pen. Believe it or not, I was beginning to panic.

I began again. The same papers, the same drawers, the same pockets were gone meticulously through. The bureau was moved out again, the carpet rolled back, and I even looked under each piece of furniture that was anywhere near. Then I did panic, and I really mean by that that I was ready to believe in the supernatural. That pen had disappeared and it was in none of the places it could possibly be!

That was precisely how it was with the case. Everything had been done, and yet we could see no daylight. Everything had been done twice and it had been a waste of time. But there was more to it than that, and Wharton was feeling the same tension and the imminence of something more deadly even than murder. It was as if in the now settled quietude of the case we could sense a working somewhere beneath, and all the time we were hemmed in by forces wholly beyond our control. Something was due to happen. What, we didn't know, and all we could do was to await the happening. Even if meanwhile we tried some possibly new opening, it was only as if we anticipated the futility it ultimately proved to be.

The pen? you say. What happened to the pen?

I'm glad you mentioned that, because the analogy continues. I found that pen. My bureau has what is known as a well. You push back a section behind the flap and there is the sunken well instead of a top drawer. I had forgotten that I had looked for something in the well, but there the pen was. It had been lying by the edge and my sleeve must have touched it, and into the well it had gone. Then I had closed the well and resumed my work until the moment when my fingers went out to pick up the pen again.

That was how it was with the case on that forenoon when Wharton and I were in his room at the Yard, and wondering as usual where next to turn. The buzzer went as it so often did, and George's hand went mechanically to the receiver. But then he gave a little startled movement. Any bit of hope could startle us now.

"Put him through," he said curtly.

"Drane," he told me, and was listening again.

"Yes," he said. "This is Wharton. . . . You've what! . . . I see. . . . Yes, we'll be there as quick as we can make it. . . . Yes. . . . Goodbye."

He was on his feet at once.

"Calne," he said. "They've found his body."

CHAPTER XV
NEARER THE TRUTH

THE BODY had come ashore at Leete's Bay, a tiny cove some ten miles north of the mouth of the Creek, and it was to Leete's Bay that we went. A hamlet is there of the same name as the cove. Calne's body was in a wooden bungalow that had been blasted by a bomb.

Drane was waiting on the one road that entered the hamlet from the west. Calne's body was little more now than a skeleton, he said, but there wasn't any doubt that it was he. The sodden clothes were right and there had been papers to identify him in the sodden wallet, even if they too had been almost pulp. He hadn't disturbed them too much, he said. Wharton would want to send them to the Yard.

I drew up the car outside the bungalow. The man who had found the body was there, and we all went inside. I stayed no more than a few seconds. The sight of a bony something above a soggy shape that had been a clothed body and the stench of chloride were too much for me. When Wharton began prodding what had been a head I made my way quickly out to the fresh air again. Once I should have been violently sick. Now I lighted my pipe and waited.

It was a quarter of an hour before Wharton and Drane emerged. Wharton was rubbing his hands as if he had just washed them, and a faint smell of chloride still hung about him.

"What killed him?" I said.

"Don't know," Wharton told me. "There's no injury that I can see to the skull."

We went the few yards to the one pub, and there he did some telephoning. Then he was telling Drane that the Home Office expert would be coming down at once. That'd be better than getting what there was of Calne up to the Yard.

"We've got to get the whole thing nicely docketed and tied," he was telling Drane. "Doesn't matter if it was only an accident; he's still got to be wrapped in red tape. Now that matter of the tides. I don't think we should rely too much on what that fellow was telling us."

I gathered he meant the man who'd found and brought in the body. Drane protested that that fisherman knew the coast like the palm of his hand, and then he was hedging. Maybe another opinion or two would be just as well.

"Jack Winder," Wharton said, then shook his head. "He may be a bit biased. Tell you what, Travers. You get along and see that coastguard at the Point. I'll have to wait here. And you might as well fix rooms for us at Ninford Wheatsheaf. That'll be as central as any. I'll join you there some time tonight."

So I went back to Ninford. The weather had turned fine again, but it was no longer summer but autumn. There was a feeling of something that had irretrievably gone. The evenings would be chill and the mornings misty, and even on that pleasant afternoon the air had the faint scent of rotting leaves.

When I left the Wheatsheaf I moved the car more slowly on. There was still plenty of time before dusk and I felt that the open country would be better than a long wait for Wharton at the pub. At the wood yard I caught the tang of wood sap and by the lane there was still the heap of logs that had been there all those weeks ago—or so it seemed—when I had last passed. But the road was deserted except for the one woman whom I passed on the one bend, and she was hurrying towards Ninford.

I walked across the sand and shingle of the track to the cottage and I was thinking of the morning I had been there last and Calne and the coastguard's wife and how deftly she had seen to his wounded skull. But I didn't think about that for very long, and I quickened my steps to the door.

There was no one there. I went round to the front and I peered through windows, and then I knew that the coastguard was out. I also knew that my bat eyes must have let me down, for it must have been Mrs. Morris whom I had met on the road. But I walked round to the shed to make sure that Morris was not there, and it was then that I saw the streak of red.

There was a pile of sawn logs, stacked neatly against the wall. At the end of one of those logs was a redness, and when I came more close I knew I was seeing the end of that log which had once saved Calne's life. The redness was the private marking of the wood yard. Wharton had told me all that.

I was moving away; in fact I was half-way back to the car when I had a curious feeling. It was something to do with the tides, and then I knew what it was. That piece of timber had come from the wood yard. It had fallen into the creek when being unloaded, or at some other time, and had been carried out to sea. That Friday night we had been entering the Creek on an incoming tide, and so—luckily for Calne—the tide had carried the piece of timber back. And all that—or so it seemed to a landsman like myself—was the kind of information that Wharton wanted. So I went back to the shed and helped myself to that log.

I pulled up at the wood yard and walked through along the sawdust track. There was the shine of a circular saw and a couple of men were moving timber off a miniature rail track. Immediately to my left was a tin building with a corrugated-iron roof. It looked like the office. A clerk was working in the room I entered and he fetched the manager from a room inside.

I showed him my credentials and explained about Calne.

"You've found him then?" he said, all interest at once.

I told him as much as was expedient and explained about the tides. We had been walking towards the car and I showed the section of log.

"That's ours all right," he said. "Where'd you get it?"

I said that was secret, for the moment.

"It's been in the water!" he said. "That's funny."

"Why is it funny?" I asked him.

"Well, how could it?" he said, and was motioning towards the very first pile of logs past the main entrance. "They're all local stuff. Drawn here and dropped here and stacked where you see them. Here's the mark, look, like the one on this end of yours. There's only one solution. Someone must have helped himself to one and walked off with it."

I assured him that wasn't so, and I knew he didn't believe me. He was asking again how the devil the log could have got into the Creek. All that stack of logs was intended some day for gate-posts. And they were in assorted straight lengths. They were really the property of the War Agricultural Committee.

Finally I was telling him not to worry. He said damn the log and he wasn't worrying, and damn the War Agricultural Committee too, if it came to that. We had a laugh and I asked about tides. Suppose a length of wood like one of those potential gateposts *had* got into the Creek, what would have happened to it? He said it depended on the tide. If the tide was going out, naturally it would have been carried out to sea. But it depended on the state of that tide. It mightn't have been carried very far. Then the incoming tide would have carried it back or it might have deposited it against a mud flat.

I saw all that, and it didn't much help.

"This is the point we want cleared up," I said. "It's really a very simple one. This side of the Creek. A piece of timber is carried right away by the tide. Where's it enter the open sea?"

"It goes in the channel between the Flat and the Point," he said. "Then it depends on the tide whether it gets washed ashore or out to sea."

"And if the same timber is dropped, say, at Walker's Ferry, what happens to it then?"

"What happened to Mr. Calne?" he said. "He got carried towards Leete's Bay. That's what'd have happened to a piece of timber."

"I get you," I said. "In so many words, there's a twin current. One leaves the Creek north and the other south."

That seemed to be it. Again in my layman's language, and I thanked him and moved the car on. Later, I said, we might ask him to sign a statement, just as a matter of form. But it was now too late to catch the coastguard's wife, so I drew the car up just short of the fork and lighted my pipe and sat in the already lowering sun on a roadside bank. It was only then that I began to see the full significance of what I had just been told. Soon I was prowling restlessly up and down the lane. Even when at last I moved the car on again, I was egg-bound with a most tremendous idea.

The late afternoon had gone and evening was coming on, and in my room at the Wheatsheaf I was driven almost crazy by the oppression of that same idea. I had my evening meal and I chewed it almost mechanically. I got a pipe going and became aware of the usual noises from the bar. I slipped out of the side door and took a walk. I came back. Wharton had rung up to say he mightn't be at Ninford till ten o'clock, so I sat on with a pint and watched a game or two of darts. But it was somehow all unreal. I was in one world and yet in quite another. I was there in a moment of the present. And yet I wasn't. I was in a moment of the past.

Closing time came and with it Wharton.

"My God, I'm tired!" he said, and I fetched him a double whisky.

"Nothing more tiring than hanging about," he said. "And there's not much to tell you. The skull's definitely not fractured. There may be a displacement—very slight—of the larynx, but it'll be hard to establish. He doesn't appear to have been drugged or anything like that."

We just discussed, not too seriously, how Calne could have met his death by sheer accident, and, of course, we got nowhere. Perhaps we were only talking from force of habit. He asked me how I'd got on and I said I had what he wanted, but he didn't seem interested. I had a whisky myself and he had another, and then we went up to bed. I knew I shouldn't sleep, and I didn't—at least not until very late. That idea of mine had boiled itself down to one simple thing. If I had been David Calne and had wanted to kill Guy Pallart, how would I have done it. And always there seemed no possible way. The mass of evidence was wholly against it. By no conceivable chance could Calne have been in Ninford at the time when Pallart was killed.

I fell asleep. I dreamed, but not about Calne—unless you can call the *Avocet* the Case. It doesn't matter what queer juxta-position of impossible time and circumstances composed my dream. It may not have been the *Avocet* after all about which I dreamt. I dreamed about a boat and it had a diesel engine and it had a gigantic main-mast, and now it had one and then it had only the other.

Then I woke. It was broad daylight. I hooked on my glasses and looked at my watch. Half-past seven, and an hour yet to breakfast. Then suddenly I was out of my bed and making for George's room. He was still sound asleep and I shook him gently by the shoulder. He rolled over, and blinked.

"Oh, it's you, is it?"

His eyes opened wider.

"What's the matter? Something happened.?"

"Yes," I said. *"Calne killed Pallart and I think I know how he did it."*

"It's gone beyond theory, George," I said. "Certain things that we know happened, can't fit in any other way. If you don't mind, I'll put myself in Calne's place. That's the way I happened to work things out."

The first thing I'd have done, I said, was to get hold of a small amount of benzedrine—the stuff that the lead-swingers and draft-dodgers use to fake a bad heart. Or it might have been nicotine. Next I would hunt round for a convenient piece of drift wood, and when nothing of the right size turned up, I would naturally turn to the timberyard and sawmill. There I would see stacks of various kinds of weights and lengths by the roadside and I had only to mark a convenient piece down.

The next thing would be to come along on any reasonably dark night with the car. As it was an American car with a back like the end of a house, I could get my piece of timber well in, and if the back didn't close quite up, that wouldn't matter a great deal in the dark. I should have ascertained by ringing him up just where the coastguard was going to be, and when I got past the track to his cottage, I'd have humped that timber on my shoulder towards the sea and hidden it in a well marked spot. So much for the preliminaries.

"How high is the *Avocet* above the water, George?"

"Five or six feet," he said. That bit about the length of timber had got him interested. He hadn't even accused me of having one of my scatter-brain theories.

The next thing, then, I said, was to get a length of fine but very stout cord or rope, about twelve feet long and make it into a handy coil. That coil could be secreted in a cabin near the lavatory on the *Avocet*. Everything would then be set. Nothing else in the way of apparatus would be required, except perhaps a safety-razor blade carried in the pocket.

Knowing that Pallart was at Ninford, and even perhaps that he had guests, I'd then ring him in a friendly sort of way. At the tail end I'd casually mention a proposed cruise and ask what about it. If I did manage to kill him, I could always say that it had been he who had proposed that cruise. But as it happened, he was very keen, and the following morning he duly turned up with his man as arranged and three guests. Just before we went aboard I should put my telephone out of order. The scheme I had in mind wouldn't work so well if the coastguard knew too quickly.

The day would pass off very well indeed, with everybody interested and happy. I have arranged a dinner at Dovercourt in order to delay the return. It was essential that it should be dark by the time we reached the mouth of the Creek. Jack Winder would be in the little wheelhouse, and he would have the *Avocet*'s speed reduced as she made the turn towards the channel. So much for planning.

The *Avocet* will turn at any minute, I said. I know that coast. I can see shore lights and the light from the coastguard's cottage. I have gone to the lavatory, ostensibly, and have that coil of rope under my jacket. It is dark on deck and I give orders to take chairs and things downstairs. I send Kales for the binoculars so as to ensure that he'll come on deck again.

And so to the six rings which Winder told us about. The six rings just below the deck to which a sheet could be tied in bad weather.

I have a choice of six rings, three on each side, and yet I haven't. I daren't use the two forward ones because I should be very near Jack Winder. The two aft are not so good, because they are more visible if one looks over the side of the boat. The two amidships are ideal because the boat tapers sharply in. I choose, and quickly, which one is handiest and I slip the rope through, *double*. The weight of the ring keeps it close against the side and it trails in or just above the water.

The moment has come. The boat checks, and slows and begins its turn. I quickly grab the rope, give a holler and go overboard. It isn't too wild a holler but it must be heard by Kales, for I have seen him coming on deck. Where Pallart is I don't know, but he is somewhere aft and he couldn't see me in any case. And the moment I am overboard, I and the rope are invisible. I hit the water and draw myself hand over hand beneath the boat. It is the boat that takes me to the Ferry. And as soon as we're nearly there, I simply pull one end of my rope, it slips through the ring, and I get ashore. If by any chance I'm discovered before I have only to pretend I've been playing some elaborate practical joke.

I am soaking wet, but it is a warm night, and all I suffer is a certain amount of discomfort. At once I make for Ninford and I cut across the fields and over the meadow bridge to the Old Vicarage. I may have to get into Pallart's bedroom. I shall certainly have to improvise. I stun him and strangle him. Then I make my way on foot towards the coastguard's cottage.

Now I have all night on my hands and I can choose the right moment for each operation. I cut the back of my skull with the razor blade and let it bleed freely. I uncover my oak log and carry it down to the sea and then swim the hundred or two yards to the Flat. I can either swim round it or hump my log across it. As the latter might leave footprints, I swim or wade gently round, pushing my log ahead of me. I get to the mud and leave the log there and make my way up to the harder ground. My clothes and myself are in a filthy state, which is all to the good. Just before dawn I begin calling feebly for help.

I've been up all night and I look like nothing on earth. There's no need to sham more than weakness, for I look pretty ill. The coastguard's wife knows I'm ill. There's a great clot of blood on my skull and she can hardly cut away the hair. Then she puts on a beautiful dressing, which means that the doctor won't need to put on one of his own and see there isn't a contusion. Then, luckily for me, Travers comes along.

He's wondering about the accident, so I try a taciturnity act. By that I tell him in no words at all that it wasn't an accident. He even gives me the chance to tell him that it was Pallart who wanted the cruise. And so I get home where Annie is shocked at my appearance. But I do a stoical act this time. No doctors for me, though I know perfectly well she'll send for one. As soon as she leaves me alone, I take a dose of dope. The doctor ultimately comes and he soon knows my heart is behaving erratically. I play up the tired and exhausted side, and that's that. Then I begin to make a slow recovery but I let Annie know that I still have headaches.

That was all. Wharton gave a prodigious grunt, but he didn't move from the bed.

"We've got something there," he told me. "Do you know that I was wondering something myself. When there was no sign yesterday of any old contusion of the skull—I wasn't looking for that, of course. I was wondering if he'd been killed the same way as Pallart—I couldn't help thinking that that crack he'd had on the boat couldn't have been quite what he made it out to be."

"And if that manager of the timber-yard is right," I said, "then that log couldn't have been where Calne said it was. It would have drifted south, not north."

"You see the implications of all this?" he said.

"Do I not," I told him.

"I have to be at Leete's Bay at half-past nine," he said. "Time I was getting dressed. You get along to the Ferry after breakfast and have a real good look at those rings. Examine them under the glass. One of them ought to be chafed from that rope. If necessary we'll get an oxy-acetylene lamp on it and cut it out of the hull."

After breakfast I went to Walker's Ferry. Jack rowed me out to the *Avocet* but I didn't want him to see me at work, so I made an excuse for him to fetch me something from Drowton in Calne's car. I thought that perhaps Annie could be naturally curious, but there I was lucky. The ring I wanted was on the larboard side—the *Avocet* was headed up-Creek—and I rigged up a kind of rope cradle and let myself out of sight of the house over the *Avocet*'s side. The paint was definitely worn on the lower side of that ring. Not as much as I'd hoped, maybe, but worn or chafed enough.

I drew up my cradle and made a pretence of being interested in the boat generally. Then I rowed myself ashore. Annie was waiting for me and wanting to know when the funeral would be. I said I didn't know. Then she insisted on making me some coffee. Jack came back and joined us in the kitchen. We talked a lot about Calne, but there was nothing new that I learned. I was just announcing that I'd be getting back to Ninford, when the telephone went. Annie answered it, and then was calling to me.

"That you, Travers?" Wharton said. "Can't get away for a bit. The inquest's on in a few minutes. But do something for me, will you? Ask Winder—mind how you do it—why that garden had to be drained and who suggested it. I'll hold the line."

It was five minutes before I was back.

"You there?" I said. "About the garden. It's just a matter of ordinary drainage. It's in a bit of a basin, and the water always stands on it after a heavy rain. It was Winder himself who suggested draining it. It *was* drained once, he says, but the pipes were all clogged up."

"I see." He didn't sound very pleased. "Well, I'll be along this afternoon or early evening. You'll have time to get to town and back. See Calne's solicitors and get a rough idea of the will. Here's who they are."

He gave me the name and address and said I'd better come straight back to the Ferry. Five minutes later I was on my way to town. It was after twelve when I got to Finsbury Pavement, and one o'clock when I left.

Calne had left a devil of a lot of money, and it went to his sister and her two boys. There were various legacies for servants of whom I'd never heard, but the Winders were quite well treated with an annuity of five pounds each a week. If Pallart would sell Walker's Ferry, it was to go to them, and the annuity was then to be reduced to four pounds. The *Avocet* was left to a Bird-watching Society, with a sum for up-keep. The will was only a month old.

My wife was due back that night so I went to the flat and wrote a note and had a service meal. I tried to get Wharton at Leete's Bay but he wasn't there, and I had wasted a half hour. It was four o'clock when I got back to Ninford. I rang the Ferry but Wharton was not there, so I had tea at the Wheatsheaf. He had not arrived at five o'clock, but I went to the Ferry all the same.

It was half-past five when he turned up, and it was Jack Winder whom he wanted to see. Jack was to get hold of Tom Pike, but Wharton didn't say why, except that he was to bring his spade. Then he was asking me about the will. Apparently he knew the outlines already, but he had wanted everything confirmed. To me it almost looked as if he'd been anxious to get me away to town for some specious reason of his own.

Tom Pike arrived and was told to stand by. Wharton kept looking impatiently back towards Ninford and it was after six when a small military truck arrived. An English N.C.O. was driving and two hefty German prisoners got out. Both had spades.

"Right," said Wharton. "That main drain's coming up."

Winder stared, as well he might.

"The whole of it, sir!"

"Don't know," Wharton said. "We'll make a start at the sump end and see what happens."

The concreted pipes needn't be shifted, he said, and it would be enough to dig down till a spade touched them and then probe the sides. And as it wouldn't be long before it was dusk, there'd better be some light ready. That car of Calne's could be drawn up at the Wandham end with headlights ready to turn on along the trench towards the Creek, and his own car or mine could be at the other end, back to the Creek.

Jack fetched his spade and the four got to work. It was only two and a half feet down to the sump and everyone was fresh. The dusk was in the sky and the headlights went on.

THOSE HEADLIGHTS, dipped though they were, made a light around Walker's Ferry and the N.C.O. was given a roving commission to turn back any of the curious from the village. Wharton and I stood watching the work. I knew what he expected to find, and he knew that I knew, but neither of us said a word.

It was an eerie scene. Rembrandt might have painted it, or Doré made some tenebrous etching. From the sump the drain had a good fall to the Creek and with every foot the trench was deeper. The heads of the men showed as they threw out the soil and then their bent shoulders would go forward and for a second a man would be invisible. The double headlights threw tricky shadows and the sky above us was overcast with a threat of imminent rain. Every now and again Wharton would move impatiently along the line of work. Jack Winder was nearest the sump, then came a German, then Tom Pike and the other German, and there had to be a space to throw the soil out. Thirty yards were cleared, which was two thirds of the way along the garden. Wharton called a halt and Annie brought out jugs of tea and cups.

Time for a cigarette and the work began again. Rain began to fall and Annie fetched a couple of umbrellas for Wharton and me. George made his first revelation.

"Should be getting pretty near now. That's where Calne did some filling in on his own."

Ten minutes went by and there was a cry. One of the Germans said his spade was on something soft. Wharton was on the move at once.

"Out of the trench, everybody."

The four clambered out. The Germans were told to get the mud from their boots and Winder fetched the N.C.O.

"That's all," Wharton said. "You can get back to Camp when you like, sergeant. I may be seeing the Commandant later."

The truck moved off. Winder and Pike got into the trench again and Wharton was holding a torch. I leaned over him as he crouched. Suddenly Winder straightened himself.

"It's a body, sir!" He looked as scared as hell. "It seems to be underneath the pipes."

A stench was coming upwards. Wharton slipped along to his car and began scattering chloride. The pipes were smashed and Pike and Winder began moving a dark something with an upward prising of their spades. The thing was lifted to the side and Wharton grabbed it and drew it near. His torch shone full on a mud-smeared face.

"My God, sir, it's Wilkin!"

"Yes," Wharton said, and gave a nod. "Stay where you are, though, and go on digging."

A couple of minutes and Pike was saying there was something hard. More broken pipes were thrown out. His fingers went down in the loose soil and he was tugging. Winder lent a hand and then Wharton was reaching down. What he drew up was the front half of a motor-bicycle. Within five minutes we had the other half and the engine. I could see the marks where a hacksaw had severed the frame.

It was midnight when at last we got back to the Wheatsheaf. Drane's men had come and gone, and the body had gone too. But first it had been replaced and flashlights taken. Winder and Pike had been warned to keep things to themselves and they had left early. Then Wharton had had endless telephoning to do, and all I could do was hang around.

The landlord was in bed so we helped ourselves to whisky, and neither of us felt like sleep. It was the implications that worried us more than the discovery. That had been anticipated. It just had to be. Calne had killed Wilkin, and he had to dispose of the body, and he was not such a fool as to dump body and bicycle in the Creek where dredging might bring them to light. It is true that Calne had not suggested the draining.

That drain had just happened to be there at the right time, and it had given Calne his idea.

What did Wilkin know?

George was of the opinion that Wilkin had seen the actual killing of Pallart. I didn't think so. I said it wasn't necessary. Calne would have had to get rid of Wilkin in any case.

"Begin at the Wilkin end," I said. "Calne employed him to spy on Pallart. Why, we can discuss later. Very well, then. As soon as Pallart was murdered, Wilkin must have had ideas, even if he didn't see a thing that Friday night. Calne simply daren't let it be known that Wilkin had been his planted spy. He couldn't have explained it away. And I'll bet that Wilkin didn't let Calne know just how much he knew."

Wharton proceeded along the line of subsequent events. We knew that Wilkin came to see Calne, for I was at the Ferry when he called. Calne arranged with Wilkin that night that Wilkin should either give in his notice at the Old Vicarage or get himself sacked. Wilkin was to come back the following night and Calne would then pay him off with a hundred pounds. Wilkin would of course have his own ideas about putting on the screws at some later convenient moment. Calne went to Colchester and drew the money. He got Annie and Jack out of the way by giving them the evening off. Wilkin arrived after dark as arranged and he was cracked on the skull and strangled before he knew it. The motor-bike was hack-sawed and partly stripped, and it and Wilkin were five feet down at the bottom of the ditch *beneath* where the pipes would run. Next morning Calne was up early and amusing himself by laying pipes and doing some filling in. Wilkin and his motor-bike had disappeared for good.

But why had Calne employed Wilkin—that was the vital question, and, try as we might, we could find no answer.

"Very much of a coincidence Wilkin being a gardener, wasn't it?" Wharton said.

"He wasn't a gardener," I told him. "He was an amateur like you and me. He knew what the average man knows, which was enough to get him through. Pallart himself told me that Wilkin was a dud gardener, but the best he'd been able to get."

I asked if Calne had been murdered or was his death an accident. Wharton could only say that the open verdict had been correct. It would never be known how Calne had died. It was true that a displaced larynx often occurred in manual strangulation, but nothing could be proved. It might even have been suicide, though there we both agreed that suicide by drowning was a curious way out for Calne. And he'd left no suicide note.

I recalled that Regency talk and we went carefully over it. Pallart had said he was going to commit a murder, or what he preferred to designate an act of justice. He said he would give the victim due warning.

"Why wasn't it Calne whom he was warning then and there?" Wharton said.

"But Pallart didn't kill Calne," I said. "He had the chance to kill him on the boat and he didn't do it. I don't believe Ungler's disclaimer. I believe that Pallart was definitely of the opinion that Kales-Ungler had tried to kill Calne—that 'accident' business—and was genuinely annoyed about it."

"But why should Ungler kill Calne?"

You can see how argument was getting us nowhere? All we were doing was to put up a skittle, knock it down, and then put up another.

"If Calne thought that Pallart was going to kill him, that gives a reason for Calne getting his own blow in first," Wharton said. "There's no argument about that. Calne definitely did kill Pallart."

"How did Calne know it?" I said. "That Regency talk was vague as could be. I could never have dreamt that Pallart was talking at Calne through me."

"He knew it through Wilkin."

"But what could Wilkin have found out?"

"Why ask *me*?" Wharton said. "Maybe he found out plenty. We'll never know. And there's no one left to tell us. Even Ungler wouldn't know."

"Wilkin would have told Calne about the German prisoner I saw on the Wednesday night," I said. "Calne may have guessed on the boat that Ungler was that prisoner."

"How's that help," demanded Wharton. "Why should the arrival of a German prisoner make Calne decide to bring things to a head?"

So back we were at Ungler. Was his story true or untrue? Not that it mattered much. If Ungler couldn't be induced to give us the true answer, then we were where we'd started from. Finally we decided to call it a day. We'd gone all the way back more than once, and my head was muzzy from concentrated thinking. Maybe the night would bring counsel, George said, and I did some wishful thinking to match that optimistic hope.

I woke late and still far from clear-witted. George was irritable, which showed that the night had brought nothing at all. And he had a long trying day in front of him, with me, as it turned out, tagging at his heels.

That night we were at it again, and we did find a real starting point. It didn't lead us to the truth because we were to have an astounding short cut, and yet I must say this. Even if that short cut had never presented itself, I think we should have worried away till we arrived at the truth, or as near the truth as makes little difference. But to get back to that starting point.

It had led us next day to Hallwell and we heard again of the lawyer's protests over the rent of Walker's Ferry, and of Pallart's flippant dismissal of the idea that he was being far too generous. We heard too that it had been Pallart who had requested the lawyer to put him up for the Regency.

You see where that got us? Pallart didn't know Calne but he knew of him. He decided that the best way to make his acquaintance was at the Regency, where a meeting could be devised as if by chance. Pallart would turn on the charm and approach Calne something like this.

"You're Calne, aren't you? I'm Guy Pallart. They tell me you're a great bird-watcher. I'm rather fond of that kind of thing myself. Only the worst kind of amateur, of course. It's a pity, because I happen to own the very place for that sort of thing. Handy for Norfolk and everywhere."

And so on and so on. Then would come a bite by Calne, and Pallart telling him too that lion didn't eat lion, and the place was his for a purely nominal rent. Pallart, in other words, wanted Calne at Walker's Ferry, and he got him there.

Was it the ridiculous rent of the place that first made Calne suspicious that all was not what it seemed? Did Pallart turn on just a little too much charm? Was that why Calne employed Wilkin? The answers were—maybe. We were not to know for a day or two yet. But we did know that Calne had lied to me when he said the rent was pretty stiff. But by then Calne had his own scheme in mind and he didn't want to give me the slightest clue.

Wilkin didn't help us at all. No papers whatever were found on him and his case had disappeared. Perhaps Calne had burnt it, but it was the one thing we were never able to see. But we decided to shift our ground to town and make guarded enquiries at the Regency. We did put in an afternoon there and gathered nothing of consequence, so we called it a day and went to my flat for tea. My wife was waiting for us. She and George were old friends.

As soon as I entered I saw the letter. It had a French stamp and at once I was ripping it open. It was from Loret and in English.

> Café-Restaurant Dufour,
> 17 rue Caneton, Paris.

MY DEAR M. TRAVERS,

I redeem my promise. I return to find an old comrade of the Resistance and it is with him that I go into partnership. I think that for the money of the excellent Major Pallart I shall become rich. Also I have friends of what you call under the counter.

You will pay me the visit as we said? Believe me that you will be welcome and there is even a room which can be occupied. You will eat well with me and I think your visit will be profitable. Already I anticipate your visit.

Receive, my dear M. Travers, the assurance of my good sentiments.

GEORGES LORET.

Wharton had a look at it. He read it a second time and even then he didn't hand it back.

"There's something funny about this letter."

My wife, with amazing self-control, was saying nothing. "Something to do with a government trip to Paris," I told her. "Connected with the Ninford Case. What's wrong with the letter, George?"

"Why's he so anxious for you to come?"

"Don't know," I said.

"It can't be your *beaux yeux*—"

"And why not?" asked Bernice indignantly.

"Well, not on this special occasion," temporised Wharton. "But he doesn't mention *me*. You didn't play darts with him. You didn't talk French, and Parisian slang at that."

"Maybe you're right," I said. "Maybe he knows something about the Case and wants to get it off his mind. You, to him that is, represent the law, and I don't."

George handed back the letter.

"You're sending him a telegram," he said. "And at once. You can fly over the morning after tomorrow."

I could feel my wife's eyes on me. George cut tactfully in. Maybe I'd be taking her later, he said, and began talking about air priorities.

It was eight years since I had been in Paris, but the schedule that George Wharton had drawn up didn't give me much time for loitering. It was eleven o'clock when the taxi drew up outside the Café-Restaurant Dufour, a trim-looking place just off a main boulevard. Georges Loret must have been on the lookout for me, for no sooner was I out of the taxi than he was there. His face was all smiles, and as his left hand took mine, he was patting me on the back. I had feared for a moment that he was going to embrace me.

"It's good to see you, Georges," I said.

"And you, monsieur. And the excellent Superintendent Wharton, he is well?"

I seemed to discern a subtle irony, but I said he was well, and then we were in the restaurant and I was being introduced to Jacques Dufour, the other partner. The two told me that the restaurant was doing well. When lunch began I should see that for myself.

"Today I make a holiday," Loret told me. He took me to his room upstairs and grinned when I noticed the dartboard. But he was desolated when I said I could not possibly stay the night.

It was a magnificent autumn day and we had our apéritif at a nearby café whose owner hailed us with joy, and maybe because Loret had shamelessly introduced me as an old comrade of the Resistance. When I tried to pay, there was the good old joke of examining my note and announcing that it didn't look genuine.

We went back for lunch, as good a meal as I ever expect to eat. Loret apologised for the wine but it tasted fine to me, but then I'm not a connoisseur. During the meal we talked about Ninford. There were times already, he said, when he had an overwhelming nostalgia for the place, for there he had spent some of the happiest days of his life. I had to tell him the latest news about Susan and the Friskes and the habitués of the Wheatsheaf.

I didn't have brandy but preferred a dash of rum in my coffee. We had it upstairs in what looked like the office. It was warm and Loret sat in his shirt sleeves and the window was wide open. Sooner or later I knew he would arrive at the Case, and he did.

"It was that Calne who killed M. Pallart?" he was suddenly asking me. "That is what I see in the English papers."

There was no point in denying it. He nodded rather heavily, as if seeking the right words.

"Even before you of the police knew it, I knew it," he said. *"I knew it when the body of M. Pallart was found."*

I'm afraid I rather stared.

"How on earth did you know that?"

"There are questions," he told me enigmatically, "which it is not always—what does one say?—profitable to answer."

"But you and I are friends," I told him. "We are both men of discretion."

"I wonder," he said, and strangely enough I knew he wasn't questioning my statement. "There are many things I know." He went across to a drawer in the desk and came back with something wrapped in tissue paper. It was a French New Testament, and brand new. He had handed it to me.

"M. Travers." There was an earnestness in even those two words. "You will hold the book and you will swear to me that what I tell you is a secret?"

Somehow I knew that unless I did as he said, I would never hear a word. So I held that book and I solemnly swore, and somehow too I didn't feel any kind of a fool. He nodded as I gave him back the book.

"You excuse," he said, "if I appear to doubt your word. It is not that, I assure you." His fingers rapped against his hairy chest. "Perhaps it is myself that I satisfy. In the conscience as you call it."

In a moment or two he was beginning his story. I am not passing it on to you in the English that he used. Even if I wished I could not recall his exact words, and even if I could, then his turns of phrase and his interspersions of French would only irritate. His story too, must have taken well over an hour. I reduce it here to the barest detail and eliminate the things you already know.

And there is one other matter. I am in many ways what Mark Antony called 'a plain, blunt man'. I have no aptitude for tense description. I cannot convey to you the tremendous vitality of the man, the dramatic and the vivid in his very gestures, and how each fibre of him would seem to quiver with the fierceness of a hate or the passionate intensity of a remembrance. All those things you must imagine for yourself, and here, then, is Georges Loret speaking.

CHAPTER XVII
NOTHING BUT THE TRUTH

"I FIRST SAW Guy Pallart at Chez Victor, and this is how and why it happened. He had been to Bayeux, for it was there that his fiancée had been tortured and then shot by the Gestapo. That much he had been told. What he wanted to know were the details, and, above all, the names perhaps of those who had done it. After that would come revenge. He had money and he had time. Once he knew the men he would hunt them down and avenge her in his own way.

"At Bayeux it was recommended that he should seek out myself, for I—regarded by the Bosches as an ordinary citizen who was not unfriendly—was nevertheless the local organiser of the Resistance. I was in Paris and it was there that he found me. What I had to tell him, monsieur, was nothing to cheer the heart. But he was a stoic—my friend Pallart—and he listened.

"I knew Marie Courtold. I alone, and those above me, knew she was English. To everyone else she was the niece of my friend Armand Garnier of the Farm of the Three Oaks, and her name to us was Louise Garnier. At the farm there was wireless apparatus for sending and receiving. It was I who would give her the information; I, or perhaps Armand, for he also was not suspect.

"The man Calne I saw three times but he was never aware of me. I had received confidential word that an Englishman would operate in our district and that he was to work alone and in his own way. To the Bosches he would be a Vichy spy but it was necessary that he should gain the confidence of those Bosches. He was in Bayeux for two months before he was arrested, but it was an arrest that was intended by himself. Then one day in June, 1944, the Bosches suddenly descended on the farm at Argueil. Armand and Louise were arrested, and there was nothing that I could do. Two weeks later, monsieur, they were shot. The *maire* was there by orders of the Bosche, and other citizens including myself. It was not the first time I had been forced to witness such a shooting, but this time it was something to send a man beyond all control. Nevertheless I had to control myself. Louise could not walk and they propped her against the wall. She refused the bandages—Armand they did not bandage—and before they shot her she cried that she was English and she was not afraid. It was then that I wept, but some of the tears were tears of helplessness and rage.

"Among us was a traitor and it was for me to find that traitor, but I had no luck. We shot some of the Bosches and they took hostages. We also took hostages. We had word of a German car and we ambushed it and the driver was killed with a grenade. There was a general and him we could not persuade to speak. Maybe he knew nothing. And he was wounded and an embarrassment, so we shot him out of hand. But the other we kept.

"He was an Interpreter at Gestapo Headquarters—the man, monsieur, whom you knew as Kales. You observed perhaps that scar on his nose? The nose there is sensitive and the scar was made by a lighted cigarette. If you had seen him naked you would have seen other marks. But it was not too difficult to induce him to talk. It was he then who told us that it was that Vichy spy who had given the information that led to the shooting of Armand and Louise."

"But that is incredible!" I said. "Calne couldn't have been capable of anything so devilish. Even if he did have to prove to the Germans that he was genuine, he couldn't have done a hellish thing like that!" Then I thought of something. "He must have intended to warn them and then something went wrong."

"Pardon me, monsieur, but you are good at making excuses," he told me. "If you cannot swim and I push you into deep water, I may say to myself that in a minute I will rescue you, and everything will be all right. But suppose by then it is too late? Am I not guilty of murder?" His lip curled. "Even if it is as you say, then this Calne was guilty. M. Pallart, he makes the same objections, but he also took steps to find out the truth."

"One other thing," I said. "Calne couldn't have known she was English—at least till the moment she was shot. Was he there?"

"He was there," he told me grimly. "It was the last time that I saw him. He also must have heard what she said when she died."

His lip curled again.

"But is it proper then for a man like Calne to kill only the French like my friend Armand? Are these schemes so important that in the course of them one can sacrifice a few French?"

I hastened to say that that had never been in my mind. He seemed to accept the apology.

That brought him to Pallart's proposal, and it was one which he, Loret, was eager to accept. He would go to Ninford. Pallart would find Calne if he was still alive, and he would also find Ungler. And Pallart, as we know, found them both. Loret hadn't been optimistic about the finding of Ungler. He himself had had to bolt from Argueil and Bayeux, and Ungler had escaped, and it was fortunate that he had been taken by the English in the first stages of the landing.

With freedom as a reward, Ungler had agreed to identify Calne and to relate all he knew of the treachery that had led to the torturing and death of Marie Courtold. Over him too there hung a threat—that it would be revealed to the English authorities that he had been associated with the Gestapo. As for the scheme, once Ungler was finally at Ninford, that was simple. The summerhouse would be the court of justice. Calne would be kidnapped and would wake up to find himself lashed to that stout oak chair, and confronted with Ungler and Loret—and something from the past.

So to Calne's invitation to the cruise, Pallart was delighted, for Ungler-Kales would go, and there could be a preliminary identification. And then came that Friday night. Loret knew something was wrong as soon as Pallart came to the kitchen.

"We've got to do some quick thinking," Pallart said. Then he gave Loret a couple of sleeping tablets to be slipped into a hot drink for Richard Brace. Loret was to go to his bedroom and then come back to the lounge. Susan was reported sound asleep and the conspirators assembled.

Calne was probably dead. If he were playing some trick, then the scheme was temporarily off, for somehow he must have

198 | CHRISTOPHER BUSH

guessed something of what was in the wind. Pallart thought him
dead, in spite of Ungler's protestations. The telephone message
was concocted and Ungler was to go to town. His story had to
be rehearsed again and again. Finally, and just short of eleven
o'clock, everyone had his story pat.

"I'd better fetch that rope from the summerhouse," Pallart
said. "The chair doesn't matter. But the police will be bound to
come snooping round here in the morning."

He went to the summerhouse. Minutes passed and Loret
grew anxious. At last he took a torch and went out to investi-
gate. Then he found Pallart's body.

"Why did you think of Calne?"

I had been bursting to ask him that. He shrugged his shoulders.

"Who else could it be? Besides, soon afterwards—it was one
night in the Wheatsheaf—Jack Winder told me that Calne was
going away. He was going to Norfolk. And Norfolk, monsieur,
has many advantages as I saw by the map. Calne would be away
from awkward questioning but he would also be ready to slip
away north and to sea if anything were discovered."

Something told me that that wasn't all that he knew.

"But you told me that as soon as you saw Pallart's body you
knew Calne had murdered him."

"Yes," he said. "I heard about that strange accident of M.
Calne. So opportune an accident. But when I flashed my torch
around the verandah of the summerhouse, I saw water. Someone had crouched there. I saw wet footprints. I moistened my
finger in that water and tasted it. *It was salt water.*"

Later he had wiped that verandah clean and I didn't ask him
why. In a few minutes I was to know. Then he had taken charge
of Ungler, who had panicked. He drove Ungler to Colchester
and all the way he was going over and over again the things
that Ungler must do and say. If necessary Ungler would have to
remove that dye from his hair and give himself up at the Overy
camp. And over his head Loret still held that threat of revelation
of Ungler's connection with the Gestapo.

Ungler was left to await the train, and on a bench under the trees as he had told us. Loret then took Pallart's body to the lounge and turned on an electric fire to check rigor mortis, for at all costs the police must think that Pallart had died after one o'clock. He sat up till near dawn with the body and then took it back to where it had been found. The rest, he said, I probably knew.

There was a long silence. I reached for that Testament, and I held it in my hand as if to show that I remembered my promise.

"And Calne?"

His eyes flashed quickly on mine. They turned away.

"There are questions, monsieur, that it is inexpedient to answer with a simple yes or no. You would ask me if it was I who killed Calne?"

"Yes," I said.

Then his eyes did meet mine. There was in them that same look of icy, frightening grimness that Wharton once had noticed.

"M. Pallart was not only my employer, he was also my friend. It was an honour to be his friend. Armand Garnier was also my friend. Louise Garnier was also my friend. When M. Pallart died you knew he had been my friend, if only because of the five hundred pounds. If I had killed Calne"—he almost spat the name—"it would not have been a murder. It would not have been even an assassination. It would have been only a simple justice." His voice lowered and his eyes turned away. "It would also have been a gratitude."

He insisted on coming with me to the airport. We shook hands and in the handshake was respect, sincerity and even perhaps an affection. He begged me to come to Paris again, and to stay. To bring my wife, and perhaps Wharton. Then at the very last moment he added something else. There was a look that was almost wistful, and from quite another man—a lovable man, the man who had loved Armand Garnier and Guy Pallart and maybe Marie Courtold.

"It will be permitted, you think, that one day I come to Ninford for a holiday?"

"You'll be welcomed," I said. "Let me know in good time, and I'll be there myself."

When I saw him last he was waving as if he could still see me. A few minutes later, or so it seemed, we were over England. It was dusk before I got to the Yard. Wharton was waiting for me in his room.

"Find anything out?"

"Yes," I said. "Quite a lot. Everything, in fact."

He drew a writing-pad towards him.

"But I heard it in absolute confidence," I said. "I can't tell you a word unless you promise that nothing will ever come out."

He stared.

"You mean to say you were such a fool as to—"

"Never mind that, George," I said. "I acted for the best. That's my ultimatum, even if it means future dissociation from the Yard."

He grunted at that. Then he was demanding to know if I thought he was the sort to compound with a felony.

"Loret killed Calne. Didn't he?"

"I'm telling you nothing," I said, and then he was waving me furiously from the room.

But at about nine o'clock that night he turned up at the flat. George was trying to be honest with himself and his job. Somehow he had convinced himself that, now he was a private citizen. He didn't say so, but he knew that I knew what was in his mind. I got him comfortably seated and filled his glass.

"What was Paris like?" he began.

A minute or two later I was telling him all I had heard. He didn't interrupt, and at the end he merely nodded.

"Nothing that need come out," he said at last. "Everything works in, though. What Hallwell told us about Pallart having a new interest in life. That mistake about rigor mortis. No end of things."

Then he was wondering how Loret killed Calne. I said he would kill him as Pallart had been killed, and then he'd carry the body to the Creek.

"And Calne," Wharton said. "He must have suffered the tortures of the damned when he knew that girl was English. You bet that when he returned to England he tried to discover all about her. He could do that easy enough. And he found out she'd been engaged to a man named Pallart. That's what made him employ Wilkin. That's why there was a significance in that German prisoner that Wilkin must have reported. That's why he decided to kill Pallart first."

"Yes," I said, and freshened up his glass. "And if only Loret hadn't removed all trace of sea-water from the verandah, we'd have had that Case buttoned up in a couple of days. I don't say he did wrong. Calne was his meat, and he knew it, the moment he found Pallart lying there dead."

"We haven't done so bad," George said. He gave a bit of a chuckle and it was only because I was out of reach that he didn't dig me in the ribs. "Nothing to be ashamed of, at any rate."

"Yes," I said. "There's plenty of life in the Old Gent yet." And George positively smirked as he emptied his glass.

Just one small episode if only by way of epilogue. There came a glorious October morning, and my wife was being out for the day. I had a sudden nostalgic urge to see Ninford again, so I got out the car. I telephoned on the way so that lunch might be ready at the Wheatsheaf.

Let me own frankly that as I neared Ninford I was miserable. Nothing was, or could ever be, the same. Somehow I was wishing that I were a poet and could put into words the thoughts that lay deep down. At the Old Vicarage I even kept my eyes averted, and that was cowardice of the worst.

I lunched and had a word with those I knew and then I went on in the car to Wandham fork. But I hated the thought of Walker's Ferry and I turned the car round and headed for home. As I came round the bend and up the hill past the Wheatsheaf, I saw someone hurrying towards me. I thought at first it was a short man wearing an overcoat, so quick were the steps. Then I knew it was Susan, and I pulled up the car as she neared.

You have seen a bird on a lawn, how it scurries along and then as suddenly stops, its head on one side and its little black eyes alert. That was Susan Beavers. Then her rosy face was beaming.

"Well, if it isn't you, sir!"

"How are you, Susan?" I said.

"Can't grumble," she said, and there was quite a complacency as she added that her mother had been over ninety and she reckoned she was a better woman than her.

"I'd like to bet you'll reach a hundred," I said. "But why all the hurry, Susan?"

"Got to get the bus at the Wheatsheaf," she said. "No sense in stopping them here. Wednesday I always see my daughter at Drowton and go to the pictures."

I'd forgotten it was a Wednesday.

"Come along, then," I said, and held out my hand. "Why shouldn't I take you to Drowton?"

She got in without any help of mine, and settled herself in the bucket seat.

"What I call real comfort," she said as we moved off. "And how are you, sir, and how's everything?"

I drove the car quite slowly and we had a fine yam. She told me there was talk of the British Legion having the Old Vicarage.

"And quite right, too," she said. "I never did like that young Mr. Richard. Never would have made one like his uncle. And them British Legion ought to make a bit of life. You can't do too much for them what have been fighting for you; that's what I say."

Friske and his wife were already in, she said, but it wasn't like the old days. Then she was giving one of her delicious little chuckles.

"Reckon I'm like that woman they have on the wireless, in ITMA. It's being so cheerful that keep me going."

"And how's the hair?"

She gave me a wicked little look, and I had to laugh. That peroxide hadn't been so bad, she said, and a visit to the hairdresser had put things right.

We were getting near Drowton and I asked what was on at the pictures.

"Something I've been wanting to see," she said. "One o' them pictures about them mackwiz."

"Mackwiz?" I said, and then I got it. It was the *maquis* she meant.

"Yes," she said. "About dropping them spies over France and all them mackwiz fighting them Germans." Then she was giving a little toss of her head. "Not that you can believe half what you see on the pictures. Most of it lies, so I always reckon." Then she gave a little sigh. "Still, it do make a bit o' life. And nothing never seem to happen in Ninford."

I drove her round by a side street to her daughter's house. She thanked me and hoped I'd see her again. Her eyes popped when I told her I'd seen Loret in France and that he might pay a visit in the not distant future to Ninford.

"Can't tell you any more," I said. "I'm in a bit of a hurry."

She waved to me as I moved the car on. And I *was* in a hurry. I wanted to leave Drowton behind me if only because it reminded me so overwhelmingly of Ninford. And yet not Ninford, perhaps, but the Old Vicarage: Susan and that first Wednesday when I had seen her on the bus: Guy Pallart and what had lain so starkly behind the cynicism and the charm.

But it was of Susan that I thought last before the traffic of the suburbs took Ninford finally from my thoughts.

"Nothing ever happen in Ninford."

That was what she had told me, and I wondered what she would have said if I had told her the truth about Ungler and a dark stain on a head of lovely silvery hair.

THE END

AFTERWORD

It is Guy Pallart's conflict with his nephew, Richard Brace, which so bemused Anthony Boucher and merits a little further exploration in this afterword. Brace is the only child of Pallart's sister, who back in the Twenties had "horrified" her family when she eloped with an improvident and alcoholic music composer turned "hack conductor" (dubbed by Pallart "a bad egg"). With both his parents having passed away during the war years, young Richard Brace, who had sat out the war on account of his weak chest, launched his own musical career. By the conflict's end he had become, to his uncle's mystified mortification, a member of a northern England dance band. Not "quite the profession I'd choose for a nephew of my own," reflects Ludo, "but it is at least a step above crooning." Of crooners the usually genial Ludo confides bitingly, "I'd cheerfully witness their execution." Why on earth, modern readers may well wonder, make such a fuss over this music?

Originating in the United States during the Roaring Twenties, the term "crooner" was an appellation for male singers who vocalized American jazz standards in a decidedly sentimentalized and emotional style, while backed alternatively by orchestra, big band or piano. (The crooner's female counterparts--Doris Day and Britain's Vera Lynn, for example--were called, but naturally, "croonerettes.") Hugely successful crooners of the day included popular originator Rudy Vallee, Russ Columbo and Bing Crosby and they live on in the present day in still-active nonagenarian Tony Bennett and others. Improbable as it may seem to us, crooning initially provoked much controversy in the United States, with its detractors, like Boston's Cardinal William Henry O'Connell, thunderously denouncing the singing style as "degenerate" and "defiling." In 1932, a *New York Times* editorial complacently assured readers that "Crooners will soon go the way of tandem bicycles, mah jongg and midget golf," but this judgment, like others from the *Times* editorial board in this era (see my introduction to Christopher Bush's *The Case of the Green Felt Hat*, 1939) proved an errant one.

While crooning had become broadly accepted in the US by the early 1940s, it remained controversial in the United Kingdom, where it was deemed by many persons in high places as an unmanly art likely to demoralize British troops fighting so desperately against what seemed increasingly insurmountable odds in Africa and Asia. In March 1942 the *Daily Telegraph* published a letter from a retired lieutenant colonel and Victoria's Cross holder excoriating "crooners and the sloppy sentimental rubbish inflicted by the BBC on its listeners." The BBC's "sickly and maudlin [musical] programmes," he righteously concluded, "are largely responsible for the half-hearted attitude of so many people towards the war and its seriousness generally." Concurring with the retired officer's damning assessment of crooners and croonerettes, the BBC four months later proscribed music with "anaemic or debilitated" vocal performances by male singers, "insincere and over-sentimental vocal performances" by women singers, "slushy" sentiment or "innuendo . . . offensive from the point of view of good taste" and all songs based on "tunes borrowed from standard classical works." The latter category was included because such tunes, known as "swung" music, were considered debasing to classical music; and it encompassed even the tremendously popular "So Deep Is the Night," based on Chopin's Etude in E Major (popularly known as "Tristesse"), which was recorded in 1940 by beloved operatic tenors John McCormack and Richard Tauber. (See Christina L. Baade, *Victory through Harmony: The BBC and Popular Music in World War II*, Oxford University Press, 2012).

Over time the BBC modified its ban, which from its inception had met with a great deal of backlash, but the fact that it was promulgated in the first place reflected the deep distaste some people then held for both crooning and swung music. A great lover of classical music who included bars of his own original composition in one of his detective novels, *Dead Man's Music* (1932), Christopher Bush evidently was one of these people (as, seemingly, was Crime Queen Ngaio Marsh, judging by her 1949 detective novel *Swing, Brother, Swing*). Clearly Bush poured something of his own disdain for modern popular music into the character of Guy Pallart—"an aristocrat to the finger-tips," according to Ludo. Contrastingly Ludo deems Pallart's sadly sallow and weak-chinned band player nephew Richard Brace not "quite off the top shelf."

Not quite off the top shelf either, I suppose it is fair to say, was Roy Diven, a band leader from small town Kansas and humble parentage who during the Thirties played engagements in rowdy cities in the American southwest like Albuquerque, New Mexico and Amarillo, Texas. A versatile musician, Roy had been classically trained in the violin but with his band he now played hot licks on the trombone and saxophone. After several years in Amarillo, Roy in 1936 married a local auditor named Augusta Smith, who was my grandmother's youngest sister. The couple had one child, a daughter, in 1938, and moved to Colorado in 1942, not long after the US entered the Second World War on the side of the beleaguered British nation. In 1943 Roy died all too young at the age of 38. A year before his death, Roy, who was also a songwriter, with his wife Augusta copyrighted a patriotic tune they titled "Come on and Fight." Perhaps Guy Pallart, Christopher Bush and the Powers-That-Were at the BBC would have approved of that.

Curtis Evans

22207470R00124

Printed in Great Britain
by Amazon